Praise for
Herald of Death

"Another superb homicidal historical holiday cozy. The 'upstairs, downstairs' class difference just before WWI comes alive, as it always does in the Pennyfoot saga, in this exciting amateur sleuth."   —*Midwest Book Review*

"Kingsbury continues to delight fans with well-thought-out mysteries that will challenge and entertain for hours."
—*Debbie's Book Bag*

Mistletoe and Mayhem

"Full of wonderful characters, a welcoming home setting, and many surprises, this one is a keeper! . . . These are characters you will want to visit time and time again!"
—*The Romance Readers Connection*

Decked with Folly

"Kingsbury expertly strews red herrings to suggest plenty of others had reason to wish Ian dead . . . This makes the perfect stocking stuffer for the cozy fan in your life."
—*Publishers Weekly*

Ringing in Murder

"*Ringing in Murder* combines the feel of an Agatha Christie whodunit with a taste of *Upstairs, Downstairs*."
—*Cozy Library*

"Engaging . . . Cozy fans will be pleased to ring in the New Year with this cheerful Kingsbury trifle."
—*Publishers Weekly*

continued . . .

Shrouds of Holly

"Charming . . . Will provide warm holiday entertainment."
—*Publishers Weekly*

"Delightful . . . Starring an intrepid heroine."
—*Midwest Book Review*

"Well-crafted and surprising all the way to the last page, *Shrouds of Holly* is a pleasurable read that is sure to get you in the mood for the holidays!"
—*The Romance Readers Connection*

"Likable characters, charming surroundings, and eclectic guests continue to make this an enjoyable series. Bravo, Kate Kingsbury . . . for making this a holiday tradition."
—*MyShelf.com*

Slay Bells

"A pre–World War I whodunit in the classic style, furnished with amusing characters."
—*Kirkus Reviews*

"The author draws as much from *Fawlty Towers* as she does from Agatha Christie, crafting a charming . . . cozy delicately flavored with period details of pre–World War I rural England."
—*Publishers Weekly*

"A true holiday gem."
—*Mystery Scene*

**Visit Kate Kingsbury's website
at www.doreenrobertshight.com**

Berkley Prime Crime titles by Kate Kingsbury

Manor House Mysteries

A BICYCLE BUILT FOR MURDER

DEATH IS IN THE AIR

FOR WHOM DEATH TOLLS

DIG DEEP FOR MURDER

PAINT BY MURDER

BERRIED ALIVE

FIRE WHEN READY

WEDDING ROWS

AN UNMENTIONABLE MURDER

Pennyfoot Hotel Mysteries

ROOM WITH A CLUE

DO NOT DISTURB

SERVICE FOR TWO

EAT, DRINK, AND BE BURIED

CHECK-OUT TIME

GROUNDS FOR MURDER

PAY THE PIPER

CHIVALRY IS DEAD

RING FOR TOMB SERVICE

DEATH WITH RESERVATIONS

DYING ROOM ONLY

MAID TO MURDER

Holiday Pennyfoot Hotel Mysteries

NO CLUE AT THE INN

SLAY BELLS

SHROUDS OF HOLLY

RINGING IN MURDER

DECKED WITH FOLLY

MISTLETOE AND MAYHEM

HERALD OF DEATH

THE CLUE IS IN THE PUDDING

Titles by Kate Kingsbury writing as Rebecca Kent

HIGH MARKS FOR MURDER

FINISHED OFF

MURDER HAS NO CLASS

THE CLUE IS
IN THE PUDDING

KATE KINGSBURY

BERKLEY PRIME CRIME, NEW YORK

THE BERKLEY PUBLISHING GROUP
Published by the Penguin Group
Penguin Group (USA) Inc.
375 Hudson Street, New York, New York 10014, USA

Penguin Group (Canada), 90 Eglinton Avenue East, Suite 700, Toronto, Ontario M4P 2Y3, Canada
(a division of Pearson Penguin Canada Inc.) • Penguin Books Ltd., 80 Strand, London WC2R 0RL,
England • Penguin Group Ireland, 25 St. Stephen's Green, Dublin 2, Ireland (a division of Penguin
Books Ltd.) • Penguin Group (Australia), 250 Camberwell Road, Camberwell, Victoria 3124, Australia
(a division of Pearson Australia Group Pty. Ltd.) • Penguin Books India Pvt. Ltd., 11 Community
Centre, Panchsheel Park, New Delhi—110 017, India • Penguin Group (NZ), 67 Apollo Drive,
Rosedale, Auckland 0632, New Zealand (a division of Pearson New Zealand Ltd.) • Penguin Books
(South Africa) (Pty.) Ltd., 24 Sturdee Avenue, Rosebank, Johannesburg 2196, South Africa

Penguin Books Ltd., Registered Offices: 80 Strand, London WC2R 0RL, England

This book is an original publication of The Berkley Publishing Group.

PUBLISHING HISTORY
Berkley trade paperback edition / November 2012

Library of Congress Cataloging-in-Publication Data
Kingsbury, Kate.
The clue is in the pudding / Kate Kingsbury.
p. cm.—(A special Pennyfoot Hotel mystery)
ISBN 978-0-425-25327-4 (pbk.)
1. Baxter, Cecily Sinclair (Fictitious character)—Fiction.   2. Actors—Crimes against—Fiction.
3. Pennyfoot Hotel (England : Imaginary place)—Fiction.   4. Christmas stories.
5. England—Fiction.   I. Title.
PR9199.3.K44228C58 2012
813'.54—dc23
2012022750

PRINTED IN THE UNITED STATES OF AMERICA

10 9 8 7 6 5 4 3 2 1

To Bill, the love of my life
and the heart of my dreams.

ACKNOWLEDGMENTS

Grateful thanks to my patient, efficient, hard-working editor, Faith Black, who went above and beyond to make sure this book is all it can be. Thanks for your good eye, your sharp mind, and your comprehension of what needed to be done.

My sincere thanks to the art department for a truly great cover. You are such a talented team, and I can always rely on you to do an outstanding job.

Many thanks to my agent, Paige Wheeler, for keeping a vigilant eye on my interests. I appreciate your efforts.

Research is a big part of writing historical mysteries, and I have my good friend, Ann Wraight, to thank for sending me interesting and informative articles from my homeland. Thanks for keeping me in touch with my heritage.

The Pennyfoot Hotel mysteries would not be successful without the dedication of my many fans. Thank you for keeping the Pennyfoot Country Club and its occupants alive and well, and for your most welcome e-mails that make my day. I am truly blessed.

THE CLUE IS
IN THE PUDDING

CHAPTER
❋ 1 ❋

Pansy Watson lifted her long skirts as she crossed the court-yard on her way to the stables. Although weak sun rays peeked through the clouds, a sharp frost overnight had left patches of ice on the ground, and the housemaid deplored the feel of chilly, wet wool flapping around her ankles.

She'd been looking forward to this moment all morning. Samuel would be waiting for her, leaning against one of the stalls that housed the horses, a big grin on his face as he watched her walk toward him. She could just see him in her mind's eye, and the anticipation of their meeting quickened her step.

This was her favorite time of the year. This was when the Pennyfoot Country Club looked its best, with the glowing

Christmas trees in the lobby and the library, bright garlands of red and green ribbons adorning the stairs, and enormous wreaths of holly and mistletoe clinging to the walls.

From the boudoirs on the top floor to the narrow hallways below stairs, the fragrance of sweet spices from the kitchen and fresh pine from the woods filled the air. The smell of Christmas. It was everywhere, and how she loved it.

When the twentieth century had begun just a few years ago, she'd worried that all the drastic changes everyone was talking about would mean Christmas as she'd known it would never be the same. She'd worried for nothing. Christmas at the Pennyfoot was still as warm and exciting as it had ever been.

Bathed in contentment and an underlying excitement, she skipped across the hard ground. This could be the year that Samuel finally asked her to marry him. She had waited so long. This had to be the year.

She was almost at the stables when she heard a shout from across the lawns. Startled, she turned to face the wiry man racing toward her. She could tell long before Samuel reached her that something was wrong. For one thing, he wasn't wearing his cap. Madam was very strict on that.

Samuel was not only the stable manager, he was madam's personal carriage driver, and now that the guests sometimes brought a motorcar with them, Samuel was responsible for taking care of them, too. Madam expected him to wear his uniform at all times while he was on duty, and that included his cap.

Not only that, but Samuel never ran anywhere unless it

was an emergency. She didn't even know he could run that fast. Heart pumping, she waited for him to reach her.

When he did, he was panting so hard he could hardly get words out of his mouth. "Tess," he said, between huge gasps. "She's gone."

Pansy stared at him, the full horror of what he was saying penetrating down to her bones. Tess was Samuel's dog, rescued as a stray and the love of his life. Sometimes Pansy felt that Samuel loved that dog far more than he loved her. "Whatcha mean she's gone?"

Samuel shook his head, as if he couldn't believe the words coming out of his mouth. "I took h-her for a walk . . . this morning . . . and sh-she chased off . . . after a squirrel." He paused and held his hand over his chest, which heaved so much his fingers rose and fell with alarming speed.

Pansy struggled to make sense of his distress. "She'll come back. You know she always does."

"Yeah. She comes back for her breakfast. I always save her a sausage or bacon. I've done that ever since I found her. She always comes back for that. She's never missed." He turned his head, staring wildly in every direction across the lawns. "Something's happened to her. I know it."

Worried again now, Pansy grasped his arm. "I'll help you look for her. She can't have gone far."

Samuel shook his head. "I've looked everywhere. I can't take any more time right now. I haven't fed the horses or groomed them yet. They'll be asking for carriages soon, and I don't have any ready."

Pansy hesitated. She was giving up her midday break to

see Samuel. She had maybe ten minutes left before she had to be back in the kitchen. She so wanted to spend those precious minutes with the man she loved with all her heart. Looking into his eyes, though, she could see the pain and fear in them.

Gulping back her disappointment, she said firmly, "I'll go and look for her. I'll get Gertie to help me if I can't find her. Mrs. Tucker will just have to understand." She tried not to envision the snippety housekeeper, arms folded across her flat chest, her strident voice demanding to know why in blazes two of the housemaids had decided to take valuable time off to look for a dog.

Mrs. Tucker could be quite scary when her temper was aroused. Even Gertie had a healthy respect for the housekeeper, and Gertie was taller and a lot bulkier than Mrs. Tucker. Gertie got away with a lot of things, but in the busy Christmas season, taking extra time off wouldn't be one of them. Even Mrs. Chubb, the permanent housekeeper, wouldn't be happy about that, though she'd be a lot nicer about saying so.

But Mrs. Chubb was away at her daughter's house, and now everyone had to put up with grumpy old Tucker the Terrible, as Gertie called her.

"Bless you, luv." Samuel threw his arms around Pansy's slight body and gave her a hug. "You know how much that means to me."

All thoughts of an outraged Mrs. Tucker flew out of Pansy's mind. Samuel was holding her in his arms, and that was all that mattered. He gave her a quick kiss on the mouth and let her go. "I have to run. Just keep calling Tess's name. If she hears you, she'll bark." With a quick wave, he disappeared into the stables.

Frowning, Pansy picked up her skirts again. If she had to cross the lawns, the hem of her skirt and petticoat would be soaked. She decided instead to go through the rose garden, where a paved path would take her to the other side of the lawns and closer to the woods. Maybe she'd run into Clive Russell, the caretaker. He could help her search for Tess.

Remembering Samuel's instructions, she started calling out the dog's name as she trotted down the path. The bushes in the rose garden were nothing but sticks, and the white trellis was completely bare of the white roses that climbed it in the summer. No place for a dog to hide there.

Working her way around the front of the country club, she heard a faint barking in the distance. Relief and excitement quickened her pace, and she was running as she reached the end of the pathway.

Just a few yards away she saw a gentleman hurrying in the direction of the duck pond. Surprised, she chased after him. He had to be one of the guests, though why he was racing around the grounds in the cold she couldn't imagine.

The man disappeared behind the shrubbery, and then she heard the barking again. Louder this time. She also heard a shout, and her anxiety intensified as she sped toward the duck pond. She reached it just in time to see the gentleman wading out of the pond carrying a very wet and bedraggled dog in his arms.

"Tess!" Pansy ran toward them and cradled the shivering

dog's head in her hands. She looked up at the gentleman, into the palest blue eyes she'd ever seen. They were almost silver and seemed to pierce right through her head. She recognized him then. She'd heard he was a famous actor, come down from London to spend Christmas at the Pennyfoot.

"Is this your dog?"

The actor's voice was commanding and a little intimidating. Pansy nodded. "Actually, it's Samuel's dog. He's the stable manager. He's been looking for her for ages."

"Well, tell him he should take better care of her. She went through the ice and couldn't get out. She would have drowned if I hadn't heard her barking."

He put Tess on the ground and she immediately shook herself, sending a spray of cold water across Pansy's hand. The gentleman's trousers were soaked to the knee. She glanced up at him again and noticed his lips had turned blue.

"Thank you, sir. Samuel will be terribly grateful, I know."

"He should be. Dogs are man's best friend. Far more trustworthy and loyal than any human being." The actor bent down to give Tess a final pat on the head, then strode off at a fast pace and disappeared around the corner.

Pansy frowned at Tess, who sat with her head down, as if she knew she'd done something wrong. "Come on," Pansy said gruffly, "I'd better get you back to the stables so Sam can get you dry." She set off with the dog at her heels, thinking about the man who had rescued Tess. *A proper gentleman and a hero*, she thought, as she once more crossed the courtyard. Then she forgot about him when she saw Samuel rushing toward her.

"You found her! Where was she? Look at her! She's soaking wet."

"She tried to go skating on the pond," Pansy said, grinning at the sight of the wet dog leaping up to try and lick Samuel's face. "A very nice gentleman rescued her. He got soaking wet, too, but it didn't seem to bother him."

"Who was he?" Samuel looked across the courtyard as if expecting to see the stranger. "I'd like to thank him."

"He's a guest here. I can't remember his name, but I know he's a famous actor from London. I did thank him before he rushed off, but if you want to thank him yourself, you'll have plenty of time. He'll be here over Christmas."

"He's famous?" Samuel leaned down to pat the dog's head. "How about that, Tess? You got rescued by someone famous."

Pansy shivered as a gust of wind wrapped her skirt around her ankles. "I'd better get back to the kitchen or I'll be in trouble with Mrs. Tucker."

"You let me know if she gives you any bother," Samuel said, one hand holding onto Tess's collar. "I'll soon set her straight."

Pansy gazed up at him, her cheeks warming. How she loved it when Samuel got all protective of her. "I'll do that." With a wave of her hand she dashed off, her feet flying across the courtyard as if she were skimming across an icy pond.

Cecily Sinclair Baxter was a firm believer in positive thinking. Expect the worst and it was bound to happen, she always

7

maintained. So, in order not to tempt providence, she clung to the conviction that this season at the Pennyfoot Country Club would be disaster free, and the infamous Christmas curse would not materialize.

Since she was the manager of the club, it was her responsibility to see that her guests enjoyed a serene and entertaining holiday, and nothing must interfere with that scenario. The first indication that providence was determined to shake its fickle fist in her face was when Mrs. Chubb announced that her daughter had taken ill and her son-in-law needed her to help take care of the grandchildren.

"I know my going up north for Christmas will leave you in a bit of a mess, m'm," the housekeeper had said, her hands working at twisting her apron into a knot. "But what can I do?"

What could she do, indeed, Cecily had agreed. She'd assured Mrs. Chubb that they would manage without her, and had then rung the agency to acquire a temporary housekeeper to see them through the holiday season.

Beatrice Tucker had arrived that same afternoon. That was two days ago, and already the woman had upset just about everyone in the kitchen and more than one guest.

"I wish there was something I could do about Beatrice Tucker," Cecily said, as she handed Baxter the newspaper. "She seems to put everyone's nerves on edge."

"It's perishing cold in here." Baxter stretched his feet out closer to the fire. "I have to wonder why we chose to live down here on the southeast coast of England. That wind gets through every single crack on the building."

He had just finished his midday meal and had settled down in their suite for an afternoon of quiet solitude. Cecily knew quite well that the last thing her husband wanted was to indulge in a conversation about problems with the staff. Nevertheless, she felt it prudent to warn him of impending trouble, since he would no doubt hear of it sooner or later. Baxter was not one to tolerate unpleasant surprises.

"Yes, dear. Now about Beatrice Tucker—"

"Who the devil is Beatrice Tucker?" He shook the newspaper out and held it in front of his face—a sure indication that he really didn't want an answer.

"She's the temporary housekeeper I hired. To take the place of Mrs. Chubb."

Baxter lowered the newspaper, his face a mask of horror. "Mrs. Chubb has *left*?"

Cecily held back a sigh. "No, dear. She's gone to Manchester to take care of her grandchildren. I told you that."

"Oh, that's right." Baxter dived behind the newspaper again.

"The trouble is, Beatrice Tucker is alienating everyone, and we can't have discord in the kitchen, especially at Christmastime. It's supposed to be a season of happiness and good cheer. We must convey that to our guests at all times."

"Mm-hm."

"So, I was wondering if you'd have a word with her."

The newspaper rustled loudly as Baxter thrust it down on his lap. "Me? You want *me* to talk to her? Why can't you talk to her? After all, you hired her."

"Yes, dear. I know. But a firm reprimand about her

attitude would be so much more meaningful coming from you."

"How so?"

Cecily smiled. "You have such an imposing voice, my love."

Baxter grunted. "You just wish to avoid unpleasantness."

"That, too."

He gazed at her for a moment or two while she wondered if he would refuse, then he sighed. Shaking out the paper again, he muttered, "Oh, very well. I'll take care of it later."

"Thank you, dear. As it happens, I am terribly busy right now. I'm expecting Phoebe and Colonel Fortescue to visit this afternoon. Madeline should be here, too, to put the final touches on the decorating."

She received another grunt for an answer. Phoebe and Madeline were her best friends, and she knew for that reason alone Baxter tolerated their presence. He made no secret of the fact that he considered Phoebe a vain, empty-headed dolt and Madeline a devious sorceress.

Cecily had to admit that Phoebe was a little preoccupied with appearances, and just about everyone in Badgers End believed that Madeline's unusual powers with herbs and flowers was all the proof needed to proclaim her a witch.

As for Phoebe's husband, Colonel Fortescue, Baxter was convinced that the gentleman was off his rocker, and Cecily could give him no argument there.

Leaning over the newspaper, she dropped a kiss on her husband's forehead. "I'll be in my office if you need me."

Taking his answering grunt for acquiescence, she left the suite and made her way down the stairs to her office.

As usual, there was a stack of papers on her desk awaiting her perusal, and she reached for the first one, hoping she could make a dent in them before Phoebe arrived. Now that Baxter had agreed to confront the temporary housekeeper, there was one less problem for her to worry about. She could only hope her husband would have better luck than she had had so far.

Beatrice Tucker was a formidable opponent. Secure in the knowledge that Cecily needed her far more than she needed employment, she had made it clear that she would run things in the kitchen her way or not at all. Unwilling to risk having to host the Christmas season without a housekeeper, Cecily had withdrawn from the contest.

Perhaps she should have warned Baxter not to antagonize the woman. She'd asked him to step in on impulse, one that she was now regretting. Baxter would not mince words. Cecily picked up her pen and dipped it in the inkwell. She could only hope that the woman had more respect for men than she apparently did for women. If not, it could turn out to be a very interesting Christmas for everyone.

Gertie McBride stood in the pantry doing her best to curb her temper. The moment she'd heard that Mrs. Chubb was going to spend Christmas with her daughter's family, Gertie knew they were in for trouble. She was right.

The miserable cow who'd taken Chubby's place was rude and spiteful, and Gertie had a good mind to tell madam that she couldn't work for someone who talked to her like she was some guttersnipe off the street.

She was the chief housemaid for blinking sake. She deserved some respect. Except for the short time she was married to Ross McBride, she'd worked at the Pennyfoot for madam since she was a little kid. How dare that bloody upstart walk in there and start ordering her around like she was nothing?

She heard the sound of shuffling feet and turned around to see Pansy standing behind her, eyes red rimmed as if she'd been crying. "What's the bleeding matter with you?" she demanded, her voice sharp with irritation.

"Shshh!" Pansy jammed a finger over her mouth. "She'll hear you. You know how she goes on at you for swearing."

"So what? I've been bleeding swearing since I knew how to talk, and I'm not going to stop now. Especially for the likes of *her*." She jerked her head at the door.

Pansy's lower lip trembled. "She just told me off again. I *hate* her. I wish Mrs. Chubb didn't have to go to Manchester."

"So do I, but there's nothing we can bloody do about it now." Gertie's gaze fell on a half-full bottle of brandy on the shelf. "Maybe we should lace her tea with that brandy. She's a different person when she's been drinking. We—" She broke off as voices rose beyond the door.

"What did you do with ze plum pudding, eh?" Michel, the Pennyfoot's chef, sounded furious.

Gertie winced and lowered her voice. "His accent always

12

gets worse when he's riled up. He's going to start banging his pots and pans around any minute now."

The words were barely out of her mouth before a horrendous crashing of metal against stone rang out. "*Sacre bleu!*" Michel roared. "You 'ave taken a slice right out of ze pudding!"

The sharp, nasal tones of the temporary housekeeper answered him. "I took a slice up to Mr. Archibald Armitage's room. I heard it's his favorite Christmas treat. He's famous and he deserves special treatment."

"I don't care if he is ze king of England, he does not have ze pudding until Christmas *Day!*" Another loud crash accompanied Michel's screaming. This time it was followed by the ringing sound of a saucepan lid rolling across the floor until it gradually spun to a stop.

"I'm in charge of this kitchen," Beatrice Tucker shrieked, "and if I want to take a slice of pudding up to one of our guests then I will, and you have nothing to say about it."

"I make ze puddings, *non?* They are *my* puddings, *non?* I make them for Christmas Day, and no one, *no-o-bod-ee*, gets a piece until I say so. *Oui?*"

Pansy giggled.

Gertie frowned and shook her head at her. If the old bat heard her she'd have her guts for garters. She lowered her voice to a whisper. "Who did she say was famous?"

"Archibald Armitage. He's in room three and he's a famous actor."

"Never heard of him."

"Neither had I, but I met him this afternoon. He rescued Tess."

Gertie raised her eyebrows. "Samuel's dog? How did he do that?"

Pansy flinched as another crash from the kitchen followed Michel's rampage. "He waded into the duck pond. Tess fell through the ice and couldn't get out. Mr. Armitage carried her out. He was soaked. He must have been freezing, but all he worried about was Tess." She smiled. "He's such a nice man."

"How'd you know he's an actor? Did he tell you?"

"Nah, but I overheard Mrs. Tucker talking to him yesterday. She told him he was her favorite actor and she'd seen nearly all of his plays."

"Blimey, he must be good for her to go all the way up to London to see him."

"Well, she wasn't very happy when she met him."

"Why not?"

Pansy glanced at the door, where angry voices still yelled on the other side. "Mr. Armitage was really rude to her. He told her not to blab to anyone that he was here. He'd come away for some peace and quiet, and he didn't want no stage-struck ninny getting in his way."

Gertie snorted. "Good for him. About time someone told bossy old Tucker off. What did she say?"

Pansy shrugged. "She didn't say nothing to him. But after he walked away I heard her muttering something about getting even. She couldn't have been too upset, though, if she took him up a slice of plum pudding."

"She probably spit in it." Gertie shook her head as another round of crashing and banging hurt her ears. "Come on, let's get out of here before them two kill each other."

She charged out of the pantry, just in time to see Michel throw down his tall chef's hat and march out of the kitchen.

Beatrice Tucker stood by the table, her cheeks burning and her eyes bright with temper. "Where have you two been?" she snapped, snatching up a pile of freshly laundered serviettes. "These all have to be folded before you can start laying the tables."

She thrust them at Gertie, who managed to clutch all but two of them. They floated to the floor, and she bent to retrieve them, losing a couple more in the process.

"Now look what you've done!" Beatrice snatched the fallen serviettes away from Gertie. "These will all have to be laundered and ironed again. Go and find four more clean ones in the linen closet, while you"—she jammed the four serviettes into Pansy's hands—"go and put these in the laundry room."

Pansy took the white cloths and fled, while Gertie jutted out her chin. "It weren't my fault they went on the floor."

Beatrice crossed her arms, her thin face sucked in at the cheeks. "I'll have none of your impertinence, young lady. Get upstairs and get those tables laid this second, or I'll report your insubordination and carelessness to madam."

Gertie was about to respond with a few choice words, then with an effort, curbed her tongue. She'd be wasting her breath on the old bat, she decided. Instead, she'd take her concerns to madam. Something had to be done about Tucker the Terrible, or there'd be another Christmas tragedy in the Pennyfoot. If someone didn't kill the bleeding old hag, she'd be tempted to do away with her herself.

Carrying the serviettes, she marched out of the kitchen

and up the stairs. By the time she reached the dining room, she'd calmed down a little. She took her time folding the serviettes and placing them into their silver rings. It wouldn't do to go to madam all blustery and hot under the collar. Madam listened to her a lot better if she kept her voice low and didn't use too many swear words. Especially if Mr. Baxter was there. He didn't have no patience at all with people complaining.

Pansy wandered into the dining room just as Gertie was about to leave. "I'll be back to finish the tables," she said, as she untied her apron strings. "I'm just going to pop up to have a word with madam."

Pansy looked anxious. "Is something wrong?"

"A lot," Gertie said grimly. "But I hope to do something about that." She left before Pansy could say anymore.

Reaching the end of the hallway, she was about to enter the foyer when she heard the dreaded voice of the house-keeper. Still smarting from her recent spat, Gertie decided to wait until the coast was clear before venturing any farther.

Apparently Mrs. Tucker was talking to a gentleman, as Gertie heard his soft tone, though it was too quiet to under-stand what he was saying.

Whatever it was, it made the housekeeper laugh, which surprised Gertie. The old bat must have been at the brandy, after all.

Gertie heard the gentleman speak again, then Mrs. Tucker raised her voice in what seemed to be a farewell. "I'm looking forward to hearing the choir, Mr. Rickling," she called out.

The gentleman answered, then came the sound of the front door closing.

Gertie waited a moment longer, then peeked around the corner. The foyer was empty, except for Philip dozing at the desk. Breathing a sigh of relief, Gertie sped across the carpet to the stairs.

Climbing fast, she rehearsed everything she wanted to say. There was no telling how Madam would react to her complaints. After all, it was Christmas, and it would be hard to make do without a housekeeper. At a pinch, Gertie knew she could fill in well enough. She'd worked at the Pennyfoot long enough to know how to manage everything.

Mrs. Chubb had finished all the baking before she'd left, and Michel didn't need no supervising. As for the maids, she could handle that all right, and madam always took care of the footmen. Feeling a little more hopeful, Gertie trotted up the stairs to the top floor.

She was passing by room three when she heard the moaning. At first she thought it was the wind in the chimneys. When it was really windy the chimneys groaned like they were in pain. Only this didn't sound like no chimneys. Gertie paused outside the door of room three.

It was the actor's room. The bloke what rescued Samuel's dog. Perhaps he'd caught a cold after wading into the icy duck pond. Gertie hesitated, then gently knocked on the door. A loud moan answered her.

"Are you all right, sir? Is there anything I can get for you?"

She heard another moan, fainter now. She tried the handle and found the door unlocked. Opening it just a little, she put her mouth close to the gap. "Sir? Can I get you anything?"

This time, there was nothing but silence from inside the room.

The last thing in the world Gertie wanted was to go inside. Yet something told her she had to take a look. Very slowly, she pushed the door open.

The room was lit by an oil lamp, set really low. The awful stench coming from the bed nearly sent her outside again, but she couldn't leave without making sure the guest was all right. He was lying on his side with his back to her, his knees brought up to his chin. "Sir?" She moved a little closer to the bed. "Mr. Armitage? Are you ill?"

There was no movement, and she moved even closer, until her outstretched hand could reach the man's shoulder. Heart pounding, she shook him. He rolled over onto his back, his eyes, fixed and sightless, telling her what she'd already feared.

Archibald Armitage was quite dead.

CHAPTER

❀ 2 ❀

"Really, Cecily, I'm shocked that you would allow a stranger to conduct the carol singing. I know quite well that the ceremony is your very favorite part of the entire season, and to trust it to someone you hardly know is taking a serious risk, don't you think?"

Cecily looked at the woman seated across from her. Phoebe Carter-Holmes was, as usual, dressed to perfection. Her hat, the same deep blue as her velvet coat, swept across her shoulders, its brim laden with white doves and silver ribbons. A huge white feather curled across the crown of the hat, and diamond hat pins twinkled in the glow from the fireplace.

Phoebe sat with her white gloved fingers pressed against

her cheek, while her dainty feet, encased in white boots, rested on the fender. Her expression was one of extreme distaste, and Cecily knew why. Phoebe was put out because she had been replaced as director of the carol singers.

"I have been assured that Cuthbert Rickling is a fine musician," Cecily said, with just a tinge of reproof. "He is quite the gentleman, most accommodating, and has offered his services for our carol-singing ceremony free of charge, and I find that most generous of him."

"You don't say." Phoebe's voice was thick with disdain.

Cecily tried again. "It's the first time we've had a chance to have the church choir. As you well know, Mr. Templeton, the former choirmaster, was always much too busy this time of year to attend our little ceremony. Much as we enjoy them, this will make a nice change from the usual village carol singers. While I truly appreciate you taking on the task of organizing everything, Phoebe, I thought that having Mr. Rickling here would give you more time to take care of your Christmas presentation. You have always been so rushed before."

Phoebe tossed her head, causing her hat to tilt over her eyes. Straightening it, she muttered, "I've always managed quite well."

"Yes, you have, but having a choirmaster conducting the church choir will make such a difference and now you will be able to relax and enjoy the ceremony."

Phoebe sniffed. "Freddie said he saw Mr. Rickling buying bottles of scotch in the bar. In my opinion, people affiliated with the church shouldn't be indulging in spirits."

Cecily frowned. "He may well have bought them for Christmas gifts. In any case, were Mr. Rickling not of exemplary character, I doubt that your son would tolerate him, much less employ him to lead the choir in his church."

Phoebe uttered a scornful laugh. "My son has no perception of character. I have been appalled at times at his choice of acquaintances. One simply cannot judge a man based on Algie's recommendation."

Given that the Reverend Algernon Carter-Holmes had a questionable relationship with men in general, Cecily could hardly blame Phoebe for mistrusting his opinion. "Nevertheless," she said firmly, "I am quite satisfied that Cuthbert Rickling's choir will give us an excellent performance at the ceremony. As for his personal life, that's his business and should remain so."

"Well, all I can say is that I hope your optimism is justified." Phoebe wiggled her boots." I think—"

Whatever she was going to say was interrupted by an urgent rapping on the door. Before Cecily could summon the visitor, the door flew open and Gertie charged into the suite as if being chased by a herd of angry bulls.

Cecily took one look at her chief housemaid's face and rose to her feet. "What has happened?"

Gertie gulped, glanced at Phoebe, then blurted out, "The gentleman in room three, m'm. He has a bit of a problem." She signaled with her eyes at the door. "I think you need to see to him, m'm, if you don't mind me saying."

The sinking feeling in Cecily's stomach was all too familiar. She could tell by Gertie's face that the problem was serious. She managed to sound reasonably unperturbed when she answered her housemaid. "Thank you, Gertie. I will be along in a minute. Perhaps you'd wait for me at the gentleman's door?"

Gertie nodded, dropped a curtsey, and fled.

Phoebe said something, but Cecily's mind was racing. The gentleman in room three was Archibald Armitage, the famous actor. She'd encountered him earlier that day when he'd barged through the front door and almost knocked her over in his haste to reach the stairs.

She'd noticed at the time that his trousers were soaked to his knees and had wondered where he'd been to get into such an awful mess. Most likely he had caught a cold and needed the services of a doctor.

Phoebe got up from her chair and headed for the door. "Well, I can see you are busy, Cecily. I shall go in search of Freddie. No doubt he is in the bar, as usual. I shall return tomorrow with my entourage. We're having our dress rehearsal for the Christmas pageant in the ballroom." She clasped her gloved hands together. "I am so thrilled to be presenting our pageant on Christmas Eve this year. It will give a special meaning to the performance."

Remembering some of Phoebe's past catastrophes, Cecily could only hope that the only thing special was a disaster-free presentation. Accompanying her friend to the door, she enquired, "You will still be coming to the carol-singing ceremony, I trust?"

Phoebe smiled, her rancor apparently forgotten. "Of

course, Cecily, dear. I wouldn't miss it for the world. I suppose Madeline will be there?"

"I believe she and Kevin will attend, yes."

"I was afraid of that." Phoebe tossed her head, making the feather on her hat waft around in a lazy circle. "Ah well, we can't have everything, I suppose."

Cecily sighed. Phoebe and Madeline had been at war with each other for as long as she'd known them, exchanging barbs and insults with all the gusto of battling warriors. Yet Cecily knew quite well that should anything happen to one of them, the other would be devastated. Though they'd never admit it, of course.

"We'll see you tomorrow, then," she said, holding the door open for her friend to pass through. She was anxious to find out what the problem was with Mr. Armitage and couldn't wait for Phoebe to start descending the stairs. Once the other woman was out of sight around the curve, Cecily hurried down the hallway to where Gertie lingered outside room three.

"Now then," she said when she reached her housemaid, "what is the matter with Mr. Armitage?"

Gertie's face looked drawn, and her eyes were wide with shock. "I think he's dead," she whispered.

"I'm sure he's not," Cecily assured her, praying she was right. "He's probably consumed something to help him sleep." She glanced quickly to her left and right, making sure they were alone in the hallway. "I'll take a look. Meanwhile, go down to the foyer and quietly ask Philip to ring for Dr. Prestwick."

"Yes, m'm." Gertie picked up her skirts and ran for the stairs.

Cecily paused for a moment, drew a deep breath and quietly tapped on the door. Receiving no answer, she turned the handle and walked into the room. The first thing she noticed was the ghastly odor. Obviously the poor man had been very sick.

On the bedside table an oil lamp flickered, and an empty glass stood next to it. The bed was in shadow, and the man on the bed lay on his back. Cecily watched for a moment or two, hoping to see his chest rise and fall. When she could detect no movement, she drew closer. The man's face looked green in the oil lamp's glow, and his eyes saw nothing as they stared at the ceiling.

Stomach churning, Cecily quickly left the room and locked the door behind her.

Gertie ran all the way down the stairs, stopping just long enough to tell Philip, the reception clerk, to ring for Dr. Prestwick before dashing on down to the kitchen. In her distress she'd quite forgotten that Mrs. Chubb wouldn't be there. Instead of the plump, reassuring figure of the Pennyfoot's housekeeper, the scraggy form of Beatrice Tucker loomed over the kitchen table.

Her tinny voice rapped out at Gertie, splintering the housemaid's already shattered nerves. "Would you *kindly* remember to enter the room in the proper manner. This is a kitchen, not a school playground. Barging in here like that can cause a serious accident."

"There's already been a serious accident," Gertie snapped, "and there'll be one more if you keep talking to me in that tone of voice."

The housekeeper threw down her carving knife and flung a hand out at Gertie. "That's *enough*! I will not take this kind of abuse from a common housemaid. I will go this minute and report your abominable behavior to madam."

Trembling with a mixture of anger and shock, Gertie stood her ground. "Madam's a little busy right now. She's got a death on her hands."

Already marching halfway across the kitchen, Beatrice halted, her beady eyes raking Gertie's face. "What did you say?"

Gertie took a step toward Beatrice and jutted out her chin. "I said, madam's got a death on her hands. Archibald Armitage is lying dead in his bed."

It seemed for a moment that Beatrice couldn't believe what she'd heard, then her face crumpled. "Mercy me. He was only thirty-three. What happened to him?"

"How the flipping heck should I know?" Gertie looked over at Michel, who stood at the stove, one hand holding his chest. "Looks like the Christmas curse turned up again."

Michel muttered something and drew a quick cross on his chest.

Beatrice made an odd sound in her throat. "What do you mean, the Christmas curse? What sort of curse?"

Beginning to feel a little calmer now that she had the upper hand, Gertie shrugged. "It happens every Christmas. Someone dies." She leaned forward and lowered her voice to a menacing tone. "Sometimes more than one."

Fear raced across Beatrice's face, then she drew herself up to her full height. "I'm sorry to hear about Mr. Armitage, but we have work to do, and standing around here gossiping is not going to get it done. You're supposed to be upstairs laying the tables, Gertie. Get back up there this minute and get it done. When you're finished you can fill the coal scuttles for the stove."

Gertie resisted the urge to stick out her tongue. Instead, she rolled her eyes at Michel, who still seemed in a trance, then turned her back on Beatrice and marched out of the kitchen.

Pansy was in the dining room when she reached it moments later. She was polishing the silver salt and pepper shakers and looked up when Gertie hurried over to her. "Where have you been?" she demanded, as Gertie tied on her apron. "It's getting late and we've still got half the tables not laid yet."

"Sorry." Gertie picked up a handful of silverware from the tray and started setting out the knives and forks. "I've got some bad news."

"What is it?"

"Well, you know that nice man what saved Samuel's dog?"

"The actor?" Pansy looked worried. "What about him?"

"He's dead."

With a muffled cry, Pansy dropped the shaker she was holding, spilling salt across the tablecloth. "He's what?"

"Dead." Gertie picked up the shaker and put it back in its cradle. "I just came from his room. He was lying on his back, staring at the ceiling, only he wasn't seeing nothing. Madam's with him now."

"Oh, no!" Pansy scooped up salt in her fingers and tossed it over her shoulder. "What happened to him?"

"Dunno. Philip's ringing the doctor right now. I suppose we'll find out sooner or later."

Pansy grabbed Gertie's sleeve. "You don't think he got pneumonia or something from wading into that pond after Tess, do you?"

"I don't think so. I think it would take longer than that."

"He could have had a heart attack from the cold."

"Yeah, I s'pose he could've."

Pansy's eyes filled with tears. "Samuel will never forgive himself. He'll think it's his fault."

"How can it be his fault? He didn't tell the stupid bloke to go in the pond."

"No, but if it hadn't been for Tess . . ."

"Then it's the dog's fault. Besides, we don't know that's what killed him, do we."

"No, but—"

Gertie dragged a handkerchief from her pocket and handed it to Pansy. "Here, dry your bleeding eyes. Don't let the old battle-axe see you like that. She'll be screaming at you to stop acting like a baby."

"That poor man." Pansy picked up another shaker and started polishing it. "I felt sorry for him being here all alone for Christmas. I even thought it would be nice if he and Lady

Bottingham would get together over Christmas. She's here all alone, too."

Gertie uttered a short laugh. "Lady Bottingham? She's much too posh to keep company with a common actor. Even if he was famous."

Pansy scowled. "Well, I think she's lonely. She's got to be at least thirty years old or so, but she doesn't have a husband. I wonder why."

"Probably couldn't find one good enough for her."

"That's sad. Anyway, it would have been nice for her to have a gentleman companion to spend Christmas with and maybe she wouldn't have minded that he was only an actor. He was a very nice gentleman. Not many men would wade into icy water to rescue a dog."

"Well, it's too late now. Archibald Armitage is gone, and let's hope he didn't die from some horrible mysterious disease that we could all catch."

Pansy uttered a shrill shriek. "What? What sort of disease?"

Gertie shrugged. "I dunno. It could be anything. Consumption, scarlet fever, measles, diphtheria, the plague . . ."

Pansy looked ready to cry. "I got really close to him today. I might have caught a disease from him."

Gertie patted her shoulder. "Don't worry. Dr. Prestwick will find out what he died of, and if it's catching he'll know what to do."

Pansy looked unconvinced, and Gertie felt uneasy about it, too. What if the whole country club was quarantined?

That would spoil Christmas really good. Deciding that worrying about it wasn't going to help much, she shook off her anxiety. "Come on, let's get these bloody tables done. I've got to fill the coal scuttles yet, and I don't want to do it after it gets dark. That coal shed is blinking creepy in the dark."

Pansy started shoving the salt and pepper shakers onto each table so fast they rattled in their holders. "I'll have to go and tell Samuel what's happened when we're finished here. It's better that he hears it from me."

"Good idea." Gertie laid a serviette beside a row of silverware. "In the meantime, help me think about what I can get for Clive for Christmas."

Pansy looked at her in surprise. "You're buying him a Christmas present?"

Pleased that she'd taken her friend's mind off the actor's death, Gertie nodded. "Yeah, well, he always makes such lovely things for my twins at Christmastime."

"That's because he likes making things with his hands. He's good at it."

"Yeah, he is. But it's more than that." Gertie paused, her gaze on the tables but her mind seeing Clive's big grin as he swept James or Lillian up into his brawny arms. "He's been like a father to the twins. They miss not having a father around, and Clive's sort of stepped in the gap."

"He's another one that makes me wonder why he never got married and had children of his own."

Gertie had often wondered the same thing, but that wasn't something she wanted to discuss with anyone but Clive himself. "Anyway, I thought I should give him something this year. I just don't know what."

"I dunno. What would you give a caretaker?"

Gertie frowned. "He's a man as well as a caretaker. There has to be something he'd really like."

Pansy dropped the last set of shakers onto a table. "Maybe a new pipe?"

"I've never seen him smoke a pipe."

"Just because you haven't seen him doesn't mean he never smokes one."

Gertie shook her head. "Doesn't sound like something he'd want."

"Then what about a bottle of whiskey? That seems to be a popular Christmas present. I saw Lady Bottingham coming from the bar yesterday carrying a bottle."

Gertie raised her eyebrows. "Maybe she was taking it to her room to drink it herself."

"Well, it had holly and ribbon tied around the neck, like she was ready to give it to someone."

"Yeah, but the barmen always do that to all the bottles they sell at Christmastime."

Pansy headed for the door, pulling off her apron as she went. "Well, I'll ask Samuel if he knows what to give Clive. He's a man so he should know. I'm going now to tell him about Mr. Armitage."

"Tucker the Terrible is going to want to know where you are."

Pansy paused at the door. "Oh, bother. I forgot about her."

Gertie grinned. "Don't worry, I'll tell her Lady Botting-ham asked you to take up a hot water bottle."

Pansy blew a kiss. "You're a love, Gertie. Ta ever so!" With that she rushed through the door and disappeared into the hallway.

Shaking her head, Gertie finished laying out the silver-ware and serviettes. Pansy's comment about Clive had started her wondering again. For months now, she'd been on the verge of asking Clive about his past. Despite spending quite a bit of time with him, she still knew nothing about his life before he came to the Pennyfoot.

Every time she thought about asking him, however, some-thing always cropped up to interrupt her. Maybe if she made a determined effort to find a moment to ask him, he could finally satisfy her curiosity. After all, he knew all about her and Ian, the father of her twins. He knew that she'd married Ian and didn't find out he was already married until it was too late.

She'd also told Clive about Ross McBride. The Scottish bagpiper had been a lot older than her, and she'd married him more for the sake of her twins than anything. Ross had been kind to her and her children, and she'd missed him when he died.

Now there was Clive. She wasn't quite sure how she felt about him. He made her laugh and made her feel good when she was with him. He was a big man, both in size and heart, and would make a wonderful father for the twins.

She had to wonder, though, why such a man wasn't already married and surrounded by his children. Why an intelligent, wise, clever man like Clive should be working as a caretaker. She couldn't help feeling that the reason he didn't talk about his past was because he had something to hide. Maybe that was why she kept such a tight rein on her feelings for him.

Or maybe it was simply that she couldn't bear to be hurt again. Ian's betrayal had devastated her. But then she'd met Ross and was at peace for a while. Until after he died, and she'd met Dan. For the first time in her life she'd been really in love, deeply in love.

Only he hadn't loved her back. Not enough to put her and the twins above his own wishes. He'd wanted to uproot them all, take them back to London to live. She couldn't do that to her children. Dan, she'd realized, belonged to a different world—a sophisticated, cultured, toffee-nosed world where she didn't belong. It hadn't taken much soul-searching to know where that would have ended up. Oh, but how it had hurt to turn him down.

Gertie took one last look around the dining room, then with a satisfied nod, headed for the door. Maybe she was destined to spend the rest of her life without a man and a father for her twins. And that was sad.

Having risked the wrath of Tucker the Terrible to be alone with Samuel, Pansy was quite disappointed to see his assistant, Gilbert Tubbs, in the stables, helping him wash the motorcars. Tess lay close to Samuel's feet, her head resting on her paws.

Samuel gave her his usual greeting—a hug and a kiss on

the cheek. "'Allo, luv," he said, leaving one arm around her. "Whatcha doing here? It's almost dinnertime, isn't it?"

"Yeah." Pansy snuggled up to him. "I'm supposed to be in the kitchen now, helping dish up the soup and vegetables. Mrs. Tucker would box my ears if she knew where I was right now."

Samuel looked worried. "Then you'd better be off with you. I don't want to get you into trouble."

Gilbert straightened up, a polishing cloth in his hand. He was a good-looking man, with dark hair and bright blue eyes that always seemed to be laughing. He was taller than Samuel, and bigger built. When he smiled, like he was doing right now, two dimples dug deep into his cheeks. "Well, look who's here! If it isn't the most beautiful girl in Badgers End come to visit us." He winked at Pansy, making her blush.

"Take no notice of him," Samuel said gruffly. "He talks to all the girls that way."

Pansy tossed her head. "I know that. He doesn't fool me for one second." Secretly she liked the things Gilbert said to her. It made her feel pretty, though she'd never admit as much to Samuel. "I didn't come here to talk to him, anyway. I came to tell you something." She looked up at him, her heart skipping a beat when he smiled down at her.

"All right then, luv. What did you want to tell me?"

She hesitated, not sure now how to break the news. Maybe it wasn't a good idea just to blurt it out. Maybe she should have waited and let Samuel find out from madam or someone.

Both men were looking at her now, waiting for her to

speak. Taking a deep breath she said a little unsteadily, "You remember the gentleman that rescued Tess?"

Gilbert's grin faded, while Samuel looked puzzled. "Of course I do. How could I forget? He saved my Tess's life."

At the mention of her name, the shaggy dog lifted her head.

"Yes, I know." Pansy's voice wobbled, and she gulped. "Well, he was a famous actor called Archibald Armitage."

Samuel looked down at Tess. "You were rescued by a famous actor, Tess. Maybe he'll put you in one of his plays."

"I don't think he's going to be doing that." Pansy bit her lip. "He's . . . he's . . ."

Samuel hugged her tighter. "What's the matter, pet? What's wrong?"

Pansy let a tear slide down her cheek. "He's dead, Samuel. Gertie found him dead in his bed."

The shocked silence that followed was eventually broken by her sob.

Samuel looked stunned, while Gilbert raised his face to the ceiling.

"Dead?" Samuel dropped his arm and half turned away from her. "What happened? How did he die?"

Worried about Samuel's reaction, Pansy shook her head. "I don't know. Madam has sent for Dr. Prestwick so we'll probably know soon. I wanted to tell you before you heard it from someone else."

Samuel shook his head. "I didn't even get a chance to thank him. I was going to do that in the morning."

"I know." Pansy hugged his arm. "I'm so sorry, Samuel. He was a good, kind man and didn't deserve to die all alone in a hotel room."

Gilbert snorted, making them both stare at him in surprise. "Good man, my arse."

"Here!" Samuel glared at him. "Watch your language around a lady."

Gilbert raised his eyebrows. "Sorry. After listening to Gertie mouthing off, I thought Pansy was used to it."

Samuel took a step toward him. "Not while I'm around and not from you."

Gilbert held up his hands in submission. "All right, all right. Don't get your knickers in a twist. I didn't mean anything by it."

Pansy, however, wasn't about to let it drop. "What did you mean, about Mr. Armitage? He was a very nice man, and you shouldn't speak ill of the dead."

Gilbert crouched down by the motorcar and started polishing it again. "Maybe not, but Armitage was not a good man by any means. He was a thief and a liar."

Pansy took a step forward. "I don't believe you. How would you know, anyhow?"

Gilbert shrugged and dropped the polishing cloth into a bucket at his side. "Never you mind." He looked up and grinned at her. "Don't worry your pretty little head about it, sweetheart."

Samuel scowled. "It's time you were off," he said, nodding at the doors. "You're finished for the day."

Gilbert stood and touched his forehead with his fingers. "Yes, sir. See you tomorrow." With another wink at Pansy, he strolled through the doors and out into the dark night.

Samuel grunted. "Cheeky blighter. If we weren't so busy I'd tell him to bugger off and not come back."

Feeling cold all of a sudden, Pansy hugged herself. "I can't believe what he said about Mr. Armitage. He waded into that icy pond to save Tess and might well have caught cold and died from it. How could a man like that be a thief and a liar? I think it's Gilbert what's lying, that I do."

Samuel shrugged. "I suppose we'll never know. I'm sorry the bloke is dead, though. I did want to thank him for saving Tess's life."

Tess raised her head again and whined. Pansy dropped to her knees beside the dog and hugged her. "No matter what they say," she said softly in the dog's ear, "*we* know that Mr. Armitage was a good man, don't we."

Samuel laid a hand on her shoulder. "Thanks for coming to tell me. You'd better get back to the kitchen, before that old crow comes looking for you."

Pansy snorted. "I'm not afraid of *her.*"

Samuel pulled her to her feet and dropped a light kiss on her lips. "Maybe you're not, but I am. I don't want her complaining to madam that I'm keeping the maids entertained in the stables."

Pansy raised her eyebrows. "Maids?"

Samuel grinned. "Well, one. The best, most beautiful one."

Pansy gave him a shove. "Go on with you." She was smiling as she left him, and in spite of her sorrow over a kind man's death, her smile lasted all the way back to the kitchen.

CHAPTER
✿ 3 ✿

Seated by the fire in her suite, Cecily waited anxiously for Kevin Prestwick to finish his examination of Archibald Armitage. Kevin had been her doctor for many years, and at one time had been a strong suitor for her hand before Baxter had captured her heart. Although Kevin was now happily married to Madeline, Baxter was never fully comfortable when the doctor was in their company. The relationship between the two men was fragile, though they had often worked together when necessary in the pursuit of a villain.

Right now Baxter was pacing back and forth in front of the fire, hands behind his back. A sure sign he was deeply troubled.

"I don't like this," he muttered. "I don't like this at all."

"No one likes a death in the house," Cecily murmured. She sat close to the flames, embracing the warmth on her knees through the thick wool of her black skirt. "It is unfortunate, to say the least. I hope it won't dampen the Christmas spirit for everyone."

Baxter paused and looked her in the eye. "I just hope it isn't the dratted curse popping up again."

Cecily felt a twinge of anxiety and laced her fingers in her lap. "I'm sure whatever happened to Mr. Armitage was caused by some illness. I just hope it isn't contagious."

Baxter's eyebrows shot up. "Good Lord! I hadn't thought of that. That would be worse than if he'd been murdered."

Cecily fanned her face with her hand. "Please, Hugh, don't even mention that word. I refuse to think that we have another killer on our hands."

A tap at the door snatched her attention away from her husband. "Come in!"

Kevin appeared in the doorway, a frown marring his pleasant features. "I'm finished with my examination."

"Do please come in, Kevin." Cecily got up from the chair and hurried over to him. "Tell us, please, what was the cause of Mr. Armitage's death?"

Kevin walked into the room and gave Baxter a wary nod. "Well, I can't be certain until I've done a further study in my surgery, but all symptoms appear to point toward a case of severe poisoning."

Cecily gasped, one hand over her mouth. "Food poisoning?"

Kevin shrugged. "It's hard to say at this point. I may

know more later. If I have something more definite, I'll give you a ring."

"Dear God." Baxter strode over to his wife and put a hand on her shoulder. "Please inform us of the results as soon as possible. If it is food poisoning we will need to take steps right away."

Cecily raised her hand to cover her husband's. "Mr. Armitage has taken all his meals in the dining room. If it is food poisoning, then the rest of my guests will be affected."

Kevin frowned. "Has anyone else complained of feeling ill?"

"Not as far as I know."

The doctor glanced at Baxter. "You have both taken the same meals as your guests?"

Baxter nodded. "I feel quite well." He squeezed Cecily's shoulder. "How about you, my dear?"

"Perfectly well, thank you." Cecily felt a glimmer of hope.

"That's a good sign." Kevin turned toward the door. "I've asked two of your footmen to assist me in removing the body. I'll ring you the minute I know more."

"Thank you, Kevin." Cecily accompanied him to the door. "We will see you in any case at the carol-singing ceremony, I believe?"

"Wouldn't miss it. Our nanny will be taking care of Angelina while we attend the evening. Madeline and I are looking forward to it. Where is she, by the way?"

"I believe Madeline is in the library. She wanted to add a few things to the Christmas tree."

"Then I shall look for her there." Cecily smiled as he gave her a quick salute, then closed the door behind him.

Baxter stood with his back to the fire again, watching her with a frown on his face. "What if it is food poisoning?"

"Then we have a lot more to worry about than Mr. Armitage's death."

Baxter let out a mournful sigh. "Just when I was beginning to hope we had escaped the curse this year."

Cecily joined him at the fire. "Cheer up, my love. At least we don't have to hunt for a murderer, and so far no one else appears to be ill, so let's hope that Kevin finds the answer and that it has nothing to do with food poisoning."

Baxter looked hopeful. "I suppose he could have eaten something else that didn't come from the kitchen."

Cecily sat down and reached for her needlework bag beside her chair. "I can't imagine what it would be. I don't think Mr. Armitage left the premises at all since he arrived late yesterday. I saw him in the building several times myself."

"Ah well, we shall know as soon as Prestwick rings. Then perhaps we can stop worrying about it."

Until then, Cecily thought, as she deftly threaded an embroidery needle, *she was going to worry a great deal*.

"Food poisoning?" Gertie almost dropped the tray of soup dishes she was holding. She put it down on the nearest table and glanced around the dining room to make sure they were alone. "Are you telling me that man died because of something he ate?"

Pansy nodded, her face white with fear. "I was passing by

madam's suite on my way to take Lady Bottingham a hot water bottle, and the door was open. I heard madam say something about food poisoning."

"Blimey." Gertie shook her head. "What do we do now? We're supposed to be serving dinner any minute now."

"I know. Mrs. Tucker just sent me up to ring the dinner bell."

"Does she know about the food poisoning?"

Pansy shivered, clutching her shoulders as if she were freezing. "I told her and Michel. I thought Michel was going to have a fit. He was shouting swear words in French and crashing his saucepans around, and Mrs. Tucker was yelling at him and at me. It was awful."

Seeing Pansy's eyes fill with tears, Gertie silently cursed the temporary housekeeper. "Well, never you mind, luv. It wasn't your fault the man died. That old bat had no right to yell at you. Go and ring the dinner bell, and we'll get everything served up, then we'll worry about what to do after that."

Pansy went on shivering. "What if the dinner's poisoned? It will be our fault if everyone drops dead. How are we going to know what's safe to eat?" She wiped her lips with the back of her hand. "I'm never going to eat another thing in this place. It's all *her* fault." She jerked her head at the dining room door. "I wish Mrs. Chubb hadn't gone away. She would never have let anyone be poisoned."

"Shshh!" Gertie put a finger to her lips. "We don't want everyone to know, do we. They'll be panicking and leave. Then we'd have no Christmas."

43

Pansy's voice rose to a wail. "How can we have a Christmas with everyone dying of food poisoning?"

Deciding that a firm tone was needed, Gertie sharpened her voice. "Pansy, shut your gob. We don't know that it was something from our kitchen what poisoned him. If it was then everyone would be dying by now, including you and me. I don't know about you, but I'm not dead yet, and you look lively enough."

Pansy hiccupped. "Yeah, I suppose. I'd better go and ring the dinner bell." She headed for the door, flinging words over her shoulder. "I'm still not eating nothing until I know for sure."

Gertie watched her go, her uneasiness growing. If it was something from the kitchen, how were they going to tell what it was? As far as she knew, all the guests had eaten the same food ever since they got to the club.

The sound of the dinner bell echoed down the hallway, and she took a quick look around to make sure all the tables were in order. Just then two maids hurried in, both carrying matches. One rushed around the tables lighting candles, while the other lit the oil burners underneath the warming dishes on the sideboard.

Pansy tore in a moment later, still looking as if she was ready to cry. "They're coming," she called out as she flew over to her station by the window.

Moments later the first guests walked through the door. Sir Reginald Minster and his wife were followed shortly after by Lady Winifred Bottingham. She wore a swirling pink feather in her hair, and her pink silk gown glittered with tiny sequins as she passed by the gaslights.

She was a striking-looking woman, with her red hair and slender figure. Staring at her, Gertie had to wonder again why the woman had never married. Lady Bottingham was a lot prettier than most of the women in the room. Certainly better looking than Lady Henrietta Minster, who was short and dumpy and clung to her husband's arm as if afraid to let go.

Pansy soon had everyone seated, and after that Gertie had no time to think about anything. Her head was too busy trying to keep up with removing empty dishes and replacing them with filled ones, seeing that everyone who wanted them had seconds, and making sure that no one waited too long for the next course.

When she finally had time to breathe, she took another good long look around the room. After a quick count she assured herself that everyone, with the exception of Mr. Armitage, was present and appeared to be quite healthy. So, it would seem that whatever had poisoned the actor, it probably hadn't come from the kitchen.

She was halfway across the room when she remembered something. Something so shocking, she stopped short with a sharp cry.

She hadn't realized anyone was behind her until the maid slammed into her back, sending her forward into the chair upon which Lady Henrietta Minster was seated.

The aristocrat was in the act of finishing her sherry. The

glass never reached her lips. Instead, the dark red liquid leapt down the front of Lady Henrietta's gown.

Hearing the shriek, Gertie thought at first that she was looking at another victim of the food poisoning. Until she saw the dismay on the woman's face, and the stain spreading across her bosom.

The maid who had bumped into Gertie was whimpering. "I'm so sorry. So dreadfully sorry. I didn't know Mrs. McBride was going to stop so quick and I just—"

Gertie turned to her. "It's all right, Maisie. I'll take care of this. It wasn't your fault."

Behind her, Lady Henrietta cried, "Just look at this! Whatever am I going to do?"

Turning back to the table, Gertie met the woman's accusing stare. "I'm awfully sorry, m'm. I'll have the laundry take care of your gown and I'll fetch you another glass of sherry."

"I don't *want* another glass of sherry!" Lady Henrietta's voice rose to a loud wail. "This is a Paris original! It's *silk*. You can't clean silk in a *laundry*!"

Gertie opened her mouth to offer another apology but before she could speak, Sir Reginald rose to his feet. Laying a moist palm on Gertie's shoulder, he leaned forward until his face was just a few inches from hers. "Please don't worry, m'dear. It was just an unfortunate accident, that's all." Still holding Gertie's shoulder tight enough to make her wince, he turned to his wife. "We really don't want to make a fuss." He lowered his voice to a distinct warning. "Do we, *dearest*."

His wife lowered her gaze to her lap. "No, of course not," she whispered.

"Then I suggest we retire to our suite where you can change into another gown."

"Yes, dear." Avoiding everyone's gaze, Lady Henrietta rose to her feet and scurried from the room, her husband close on her heels.

The minute the door closed behind them, the buzz of conversation resumed, and Pansy rushed over to her. "What happened? Whatever did you do to upset her like that?"

Gertie shook her head. "Never mind that now. I have to talk to madam right away. I'll be back as soon as I can." Before Pansy could protest, Gertie sped over to the door and out into the hallway.

"You're not eating your dinner," Cecily observed, giving her husband a stern look. "Are you not well?"

Seated at the small table in front of the fire, Baxter gazed down at his plate of roast duck, roasted potatoes, and carrots with a scowl of distaste. "I don't have much of an appetite."

Cecily sighed. Normally during the Christmas season they took their meals with the guests in the dining room. After the upset of Mr. Armitage's death, however, neither one of them had felt up to socializing, and had chosen instead to have dinner in their suite.

Still, Cecily felt guilty for abandoning her guests and was hoping to persuade Baxter to at least join them in the ballroom later. Judging from his morose expression, it seemed unlikely that he would agree.

She was about to attempt a plea when a sharp rapping on the door turned her head.

"Drat," Baxter said, pushing his plate aside. "Now what?"

Cecily raised her voice. "Come in!"

The door opened and Gertie charged into the room, barely dropping a curtsey before saying breathlessly, "I've got something I have to tell you, m'm."

Baxter grunted. "I suppose it's too much to ask that you address both of us before blurting out whatever it is you have to say?"

Gertie dipped her knees again. "Sorry, sir. Good evening, Mr. Baxter. You, too, m'm."

Cecily rolled her eyes. It was obvious Gertie had something important to say. Niceties could wait. "What is it, Gertie? Don't tell me someone else is ill?"

"No, m'm. Not that I know of, anyway."

Cecily's shoulders slumped in relief. Nothing could be worse than that. Could it? Eyeing her housemaid warily, she waited for her next words.

"It's Beatrice Tucker, m'm."

"Oh, good Lord." Baxter shoved his chair back. "Can't you settle these petty squabbles in the kitchen without barging in here and interrupting our meal? We've heard nothing but complaining and whining from everyone since that woman got here. It's Christmas for heaven's sake. Can't you get along for a few more days?"

Gertie squared her shoulders. "Begging your pardon, Mr. Baxter, but Mrs. Tucker is an overbearing, mean-mouthed old bat who finds fault with everything we say and do. It's bloody hard to get along with someone like that."

"Well, it's too late to get anyone else now, so you'll all just have to put up with her."

"Yes, sir. We're trying to do just that." Gertie turned back to Cecily. "I'm sorry to interrupt your dinner, m'm, but there's something you should know about Mrs. Tucker."

Ignoring her husband's growl of disgust, Cecily nodded at Gertie. "If it's something you can't handle, then you'd better tell me."

"Yes, m'm." Gertie sent Baxter a swift glance, then moved closer to Cecily. "It's about Mr. Armitage."

Cecily could tell from Baxter's expression that now he was all ears. Anxiety made her voice sharp when she said, "Go on, Gertie."

"Well, m'm, it's like this. Pansy happened to hear you mention food poisoning, and at first I thought it must have been something from the kitchen, but nobody else seemed to be ill so then I thought perhaps Mr. Armitage ate something that nobody else did."

"What in blazes does that have to do with Mrs. Tucker?" Baxter demanded.

"I'm coming to that, sir." Gertie cleared her throat. "It seems that Mrs. Tucker really liked Mr. Armitage. She went all the way to London just to see his plays. But when she met him here at the Pennyfoot, he was sort of nasty to her and it upset her."

Baxter started to say something but Cecily gave him a warning look and he shut his mouth.

"Anyway," Gertie went on, "right after that Mrs. Tucker sent up a slice of Christmas pudding to Mr. Armitage. Michel was really put out about it, and he said no one was to have any until Christmas Day, but Mrs. Tucker said it was her kitchen and she could do what she liked and that Mr. Armitage was famous and deserved special treatment and—"

Cecily hastily interrupted. "So you're saying that Mr. Armitage was the only person to eat some of the Christmas pudding?"

Gertie looked relieved. "Yes, m'm. That's exactly what I'm saying. It just seems strange to me that Mrs. Tucker could be cross with Mr. Armitage one minute and be sending him up special treats the next."

Baxter muttered something and turned to stare into the fire.

Ignoring him, Cecily smiled at the maid. "Very astute of you, Gertie. Thank you."

"Yes, m'm. Can I go back to the dining room now?"

"Yes, of course, and Gertie?"

The housemaid paused at the door. "Yes, m'm?"

"Not a word of this to anyone. Understand?"

"Yes, m'm. Of course." Again she dipped her knees, then shut the door quietly behind her.

"Not again," Baxter muttered. "Is she trying to tell us that woman deliberately poisoned Armitage? If so, then it's murder."

"Now let's not jump to conclusions." Cecily got up from her chair and joined him at the fire. "Mrs. Tucker didn't make the Christmas puddings. Michel made them. Though I hardly think he's capable of putting poison in them. Unless something got into the mixture accidentally. Maybe rat poison. I know Mrs. Chubb keeps a supply in the pantry. If so, then it's not murder at all, but simply a very unfortunate accident."

"Then we'd better get rid of the rest of the pudding, before someone does eat some of it. In fact, it would be a jolly good idea to get rid of all the puddings."

Cecily sighed. "I'll have Kevin test it first. Michel won't have time to make more and Christmas Day would be unthinkable without the puddings. We'd lose that whole tradition of carrying flaming puddings into the dining room. It's the grand finale to the entire meal."

Baxter grunted again. "What would you rather have? Flaming puddings or dead guests?"

"Well, when you put it like that."

"As I thought. Get rid of the puddings. I'll tell Mrs. Tucker myself." He started for the door.

"There's just one thing."

Pausing, he looked back at her. "What's that?"

"Well, let's suppose, just for instance, that Mrs. Tucker did put something in Mr. Armitage's pudding. How would we know unless Kevin tests it?"

"Good point."

"Then again, she could have simply put something in the slice she sent up to him."

He frowned. "I know she's a bit of a tyrant, but do you really think she's capable of murder?"

"Everyone is capable of murder." Cecily sat down on her armchair. "I've told you that before."

Baxter walked back toward her. "Yes, you have. I sincerely hope that this time you're wrong."

"About everyone being capable of murder?"

"About Mrs. Tucker. I was really looking forward to a nice peaceful Christmas for a change."

Cecily stared into the glowing coals in the fireplace. "I'm afraid, my love, that seems rather unlikely. The Christmas curse prevails."

Baxter raised his chin to stare at the ornate ceiling. "Damn the Christmas curse. One of these days it will be the end of the Pennyfoot Country Club."

Cecily held back a cry of dismay. "I hope and pray that you are wrong."

Baxter didn't answer but turned away with an expression on his face that worried her. It wasn't the first time her husband had indicated that the demise of the Pennyfoot would be a blessing in disguise. She was hanging on to her profession by a thin thread, and it wouldn't take much for Baxter to put his foot down once and for all and put an end to her association with the country club.

And that would be the biggest tragedy of all.

Gertie had barely put a foot inside the kitchen before Beatrice pounced on her. "What's this I hear about you spilling sherry all over Lady Henrietta's gown?"

Gertie slammed her tray of dirty dishes down on the counter so hard the knives leapt off the plates and bounced onto the floor. "Who told you that?" she demanded, ready to split open the head of whoever had told on her.

Beatrice folded her arms. "Never mind who told me. Just rest assured that the cost of a new gown will be deducted from your salary."

Scowling, Gertie scooped up the knives from the floor. "Well, you don't pay me. Madam does."

"So you think I should speak to madam about this?"

Gertie scowled. "Do what you want. It weren't my fault, anyway. I got pushed into the table by someone else. Besides, Sir Reginald was very nice about it. He said as how it were an accident and not to worry about it."

Beatrice turned away and started wiping down the kitchen table with a wet tea towel. "Well, it's more than you deserve. It's my opinion that you should pay for a new gown and I'm sure madam will agree with me. Lady Henrietta has had enough tragedy in her life. She doesn't need an upset like this."

"What does that bloody mean?"

"Nothing that's any of your business. But if you must know, the Minsters have suffered a dreadful tragedy at the hands of an unscrupulous scoundrel, and they have not yet recovered from it."

Gertie stared at her. "How do *you* know that?"

"Someone who knows them told me."

"Who?"

"Never you mind." As if realizing she'd said too much, Beatrice snapped, "Get busy with those dishes, young lady, or you'll be here all night."

Still smarting, Gertie fetched a cauldron from the stove and set it in the sink. Turning on the tap, she watched the water pouring into the huge container. Intrigued by the snippet of news she'd heard about the Minsters, she wondered who had told Beatrice about the aristocrats. She wouldn't have thought the housekeeper moved in those kinds of circles.

Then again, as housekeeper, she probably served in an aristocrat's house, where everyone downstairs gossiped about the upstairs crowd. Too bad the old crow was such a miserable old bugger. She probably had all sorts of juicy stories to tell.

Sighing, Gertie hauled the cauldron out of the sink and heaved it over to the stove. All she could hope was that Beatrice Tucker forgot about her paying for the gown. That would surely put an end to her Christmas shopping.

CHAPTER
4

The following morning Gertie was the first one to arrive in the kitchen. She'd been woken up earlier by her twins. Their excitement over the long-anticipated visit from Father Christmas had kept them from sleeping, and since they were all in the same room, Gertie had little choice but to wake up with them.

After getting them settled with Daisy, their nanny, Gertie decided to get a head start. She was anxious to find out what was going to happen to the old bat now that she'd told madam about the Christmas puddings.

In spite of the numerous pots and pans hanging on the walls, the kitchen looked bare when she walked into it, in stark contrast to the rest of the country club. Madeline

Prestwick had been lavish with the decorations, as always, but the downstairs part of the Pennyfoot was left to the staff to decorate.

The maids had hung paper chains along the hallway and dangled mistletoe at either end, no doubt hoping for a quick smooch from one of the footmen. Gertie was way past such hanky-panky, though she wouldn't mind meeting Clive under a bunch of mistletoe.

Quickly curbing the treacherous thought, she looked around the kitchen. Someone had put some sprigs of holly tied with red ribbon on the shelf above the ovens. On either side of the holly, a red candle nestled in a silver candlestick, while a paper angel graced each end of the shelf.

Gertie smiled, wondering who had taken the time to do all that. It couldn't have been Tucker the Terrible, she wouldn't have wasted her time that way. It must have been one of the maids.

Walking over to the sink, she saw a tray of cups and saucers waiting to be washed and dried. She reached under the sink for the heavy cauldron and set it under the tap. After filling it with water, she hauled it over to the stove. The ashes in the boiler still glowed red, and she added coals a few at a time until they began to smolder and burn.

By the time she'd brought the butter out of the pantry to soften it, folded all the serviettes and polished all the silverware, the water was hot enough to wash the dishes.

Gertie filled the sink, added soap, and then plunged the china into the hot water. The old bat would be surprised to see everything done, she thought, smiling to herself at the vision of Beatrice Tucker thanking her profusely for getting off to such a good start in the morning.

Fat bloody chance of that. The miserable cow would probably look for something she'd done wrong, like not polishing a fork properly, or leaving a corner sticking out from a serviette.

Her grin fading, she swished a teacup around in the soapy water and ran a dishcloth around the rim. If there was one thing she found hard to do, it was keep a secret. Especially one as juicy as the one she was bursting to tell Pansy. What if Tucker the Terrible had murdered Mr. Armitage? They'd take her away, of course. Then they'd have peace and quiet in the kitchen again.

If she could be sure Pansy would keep her mouth shut, she'd tell her. But chances were Pansy would go blabbing to Samuel, and before you knew it, the secret would be all over the Pennyfoot. No, better keep quiet about it, rather than risk upsetting madam.

Annoyed with herself for dwelling on it, she concentrated on thinking about something else. What to get Clive for Christmas. He'd already told her he was making something for the twins this year. Every year he made them something different, each better than the last. One year it was a tree house. Last year a rocking horse. She couldn't wait to see what he had in store for them this year.

How the twins loved Clive. He was so good to them, too. Gertie sighed as she stood the dripping teacup on the draining board and reached for another one. If only she could sort out her feelings for him. One way or another. It was this going back and forth that bothered her so much. When she was with him all she could think about was how happy she was in his company. Then, when she wasn't with him, all the doubts came flooding back.

The sound of the kitchen door opening cut off her thoughts. Michel sailed across the kitchen with a jaunty wave of his hand. "Bonjour, mon ami!"

Gertie gave him a wary look. One never knew what kind of mood Michel would be in from one minute to the next. Most of the time, he took a delight in insulting everyone, though he kept insisting he was merely joking.

Once in a while he'd disappear into the pantry and everyone knew he was at the brandy bottle again. You could always tell when Michel was drunk. He'd lose his French accent and start talking Cockney, which was the accent he'd grown up with in the first place.

The guests all thought he was French, and madam preferred to keep it that way, though she would never actually lie about it. If anyone asked her, she'd be deliberately vague about how he came to be working for her at the Pennyfoot.

Only Gertie and Mrs. Chubb knew that she gave Michel the job after he came out of prison. He'd spent eight years in there for burning down a gentleman's club after he'd been thrown out because he didn't talk and dress proper. Lucky for him he didn't kill anyone, or he'd still be there.

Right now, Michel seemed to be in a good mood for once. He was humming to himself as he whisked pots and bowls out of the cupboard. The humming soon stopped when Beatrice Tucker shoved the door open.

Gertie could feel all the muscles in her back go tight when the housekeeper snapped, "Where's Pansy? She should be in here by now."

"I'm right here, Mrs. Tucker." Pansy appeared in the doorway, a nervous smile plastered on her face.

"Get to work. You're late." Beatrice headed for the pantry. "And Gertie, the boiler needs more coals." She disappeared inside the tiny room and shut the door firmly behind her.

Michel scowled at the pantry door and slammed a lid down on a saucepan. "Bonjour to you, too," he muttered.

"I already put the bleeding coals in the flipping boiler." Gertie thumbed her nose at the pantry door.

Pansy rolled her eyes. "Looks like another fun-filled day in the kitchen to look forward to."

"Yeah, well, maybe not for much longer." Gertie clenched her teeth as soon as the words were out of her mouth.

"What do you mean?" Pansy walked over to join her at the sink, a dish towel in her hand. Reaching for one of the cups, she added, "Is something bad going to happen?"

Cursing herself for the slip of her tongue, Gertie shrugged. "Not that I know of."

"Then what did you mean?"

She might have known Pansy wouldn't let it go. She was still trying to think of an answer when Michel unexpectedly came to her rescue.

"She means that as long as that *cochon* is in charge, we have no fun at all, *non?*"

Gertie sent him a grateful smile. *"Oui."*

Pansy raised her eyebrows. "Hark at you, talking French now."

Gertie was about to answer when Beatrice stormed out of the pantry. "What happened to the butter? I distinctly remember putting it on the back shelf in the pantry and now it's gone."

"I brought it out to soften it for you," Gertie said, wishing now she hadn't bothered.

"Well, you might have said. I wasted all those minutes looking for it." Beatrice marched across the kitchen to the table and picked up the butter dish.

"If you'd used your bloody eyes you would have seen it," Gertie muttered under her breath.

Standing close by her side, Pansy giggled.

"What did you say?" Beatrice's voice cut across the kitchen like a blast of hail.

"She said she brought the butter out to help you," Pansy said, earning a look of gratitude from her friend.

Beatrice grunted. "Well, next time, tell me. Oh, and Michel, you'll have to make more Christmas puddings."

Gertie's hands stilled in the water. Behind her, she could almost feel Michel's temper rising.

"I do *what?*" The chef sounded dangerously quiet.

"You'll have to make more Christmas puddings. I burned the other ones in the stove."

"You burn *my* puddings in ze stove?"

Gertie nudged Pansy and turned around to enjoy the show.

"Yes, I did. It occurred to me that Mr. Armitage might have been poisoned by something in the pudding I sent up to him. I thought it prudent to destroy all of them and make new ones."

Michel brought the saucepan he was holding down hard on the stove, sending a splintering crash across the room. His voice gradually rose, getting louder and louder until he was practically screaming. "*I* make the puddings! Me, Michel the chef! There is no poison in my puddings. You burned fifteen *perfect* Christmas puddings." He paused for breath, then added in a dangerously quiet tone, "I hope you took out ze silver thrupenny bits before you destroyed my puddings."

Beatrice tossed her head. "Of course I did. I'm not stupid. Though if you ask me, it could have been the thrupenny bits that poisoned Mr. Armitage. I never did think that tradition was very hygienic."

"My thrupenny bits," Michel said, emphasizing each word, "are as clean as your boiled tea towels. Cleaner. I do not make more puddings! If you want more puddings, then you bloody well make them yourself!"

This last was delivered with a strong Cockney accent that obviously took Beatrice by surprise. Her jaw dropped as she watched Michel stalk across the kitchen, flinging his hat to the floor before he disappeared through the door.

"Now you've bloody gone and done it," Gertie observed.

Pansy stood with her hand over her mouth, her eyes bright with subdued excitement.

Beatrice sent them both a look of pure contempt. "Mind your own business and get back to work," she snarled, then dashed out the door in hot pursuit of the angry chef.

"Where do you think Michel is going?" Pansy picked up another cup and started drying it with the dishcloth.

Gertie shrugged. "Probably going to complain to madam. I hope for his sake Mr. Baxter's not there. He's a bit liverish when it comes to complaints."

Pansy shook her head. "Why would Mrs. Tucker burn all those puddings? Do you really think they were poisonous?"

"I don't know. I—"

She broke off as the door opened and Dr. Prestwick walked in. He stood just inside the door, looking around as if he expected to see more people in there.

Gertie pulled her hands out of the water and dried them on her apron. She really liked Dr. Prestwick. Not only was he easy on the eyes, with his fair curly hair and roguish smile, but he was a real gentleman. Always treated her as if she were just as good as any of the posh ladies that crowded his surgery every week. And everyone knew that most of those ladies were there with pretend ailments, just so's they could be in the doctor's company once in a while.

The whole village had been shocked when the good doctor had married Madeline Pengrath. There wasn't anyone in Badgers End who didn't know that Madeline had special powers. She used her herbs and flowers to cure everything from the sniffles to the gout, and Gertie knew at least a dozen gentlemen had gone to Madeline to help them with their marriage problems.

It had just seemed strange to people that Dr. Prestwick, a man of science and medicine, would marry a witch, even if she was the most beautiful and kindest person you'd ever want to meet.

Gertie smiled at the doctor as she hurried toward him. "Is there something I can help you with, Doctor?"

Kevin Prestwick looked a bit anxious when he turned to her. "Actually, I was looking for Mrs. Tucker. Mrs. Baxter sent me down here to take a look at the Christmas puddings." His expression changed, as if he was aware he'd said too much.

Gertie knew why he was there, but aware of Pansy hovering at the sink, couldn't tell him what she knew. "Oh, I'm sorry, Doctor." She cleared her throat. "I'm afraid the puddings have gorn."

Kevin stared at her, his eyebrows arched in surprise. "Gone?"

"Gorn, sir. Bloody burned in the boiler, they were. Mrs. Tucker got rid of them." She stared hard at him, willing him to read her mind. It was her strong opinion that the housekeeper had burned the puddings to get rid of the evidence. There was no doubt in her mind that the old bat had poisoned one of them and had disposed of the others to make it look like there was something wrong with all the puddings.

Kevin stared back at her for a moment longer, then murmured, "Why would she do that?"

"Why, indeed, sir," Gertie agreed with relish.

Pansy piped up from the sink. "She thought there might be something in them what poisoned Mr. Armitage."

"Did she now." Kevin seemed to think about that for a moment, then with a nod, he twisted around and headed out the door.

Pansy stood staring at the door, her face creased in a frown. "What was all that about?"

Gertie wandered back to the sink and dipped her hands once more into the gray water. "How should I blooming know?"

"Why would Dr. Prestwick want to look at the puddings . . . oh!" Pansy dropped the saucer she was drying, and it clattered noisily on the counter, though luckily it didn't break. Her voice was hushed when she added fearfully, "They think Mrs. Tucker poisoned Mr. Armitage on *purpose?*"

"Shshh!!!" Gertie threw a glance at the door. "We're not supposed to say anything about it."

Pansy's eyes widened. "Crumbs, we'd better be really, really careful what we say to her. If we upset her she could poison us, too."

"Will you be bleeding quiet!" Gertie gave her a stern look. "If this gets out madam will think I blinking told everyone and then I'll be in trouble."

"All right, I won't say nothing." Pansy picked up the saucer she'd dropped and examined it for cracks.

"Not even Samuel."

Pansy swung around, her eyes wide. "But we should warn him about Mrs. Tucker. She might poison him, too."

Gertie stared at her. "Why would she want to poison Samuel?"

"I dunno, but when I went into the stables to see Samuel the other day, Mrs. Tucker was in there talking to Gilbert Tubbs, and when she saw me she asked me where Samuel was and she sounded really angry."

Gertie rolled her eyes. "That doesn't mean she wants to bleeding kill him, twerp. She sounds angry all the time."

"But—"

Gertie crossed her arms. "You don't say nothing about this to *nobody*. Not even Samuel. Got it?"

Pansy sighed. "All right. Not even Samuel."

"Promise?"

"Yes, I promise."

"Swear on your mother's grave."

Pansy looked mournful. "I don't have no mother."

"You did sometime. Somewhere."

"How do I know she's in a grave?"

"Why else would you end up in an orphanage?"

Pansy stared hard at the saucer. "I don't know."

Sorry she'd brought up the subject, Gertie put an arm around her. "Never mind, luv. You've got me, and madam, and Mrs. Chubb. We're your family now."

Pansy managed a wobbly smile. "Yeah. The best family I could have, too."

The door swung open just then and Beatrice swept in, her face red and her eyes blazing. "Are you two still here? You should have been up in the dining room ages ago. I thought I told you to put more coals in the stove. What's the matter with you? Are you deaf or just stupid?"

Gertie turned, her mouth already forming the torrent of words to fling at the housekeeper. Just in time, she caught sight of Pansy's expression. Her friend looked terrified. It occurred to Gertie then that it might be better not to get the old bat riled up at her. Pansy was right. Tucker the Terrible might be tempted to put poison in everyone's tea.

Instead, she wiped her hands on her apron and went over to the coal scuttle. It was half-empty, and she chucked the rest of the coals into the stove and closed the door. "I'd better go and fill up the scuttle before I go upstairs," she said, and before the housekeeper could answer, Gertie was out the door and charging across the yard to the coal shed.

She had almost reached it when a deep voice called out her name. Turning, she saw Clive striding toward her, the wind ruffling his black hair. As always when she first caught sight of him, she felt a flutter of excitement deep in her stomach.

Clive wasn't handsome, like Dr. Prestwick, but he had a kind face with dark eyes that always made her feel warm inside when he looked at her. She always forgot how big and brawny he was until he was standing over her and reminded her all over again. She liked that she had to look up at him. She wasn't used to that. It made her feel protected and safe when she was with him.

He was smiling as he stopped in front of her. "Good morning, Gertie." He reached out and smoothed back a stray strand of her hair. "How are you this fine morning?"

She smiled back at him. "Better now that I've seen you."

His grin widened. "Seeing you always makes my day brighter." He bent over and took the coal scuttle out of her hand. "Here, I'll fill this for you."

"Thanks!" She watched him open the shed door and step inside, wondering if he knew that one of her least favorite jobs was filling the scuttle. Something about walking into that dark, smelly, dusty hole always gave her the creeps.

Probably because she'd once found a maid buried among the lumps of coal. Every time she shoveled the gleaming black lumps into the metal container she thought about the moment she'd spotted the maid's shoe and realized it was attached to the foot of a dead body. She'd fainted dead away, and it had been weeks before the nightmares had stopped.

Even watching Clive shovel the coal made her all shivery inside. She was glad when he'd filled the scuttle and stepped outside again into the cold, fresh air.

She held out her hand to take the scuttle from him, but he shook his head. "I'll carry it back to the kitchen for you."

If it had been anyone else, she would have grabbed it from him, insisting she was quite capable of carrying it herself. After all, there were women out there giving up their lives for women's rights and independence, and she fully supported their struggles.

It was time men realized that women were human beings, not slaves to their every whim. Women were quite capable of making decisions, changing lives and even ruling countries. All they needed was the chance to prove themselves, but men were too afraid to let them because deep down they knew they would lose their power over them.

With Clive it was different, somehow. It felt good to have him do things for her. She tripped alongside him, forgetting all her worries about food poisoning and Tucker the Terrible. It was enough to have these few minutes by the side of the man she loved.

The man she loved.

The truth hit her like a bolt of lightning. She stopped, stunned by the realization and terrified by its consequences. She had fought against this very thing for so long, determined not to risk her heart again. After all she'd been through, how could she have let this happen? What the blue blazes was the matter with her, that she had let herself fall into yet another trap?

Furious with herself, she snatched the handle of the scuttle and dragged it out of Clive's hand. "I'll take this. You've got work to do." She couldn't look at his face, for fear of what she might see there. Keeping her head down, she charged across the yard and through the kitchen door.

Beatrice looked up as Gertie barreled across the kitchen, barely stopping to drop the scuttle in front of the stove before barging through the opposite door and out into the hallway. She didn't stop running until she was at the door of the dining room. By then she was out of breath and had to hold onto the door while she got it back.

Pansy was laying tables, and looked up as Gertie stumbled into the room. "Whatever's the matter?" She dropped the spoons on the table and hurried over to her. "Are you ill?"

"Yeah, I am." Still gulping in air, Gertie leaned one hand on the nearest table. "Sick in the head, that's me."

Pansy frowned. "What are you talking about?"

"Never mind." Gathering the last of her wits, Gertie picked up a handful of silverware. "Let's get these tables laid before the old bat comes screaming after us."

"But—"

Gertie raised her hand. "I'm all right, Pansy. Just out of breath, that's all."

Pansy stared hard at her. "You don't look all right. You're all white and shivering. You must be catching a cold."

"Yeah, that's what it is." Gertie somehow summoned up a grin. "You'd better stay away from me if you don't want to catch it."

Pansy backed off, though she still looked unconvinced.

Gertie turned her back on her and started laying out the place settings. Thank the Lord for work. She needed to keep her mind off what she'd just discovered. She needed to see her twins, to remind her why falling in love with Clive Russell was absolutely the worst mistake she could ever make. She needed to remember how she felt when she found out that Ian was married, or when Ross died, or when Dan told her he was moving back to London without her.

She needed to fall out of love with Clive Russell, and the sooner the better.

CHAPTER
❀ 5 ❀

Cecily was in her office when Kevin Prestwick called on her. She had barely got a greeting out before he informed her that Beatrice Tucker had destroyed every one of the Christmas puddings.

Her first thought was utter dismay that now there would be no flaming puddings to carry into the dining room. Her second thought was that the housekeeper had something to hide.

"It means, of course," Kevin said, pacing back and forth in front of her desk, "that we have no way of pinning down the source of the poison."

Grasping at straws, she murmured, "Of course, it might

not have been the pudding that killed Mr. Armitage. It could have been something else. Perhaps the pork, though the butcher is always so careful to see that it's properly cured. Besides, I ate it myself and since no one else appears to have taken ill, I don't—"

"Cecily." Kevin stopped pacing and placed both his hands on the desk. Leaning forward he said quietly, "Armitage died from an ingestion of an arsenide compound. Commonly used in rat poison."

"Oh, my." Cecily clutched her throat. "Mrs. Chubb always keeps a supply of rat poison in the pantry. Do you think some of it could have fallen into the pudding mixture? I can't imagine that Michel would be so careless. Then again, he takes a sip now and then from the brandy bottle and—"

Once more Kevin interrupted her. "The amount it would take to kill a person that quickly would not have been there accidentally. Either Armitage had been ingesting arsenic over a period of time and it finally caught up with him, or someone put a heavy dose of the stuff into something he ate. Either way, these are very definitely suspicious circumstances."

So there it was. Much as she'd tried to suppress it, ever since she'd first heard of the death, she'd had the feeling that Archibald Armitage had been murdered. Now it was confirmed, and it was possible that her temporary housekeeper had killed him.

"Is there any way to determine whether or not the dose was administered here in the Pennyfoot?"

Kevin shrugged. "Not without evidence of the source."

"So we have no way of knowing if someone here in the

club killed him, or if someone he knew elsewhere had been poisoning him."

"Precisely. I'm sorry, Cecily. I'll ring the constabulary for you. I expect P.C. Northcott will pay you a visit this afternoon."

"No doubt." Cecily sighed. "I'll make sure no one touches anything in the room until Sam Northcott has looked at it."

"Good idea." Kevin headed for the door. "Though if the poison was in that slice of pudding and the rest of them have been destroyed, I don't know how the constable is going to prove anything." He paused and looked back at her. "Be careful, Cecily. It's possible you have a killer in the Pennyfoot. Again."

She smiled wearily at him. "Thank you, Kevin."

He gazed at her for a moment longer, then with a sharp nod of his head, disappeared out the door.

With a heavy heart, Cecily reached for the bellpull and gave it a tug. Another Christmas marred by a violent death. Much as she disliked the temporary housekeeper, she couldn't bring herself to believe that the woman had actually murdered one of the guests.

If Armitage had been poisoned here, maybe Mrs. Tucker had simply wanted to make him sick, in retaliation for his rudeness. Though even that seemed somewhat harsh treatment for such a feeble crime. Having been in service for most of her life, Beatrice Tucker should be well used to rudeness and insults from her superiors. No matter what Mr. Armitage had said to her, he surely didn't deserve such an agonizing end.

Her thoughts were interrupted by a tap on the door. Pulling herself together, Cecily cleared her brow. "Come in!"

Pansy tiptoed into the room and bent her knees in a curtsey. "You rang, m'm?"

"Yes, Pansy. I need you to tell Mrs. Tucker that under no circumstances is anyone to enter Mr. Armitage's room until I say so."

Pansy drew her brows together. "Yes, m'm. I already cleaned it up, though, if that's what you're worried about."

Cecily brushed her fingers across her forehead. "You did what?"

"I cleaned it up, m'm. It were awful, to tell the truth. I kept heaving all the time I was cleaning."

"Did you bring anything out of the room?"

"Yes, m'm. I did." She raised her chin and stared at the ceiling, frowning in concentration. "Now let me see. There were newspapers, an empty cigar box, a whiskey bottle and a glass and some books. I left all his clothes and personal things in there, though. Mrs. Tucker said we had to wait and see what you wanted to do about them. Oh, and there was the slice of Christmas pudding that Mrs. Tucker sent up to Mr. Armitage. I s'pose he never had a chance to eat it before he got ill."

Cecily raised her eyebrows. "The whole slice?"

"Yes, m'm. He hadn't had one bite of it."

Thinking hard, Cecily tapped her fingers on her desk. "What did you do with the things you brought out?"

"Mrs. Tucker told me to put everything into a pillowcase

and bring it down to the kitchen. She said the things might be com . . . cotimate . . . contimate—"

"Contaminated." Cecily frowned. "What did she do with them?"

"I think she put them out in the yard, m'm. She said she'd ask you what to do with them later."

"Very well. I want you to put everything in the coal shed for now, out of the rain. I'll see to them later."

"Yes, m'm." Pansy curtsied and backed up to the door. "Will that be all, m'm?"

"Yes, Pansy. Thank you." Cecily waved her off and stared at the telephone. With any luck Kevin would have gone straight back to his surgery. She might be able to talk to him within the hour. Right now, she needed to think.

Apparently the Christmas pudding was not the culprit in the death of Archibald Armitage. Therefore it could be that the housekeeper was not directly to blame for his death, after all. Perhaps the gentleman had been ingesting the poison for some time before he came to the Pennyfoot, as Kevin had suggested. That was quite a relief, though she would feel a great deal better if she could be certain of that. All she could do was wait for Kevin to examine the contents of Mr. Armitage's room and hope fervently that the good doctor could give her some answers.

"Not the Christmas pudding?" Standing at the kitchen sink, Gertie stared at Pansy. "Are you sure?"

Pansy nodded. "I brought down the pudding myself. It's in a pillowcase in the coal shed, along with everything else. Except Mr. Armitage's clothes and things. Mrs. Tucker said as how to leave them there."

Gertie felt a stab of disappointment. She'd had high hopes that the housekeeper would be found guilty of murder and sent to prison, thus freeing them all from the woman's bad temper and allowing them to enjoy the Christmas season.

Reluctant to give up the idea, she murmured, "Well, the old bat could still have poisoned him with something else."

"Well, I don't know what. He ate what everyone else ate."

"We don't know that." Hearing the squeak of the kitchen door, she hastily grabbed a platter and started drying it. Lowering her voice, she muttered, "Maybe Tucker the Terrible sent him up something else to eat."

"Well, if she did and he ate it, we'll never know, will we."

Gertie pursed her lips. "Maybe we can trick her into admitting she did it."

"How are we going to do that?"

Gertie shrugged. "I dunno. But I'll think of something."

"You two stop nattering and get on with those dishes!" The housekeeper's strident voice made them both jump.

Gertie turned around to face her. "We was just talking about the bloke what died," she said. "What do you think killed him? Could it be something from this kitchen what poisoned him?"

"Of course not!" The housekeeper jerked her hand, dropping the rolling pin she was holding. It clattered onto the floor, then rolled over to Gertie's feet.

She bent over to pick it up and offered it back to Beatrice.

The housekeeper's eyes glinted with temper. "Wash that thoroughly and put it back where it belongs. And if I hear any more gossip about Mr. Armitage's death, I'll report you both to madam. Is that clear?"

Gertie rolled her eyes and dumped the rolling pin into the soapy water in the sink. Too bad the old bat hadn't poisoned the actor. Now they would have to continue to put up with her over Christmas.

She couldn't wait for Mrs. Chubb to come back from seeing her daughter. If Tucker the Terrible didn't shut up screaming at them, Gertie thought fiercely, she might be tempted to put poison in the miserable cow's tea herself.

When Phoebe arrived early that afternoon for the dress rehearsal, Cecily ushered everyone into the ballroom as fast as she could manage. The last thing she wanted was for Phoebe or the members of her dance troupe to find out about the death and start speculating. Word would spread quickly throughout the Pennyfoot and, before she knew it, she'd have guests abandoning Christmas at the club.

Phoebe seemed surprised and a little put out by Cecily's haste to get rid of her. "Do you have an urgent appointment or something?" she asked, as Cecily closed the doors of the ballroom behind the last dancer.

"I have many urgent appointments." Aware that she was being somewhat rude to her friend, Cecily forced a smile. "There is always so much to do this time of year."

"Ah yes." Phoebe watched her dancers wander onto the stage and shook her head. "Look at them. I don't know how many times I've told them this is a dress rehearsal." She raised her voice and yelled at the stage. "That means *costumes*, you imbeciles! You are all supposed to be in full costume. Get backstage and *dress*! I want everyone back here, in full costume, in five minutes. Anyone who is later than that will not be performing tomorrow night. Is that clear?"

A weak and ragged chorus of, "Yes, Mrs. Fortescue," wafted down from the stage. One by one the dancers trudged off behind the curtains and disappeared.

Phoebe shook her head, making the peacock feathers in her hat dance about. "Those girls will be the death of me." She turned back to Cecily. "Speaking of death, I heard that one of your guests died in his room yesterday. That must have been a dreadful shock. He was a famous actor, wasn't he? How dreadful. I suppose the news will be in all the newspapers. Those news reporters seem to ferret out these things when it pertains to a famous person."

Cecily's dismay quickly turned to annoyance. "Who told you about it?"

Phoebe patted her arm. "My dear, please don't worry. I shan't say anything, of course. It wouldn't do for these girls to find out someone died right here in the Pennyfoot. You know how superstitious those silly girls can be. Why, I'd never get them back in here."

With an effort Cecily curbed her irritation. "I'm quite sure I can rely on your discretion, Phoebe. I would, however, appreciate knowing who it was told you about Mr. Armit-age's death."

Phoebe looked offended. "It was Madeline, of course. Freddie and I happened to bump into her on our way out. Freddie very kindly offered her a ride in our carriage, since it was raining and she usually walks all the way home. She said that Kevin would take her home and that he was here attending to Mr. Armitage, who had died in his room. I'm sure she didn't realize that it was supposed to be such a deep dark secret from me."

Cecily was quick to make amends. "Of course not," she said, tucking her arm in Phoebe's. "I just wondered who else knew besides us. After all, news of a death in the house isn't exactly conducive for Christmas cheer."

"Indeed it is not." Apparently mollified, Phoebe squared her shoulders. "It's sad, of course, passing away right at Christmastime. It seems so much more tragic, somehow. Though from what I understand, Mr. Armitage was not a very nice person. Why, I heard him myself arguing with one of your guests. Not to speak ill of the dead, but he was quite belligerent, and his language was disgusting."

Cecily raised her eyebrows. "I wasn't aware that you were acquainted with Mr. Armitage."

"Well, not personally, of course, but I certainly recognized him when I saw him. His picture was in the newspaper, together with an article that mentioned he would be spend-ing Christmas at the Pennyfoot. I'm surprised you didn't see it."

Taken aback, Cecily took a moment to answer. "I don't have time to read the newspaper, though Baxter reads it. I'm surprised he didn't mention it to me."

"Probably because he knows you would be upset." Phoebe tilted her head to one side, causing the wide brim of her hat to bounce off her shoulder. "You usually like to keep the identity of your famous guests a secret."

Sensing she was still a little peeved, Cecily smiled. "Only to the general public, Phoebe, dear. It's one of our policies, to protect our guests from unwanted intrusions." Her smile faded. "You said that Mr. Armitage was arguing with one of our guests. Do you happen know who that was?"

Phoebe frowned. "Well, I don't know his name, but he was quite a portly gentleman, with gray hair and a luxuriant mustache. His wife interrupted the argument, and I do believe he called her Henrietta."

"Ah." Cecily nodded. "That would be Sir Reginald Minster and his wife. I don't suppose you have any idea what they were arguing about?"

Phoebe made a big production of brushing imaginary specks from her skirt. "As a matter of fact, I do. I came upon the gentlemen in the lobby, and rather than pass by them while they were engaged in such a violent confrontation, I hid behind the Christmas tree until they had left."

Cecily was about to speak when a voice from the stage interrupted her. "Mrs. Fortescue? Ada can't find her head-dress. She says someone stole it."

"Nonsense." Phoebe glared up at the young woman. "Tell

her to look for it. Remind her she has to move things to find things. I'll be there in a minute and I expect everyone to be dressed and ready."

"Yes, Mrs. Fortescue." The woman turned to go, hesitated, glanced back at Phoebe, then with a shrug of her shoulders, disappeared behind the curtains.

"Such utter ninnies." Phoebe shook her head, dislodged her hat, and straightened it with a tug from both hands.

Curbing her impatience, Cecily tried again. "I'd really like to know what the argument was about, Phoebe."

Phoebe widened her eyes. "You're not usually one for gossip, Cecily. You surprise me."

Cecily gritted her teeth. "It's important."

Phoebe looked even more nonplussed. "I really don't . . . oh!" She slapped her gloved hand over her mouth. From behind it she mumbled, "Don't tell me Mr. Armitage was *murdered*?"

Cecily silently cursed her lack of caution. It didn't happen often, but once in a while, Phoebe could be quite perceptive. "I didn't say that. I merely asked what the argument was about."

Looking shaken, Phoebe stared down at the toes of her boots peeking out from under her skirt. "Well, er . . . I wouldn't normally repeat such things, but since you seem so intent on knowing, I suppose I could make an exception."

Hanging onto her patience by a mere thread, Cecily muttered, "Please do. Preferably before we are interrupted again."

"Oh, of course." Phoebe looked over her shoulder. "Well,

it was rather a delicate matter, which is why I hesitate to reveal it. It concerned the gentleman's daughter, from what I heard."

"You mean Sir Reginald's daughter?"

"Yes." Phoebe's cheeks turned a delicate shade of pink. "I really don't like discussing such things, but from what I heard"—once more she glanced over her shoulder—"the gentleman's daughter was . . . ah . . . compromised . . . by the actor and died giving birth to his child."

Cecily drew in a sharp breath. "How awful. Sir Reginald and his wife must have been devastated."

"I imagine they were. I can quite see why the gentleman was so infuriated with Mr. Armitage."

"Yes," Cecily murmured. "So can I."

Phoebe's eyes widened. "You don't think he—"

"I don't think anything of the sort," Cecily said, forestalling the rest of Phoebe's sentence. "I'm sure Mr. Armitage's death was due to an unfortunate accident." She curled her fingers into her palm and prayed that was so.

Phoebe looked as if she would argue, then she shook her head. "Yes, well, if you say so. I suppose I should go backstage and see what those silly girls are doing. They can be so destructive when they're not supervised."

Cecily had to hide a smile. Phoebe treated her dance troupe as if they were small children instead of grown adults. Though perhaps, she amended as she left the ballroom, calling them adults was possibly giving them more credit than they deserved. They delighted in tormenting Phoebe, and thanks to their considerable lack of talent, her presentations on the stage more often than not ended in disaster.

Thinking of disaster brought her back to the subject of Archibald Armitage's death. The moment she arrived back in her office she rang Dr. Prestwick, and was vastly relieved when he answered.

"The poison wasn't in the Christmas pudding," she said, in answer to his greeting. "One of my maids found it untouched in Mr. Armitage's room."

"Then we can rule that out." Kevin sounded relieved. "We shall have to look elsewhere for the source of the poison."

"Everything that Pansy took out of the room has been put into the coal shed." She paused, then added, "Could you possibly come back this afternoon and take a look? I'd like to have some answers for P.C. Northcott when he gets here."

"Of course. I can be there in about an hour."

"Thank you, Kevin. If we can eliminate as the source everything that was in the room, and seeing that no one else has taken ill, we should be able to assume that Mr. Armitage was poisoned elsewhere, should we not?"

"I should think so, though you never know with Northcott. He can be quite obtuse at times."

Cecily sighed. "Well, he should be on the brink of leaving for his annual Christmas visit to his wife's relatives. If that's so, he'll be in a hurry to settle this and more likely to accept what to me would be a logical conclusion."

Kevin laughed. "I've yet to see the day that Northcott is logical in any shape or form, but one can always live in hope."

Cecily replaced the receiver with cautious hope. If all went well, this whole dreadful business could be behind them by the evening, and she could then concentrate on providing the best Christmas season yet for her guests. If that were so, it would indeed be a blessing.

Gertie peered at the dusty bottles lined up along the shelves, trying to read the labels. She'd never liked coming down to the wine cellar. It was too dark, too cold, and had too many spiders and other nasty stuff crawling around.

The cellar had no gas lamps to light the way. In order to see, she had to light the oil lamp that hung by the entrance, and with a basket in one hand and the lamp in the other, creep down the steps to the cellar below. The smell reminded her of rotting apples and something else she didn't want to think about.

The room wasn't that big, and it was crammed with shelves from end to end. She had to walk down the aisles, looking for a dozen or so bottles of wine that Barry Collins, the publican, had ordered for the bar. As she walked, the lamp swung in her hand, sending weird shadows dancing all over the place.

She kept thinking that someone was down there with her. Someone who wasn't supposed to be. Maybe even the some-one who had murdered Archibald Armitage in his bed. The thought gave her sharp stabs of panic, and she had to fight the urge to turn and race up the steps to the daylight.

Once, not so long ago, she'd been trapped down there with a killer. She'd managed to get away from him, but the memory was as sharp in her mind as if it had happened yesterday. Ever since then, she had the creeps every time she had to go down there.

Mrs. Chubb understood that and did her best to avoid having to ask Gertie to go down in the cellar. Tucker the Terrible, of course, wouldn't listen when Gertie had suggested that Pansy get the wine. Oh, no. She ordered Gertie to go down there, and now here she was, standing in the dreaded stuffy room, trying to read the dusty labels.

Farther down a narrow corridor lay empty rooms. They'd once housed the card games that the toffs had so enjoyed, and which had been illegal all the time the Pennyfoot was a mere hotel. There was once a secret trapdoor to the rooms, but when the hotel was turned into a country club, making it legal to gamble, madam had closed off the rooms and a new floor had been laid over the trapdoor.

Now the only way to the rooms was down the corridor, and that was somewhere Gertie would never venture. The passageways had once been used by pirates smuggling everything from spirits to perfume from Europe. They led under the building all the way to the ocean. Rats had now taken up residence, and heaven knew what else. Odd sounds echoed down the corridor now and then, making Gertie jump in fright. It would take a matter of life and death for her to go down those passageways now.

She tried not to look at the entrance to them as she turned the corner of a row of shelves and started up the other side. As she did so, a large shadow seemed to move across the other end. Her heart seemed to leap right up into her throat as she stared at the far wall, blinking hard to clear her vision.

It was too dark to see clearly, but the shadow had gone, and she let out her breath. The place gave her the willies and made her imagine all sorts of things. She still had another three bottles to collect and already the basket was almost full.

It was just as well that Pansy hadn't come down, she thought, as she studied more labels. Her friend would never have been able to carry all that weight up the steps. She spotted a label she needed and placed the oil lamp on the shelf while she picked up the bottle.

As she did so, she heard heavy footsteps coming up behind her. Unnerved by the sudden sound, she let out a scream and the bottle fell from her fingers. The crash of splintering glass seemed to echo over and over again in her ears. She could smell the wine as it splashed over her shoes, and it was all she could do to hold onto the basket that contained a dozen bottles as she swung around to face the intruder.

Memories of her last encounter with a killer seared her mind. She hastily put the basket down, grabbed one of the bottles and prepared to fight for her life.

Hauling the heavy basket of linens down the top flight of stairs, Pansy wished the country club had a laundry chute that went all the way from the top floor to the bottom. There was one outside the dining room that went down into the laundry room. That's where she dumped all the soiled table-cloths and serviettes.

There was nowhere, however, where she could drop the sheets and pillowcases she took off the beds, and that meant struggling down three flights of stairs with an unwieldy basket that weighed a ton.

Grunting with the effort to raise the basket higher, she balanced it on her hip and turned the corner on the first landing. At the same moment, a footman came bounding up the stairs and onto the landing. Unable to avoid him, Pansy smacked into him, sending the basket flying out of her arms and rolling down the stairs, spilling sheets and pillowcases all over the steps.

"Now look what you've done!" She glared up into brown eyes sparkling with mischief and suppressed a groan. She might have known. Charlie Muggins was always finding an excuse to get in her way and keep her talking. More than once she'd been in trouble for being late because the cheeky young footman had stopped her from going where she was supposed to be going.

Not that she minded all that much. Charlie was always good for a laugh, and she rather liked him. If she hadn't been so head over heels in love with Samuel, she might even have accepted one of Charlie's numerous invitations to go walking with him.

Right now, however, she was in a hurry to get the linens down to the laundry room, and it was going to take her ages to pick up all that mess. She tossed her head at the footman and made her voice really stern. "Out of my way, Charlie. I've got work to do and I'm late already."

"Wait a minute." He laid a hand on her arm. "There's something I want to ask you."

She shook off his hand and tried to push past him. "I haven't got time to listen to you now."

He shifted his body so she couldn't get by him. "Just give me a minute and I'll help you pick up all that stuff. I'll even carry it down to the laundry room for you."

She squinted at him, wary of what he might want from her. "What are you up to, Charlie Muggins?"

"Nothing, I swear." He raised both hands in the air. "I just wanted to know what happened to Archibald Armitage, that's all."

She pinched her lips together and raised her chin. "I don't know what you're talking about."

"Yes, you do." He glanced over his shoulder. "I heard it from one of the maids. Gertie found him dead in his room."

Worried now that she might be blamed for letting out the news, Pansy shook her head. "I don't know nothing. Ask Gertie if you want to know."

"Gertie won't tell me." He leaned in toward her, a smile on his lips. "I know you will, though. Especially if I carry that heavy basket all the way down to the laundry room for you."

Pansy eyed the tumble of white sheets on the stairs. The basket had bounced all the way down to the next landing. It would take her ages to get everything picked up on her own. "I don't know much," she said, lowering her voice to a whisper. "All I know is that he was poisoned by something he ate in the hotel."

"That's what I thought." Charlie narrowed his gaze. "I thought I should warn you."

A spasm of fear shot down her back. "Warn me of what?"

"Not of what. Who." He looked over his shoulder again. "You see Gilbert Tubbs a lot, don't you."

Pansy frowned. "I see him when I visit Samuel in the stables. What of it?"

Charlie leaned closer. "I think he may have poisoned Archibald Armitage."

Shocked, Pansy uttered a shrill laugh. "What? Whatever makes you think that?"

Charlie took hold of her arm and drew her into the corner of the landing. "I know Gilbert. We used to go to school together until he moved to London. It was me that got him the job here as Samuel's assistant. I felt sorry for him."

"Why did you feel sorry for him?"

"I was in the Fox and Hounds one night when Gilbert came walking in. I didn't even know he was back here. The last I heard, he was doing all right for himself in the city, managing a nightclub in Piccadilly."

Pansy raised her eyebrows. "Go on! Whatever made him come back here, then?"

Again Charlie glanced over his shoulder. "Well, it turns out that Archibald Armitage swindled a lot of money out of some investors in a play. Gilbert was one of them. He lost a bundle and ended up pretty much broke. He couldn't afford to stay in the city anymore so he came back here. He begged me to get him a job here, so I did."

Still struggling to absorb what she'd just heard, Pansy shook her head. "Mr. Armitage stole Gilbert's money? I don't believe it."

Charlie shrugged. "Gilbert showed me an article in the newspaper about it. There was a court case and everything but the investors couldn't prove that it wasn't a legitimate business deal."

"Well, then, that just goes to show that Mr. Armitage didn't do nothing wrong."

"Gilbert said that Armitage took the investors' money for the play, but didn't produce it. It never made it to the stage. He trumped up a few receipts for the court, but all the investors knew he'd never spent anything on the play. He just pocketed all the money."

Pansy pouted, still unwilling to believe her hero could be so dishonorable. "Well, even if that's true, that doesn't mean that Gilbert poisoned him."

Charlie leaned in closer. "When Gilbert asked me to get him a job here, he mentioned that Armitage would be coming here for Christmas. He saw it in the newspaper. He said he'd like to fix the brakes on Armitage's motorcar so he'd end up in the ocean. I thought he was joking and I didn't think nothing of it at the time. Now that the poor bloke is dead, though, I'm wondering if that's why Gilbert wanted to work here. So as he could do something nasty to Armitage."

Pansy began to get a sick feeling in her stomach. Holding one hand over her midriff, she muttered, "I can't believe Gilbert would do something like that." But she could. She heard again the bitterness in Gilbert's voice. *Armitage was not a good man by any means. He was a thief and a liar.*

"I hope you're right." Charlie brushed his fingers across

his forehead. "I wouldn't like to think I brought a murderer into the Pennyfoot."

Pansy swallowed. She had to get to Samuel and tell him what she'd heard. "I have to go," she said, twisting around to run down the steps.

"Just be careful, that's all," Charlie said, following her down. He bent down to scoop up an armful of sheets. "You never know what that chap is capable of doing."

Pansy didn't answer. She flew down to the landing and picked up the basket. Now she could hardly wait until she saw Samuel again, and boy, was he in for a shock.

Kevin arrived as promised, less than an hour later. Cecily received him in the library, where a warm fire glowed in the fireplace. "It's getting colder outside," he observed, as he warmed his hands in front of the flames. "I wouldn't be surprised to see it snowing by this evening."

"Oh, heaven forbid." Cecily rolled her eyes. "The last thing I need now is snow. I need Mr. Rickling's choir here for our carol-singing ceremony."

"I wouldn't concern yourself. Even if it does snow, it probably won't be enough to prevent your choir from getting here."

"I hope not." Sensing his uneasiness, she started to worry. "Kevin, is there something you need to tell me?"

He turned to face her, his smile rueful. "I never could hide anything from you for long."

Worried now, she moved closer. "What is it? Is it about Mr. Armitage's death?"

His smile vanished. "I'm afraid so. I'm sorry, Cecily. I brought my test kit with me. The poison that killed Armitage was in the whiskey bottle and glass."

"Oh, my." Her hand strayed to her throat as she stared at him in dismay. "You are quite certain?"

"There's no doubt in my mind. There was enough left in the bottle to make a thorough assessment. It must have been a very large dose. Since the arsenic would have been colorless and virtually tasteless, Armitage had drunk most of the bottle without any idea that someone had tampered with it. It would have been a most unpleasant death."

"How ghastly. That poor man."

"Indeed." Kevin paused. "That's not all. The bottle bore the Pennyfoot logo on the label. It was one of the bottles brewed especially for the hotel."

Cecily felt for the armchair behind her and dropped down on it. "So someone here in the Pennyfoot must have poisoned him."

"It looks that way. I'm inclined to think that someone either presented Armitage with the bottle, or left it in his room while he was absent."

"That's possible. Our guests don't always lock their rooms when they leave."

"Quite." He paused, looking even more uncomfortable. She stared at him. "There's something else?"

"I rang the constabulary. P.C. Northcott has already left for London. The constable on duty will be here shortly. From what I understand, however, Inspector Cranshaw is also away on holiday, so at least you won't have to deal with him until after Christmas, and by then we could have all this cleared up."

Cecily cringed at the sound of Cranshaw's name. The inspector had been an adversary ever since the Pennyfoot had first opened as a hotel. Suspecting the presence of illegal card rooms hidden beneath the floorboards, he'd done everything in his power to prove his theory and had vowed to shut down the hotel once and for all.

Now that the Pennyfoot had been turned into a country club, card games were legal, and the inspector had lost a valuable tool in his quest. Nevertheless, he continued to search for reasons why the Pennyfoot should be put out of business, and his discussions with Cecily were always most unpleasant.

She was vastly relieved to hear the inspector was out of town, but the prospect of dealing with an unknown constable who could possibly share Cranshaw's views was unsettling, to say the least. "I don't suppose you found anything that might indicate who was responsible for this?"

Kevin shook his head. "I'm a doctor, not a detective. I leave all that up to you."

She sighed and leaned back on her chair. "It appears that I'll be spending another Christmas hunting down a murderer."

"If I didn't know better, my dear Cecily, I'd say that you rather enjoyed the chase."

She gave him a sharp look. His expression was quite sober,

though his eyes twinkled with amusement. She folded her hands demurely in her lap. "I'd never admit to such a thing."

"I wouldn't expect you to do so."

A sharp rap on the door compelled her to sit up. "Who is it?"

A timid voice from out in the hallway answered her. "It's Pansy, m'm. There's a constable here to see you."

Cecily exchanged a worried glance with Kevin and rose to her feet. "Show him in, Pansy."

The door opened and a young man stepped into the room, wearing a constable's uniform and carrying a helmet under his arm. He inclined his head as he came forward. "Good afternoon, m'm." He nodded at Kevin, who returned the gesture with a nod of his own.

"Constable Watkins, m'm. At your service." The constable edged as close to the fire as he could get. "I understand there's been a possible homicide here."

Cecily studied the constable with a certain amount of trepidation. He seemed hardly old enough to be a policeman. His unwrinkled face was freckled and topped with a thatch of thick, curly red hair. He seemed ill at ease, fidgeting with his helmet and shuffling from one foot to the other.

Cecily had the distinct impression that this was his first murder investigation. Given the circumstances, she would have much preferred to be dealing with P.C. Northcott. He might be a bumbler in the worst degree, but having dealt with him for so many years, she knew how to handle him. She had learned long ago to take advantage of Northcott's ineptitude and had conducted her own investigations without his meddling.

This constable, on the other hand, was a quite different kettle of fish. He was young and probably inexperienced, but no doubt eager to prove his worth to his superiors. Especially Inspector Cranshaw. That did not bode well for her Christmas season.

No doubt P.C. Watkins would insist on questioning the guests, thus upsetting everyone. That was something she had usually been able to avoid with Sam Northcott. Her only option was to find out who had administered the poison to Archibald Armitage, before P.C. Watkins disrupted the entire holiday for everyone.

CHAPTER
❀ 6 ❀

Gertie's heart seemed to stop as the bulky figure loomed up in front of her. One arm raised, she yelled, "Come any nearer and I'll knock your bleeding block off!"

The voice that answered her sent shivers down her back. Pleasant shivers. "Oh, and here I was thinking you liked me."

Feeling foolish, she lowered her arm. "Clive! You scared the heck out of me. What are you doing down here?"

"I saw you come down here and thought you could use a hand carrying this." He swung the heavy basket up as if it contained nothing more than cotton wool. "Sorry I scared you." He peered at her. "You really were frightened, weren't you?"

She nodded, feeling perilously close to tears. The rare

sensation made her blink really hard. "I nearly died down here once."

He muttered something and before she could react, he wound an arm around her shoulders and hugged her to his chest. "I'm such a dolt."

Her mind was telling her to move away from him before she made a complete idiot of herself, but her body didn't seem to listen. She sniffed. "It wasn't your fault. I just get jumpy every time I have to come down here."

"I'm not surprised. From now on, you just tell me when you have to fetch more wine and I'll come down here and get them for you."

Acutely aware of her newly discovered feelings for him, she drew back. "Ta ever so, Clive, but I'll manage." She tried to take the basket from him but he held it out of her reach.

"You can at least let me carry this up the steps for you."

Softening, she smiled at him. The shadows made his eyes seem darker, and more intense. Her heart leapt in response and she hurriedly brushed past him, heading for the stairs. "I'd better get them bleeding bottles back to the bar or I'll have Tucker the Terrible after me."

He laughed, a full, rich sound that echoed up the stairway. "You are such a tonic, Gertie McBride. Don't ever change."

Surprised, she looked back at him. "Me? Why would I change?"

He shrugged, his face suddenly serious. "People do."

She thought about that as she trudged back to the kitchen carrying the heavy basket of wine. Clive had sounded so sad when he'd said that. *People do.* Who had changed for him, she wondered, and why had it hurt him so? There was so much she wanted to know about him. About his past, and what had brought him to the Pennyfoot and a job for which he seemed far too educated and intelligent. Who was Clive Russell, really? She longed to know, yet at the same time was apprehensive of what she might learn about him.

Would it change her feelings for him? She didn't know the answer to that, but it certainly gave her something to think about.

Pansy was in such a hurry to get to the stables she failed to see the deep puddle in front of her until she was right on top of it. She made a desperate attempt to sidestep, but the heel of her shoe got caught in the hem of her skirt. Before she knew it she was sprawled on the ground with one elbow deep in the puddle of muddy water.

With her dignity injured more than her body, she scrambled to her feet and brushed off the mud and wet leaves from her uniform. Her sleeve was soaked, and the leaves had left a stain right in front of her skirt. Stomping across the courtyard, she hoped her clothes would dry before she got back to the kitchen. If not, Tucker the Terrible would make her change her clothes, and that would put her behind with her chores and cause all sorts of problems for everyone.

What she should do is go back now and get changed as quickly as possible. Her urge to see Samuel, however, was stronger than her fear of the housekeeper, and she kept marching until she reached the stables.

She could hear Gilbert talking to Samuel, and he sounded agitated. His voice rose as she drew closer, and she paused, hiding behind the wall of the stalls, so she could hear what the argument was about.

"Well, I don't care what you bloody say, that bastard deserved to die."

Samuel made a sound of disgust. "Well, I don't have time to stand around arguing with you about it. Madam wants someone to take Sir Reginald Minster into town. Take one of the carriages and meet him at the front entrance in ten minutes."

Gilbert muttered something under his breath and charged out of the stables without even noticing Pansy crouched against the wall.

Shaken, Pansy crept forward until Samuel saw her. He held out his arms and she rushed into them, closing her eyes as he hugged her. "What are you doing here?" His lips brushed her cheek. "Aren't you supposed to be getting the dining room ready for afternoon tea?"

"I had to sneak out and tell you something." Pansy snuggled up to him. "There was a constable come to the Pennyfoot a little while ago. I took him to see madam in the library." She pulled back to look up into his face. "I heard him say that there's been a homicide. That means murder doesn't it? He was saying Mr. Armitage was *murdered*."

Samuel let her go, his face frozen in shock. "Who killed him, then?"

"We don't know. We thought at first it was Tucker the

Terrible, because she sent him up a slice of Christmas pudding and it was the only thing he ate that nobody else did, but then I went and found the pudding in his room so now we don't know what killed him."

"Well, I'm sure madam will find out. She's good at doing that."

Pansy glanced over her shoulder. "What if Gilbert poisoned him?"

Samuel's eyebrows shot up. "*Gilbert?* Why on earth would he do such a thing?"

"I was talking to Charlie just now and he said that Mr. Armitage stole money from Gilbert and he took this job here so's he could fix the brakes on Mr. Armitage's car."

"That's bonkers. Charlie's full of rubbish. Gilbert would never do something like that."

"Then why did he tell Charlie that's what he wanted to do?"

"He must have been joking."

Pansy tossed her head. "What if he wasn't? What if he decided that poisoning was better than messing about with the brakes of a motorcar?"

Samuel crossed his arms. "You'd better be careful. Talk like that could get you in a lot of trouble."

Pansy tossed her head. "From who? Gilbert? I'm not afraid of *him*."

"From me." Samuel frowned. "Gilbert says a lot of daft things but he's a good bloke and a great mechanic. Not many people know how to work with motorcars the way he does. He knows them so well he can sense when something's wrong and how to fix it. More and more people are buying motorcars every day, and they're going to need people to take care of them. There's going to be a big demand in the future for people like him and me."

"So what?"

"So I won't have you going around calling him a murderer."

"I didn't call him a murderer. I just said he *might* have done it."

"Well, he didn't."

Pansy pouted. "How do you know? He's only worked here a week. You don't know nothing about him."

"I know a lot about him. We spent a couple of evenings in the pub together and talked about a lot of things."

"You went drinking with him without me?"

A dangerous gleam appeared in Samuel's eyes. "It was business."

"What kind of business?"

"Never you mind."

Fear started to creep along Pansy's veins. This wasn't like Samuel at all, to keep things from her. Confused, she threw caution aside. "Well, it *is* my business if we're going to get married."

A red spot appeared in each of Samuel's cheeks. He avoided her gaze, pretending to study the horse in the stall closest to him. "Who said we were getting married?"

Pansy's stomach seemed to drop to her boots. Fighting back tears, she declared, "You said you loved me, and I love you. That's what people do when they love each other. They get married. I've waited long enough for you, Samuel. I want to get married."

"Well, I don't."

Horrified, she slapped a hand over her mouth, unable to prevent the tears streaming down her cheeks.

As if he'd suddenly noticed her distress, Samuel's expression changed to regret. "Don't cry, sweetheart." He moved toward her, but she jerked back out of his reach. "I didn't mean never. I just meant not now."

"Why not?"

She'd mumbled the words from behind her hand, but he must have understood. He raised his chin, staring at the rafters a moment or two before answering her. "I need to save my money. I want to buy a garage for motorcar repairs and start a business. Gilbert's going in it with me. We think we could have a really successful business going in a few years. Once we're established and making money, then you and I can get married."

Disappointment, anger, and fear had sent Pansy's mind into turmoil. When Samuel reached for her she backed away from him. "No, no. I'm not going to wait for you forever. I've waited too long as it is. If I don't get married soon I'll be too old to have babies and I want babies, Samuel." The tears kept coming, and she dashed them away with the back of her hand. "If you don't want to marry me, then I'll find someone who will."

"Pansy . . ."

She didn't wait to hear what he had to say. Blinded by

tears and aching in every part of her body, she flew out of the stable and into the courtyard. It was over. She and Samuel were never going to get married now. She was going to be a spinster for the rest of her life.

Constable Watkins fixed his gaze on Cecily's face, waiting for her to speak.

She chose her words carefully. "One of my maids found one of our guests had died in his bed. I called Dr. Prestwick and he examined the patient." She looked to Kevin for help.

"Shouldn't you be taking notes?" Kevin asked abruptly.

"Oh, right-ho." Watkins pulled a notebook from his breast pocket and hunted in the other pocket for a pencil. Not finding one, he looked from Kevin to Cecily and back to Kevin again with a helpless look that reminded Cecily of Gertie's twins.

Kevin rolled his eyes and produced a pencil from his own breast pocket. "Here. You should never go anywhere without a pencil."

"Yes, sir. I mean, no sir." Looking a little desperate, the constable flipped open the notebook. "The name of the victim?"

Cecily listened as Kevin answered the constable's hesitant questions. It didn't seem likely that the policeman would understand half of what Kevin said, but eventually he seemed satisfied and closed his notebook.

"I'd like to take a look at the room, m'm," he said, walking slowly toward the door.

"I'll show him," Kevin said and followed the constable out the door.

Cecily watched him go, full of misgivings. How was she going to stop him from questioning all the guests? It had to be obvious that someone here in the Pennyfoot could have poisoned Armitage. Her mind whirled back to her conversation with Phoebe. Should she mention the argument between Sir Reginald and the actor to P.C. Watkins? Was it enough motive for murder?

Moving closer to the fire, she acknowledged that she probably should tell him. If Sir Reginald was the killer, the constable would no doubt question him first and with any luck, decide he was guilty and delay questioning anyone else. She might still be able to avoid upsetting the rest of her guests.

It seemed an eternity until Kevin returned to the library. Seeing that he was alone, Cecily stared at him in dismay. "Where's the constable? He's not questioning the guests already?"

Kevin smiled. "No, he's on his way back to the police station."

Cecily sat down on her chair. "How on earth did you manage that?"

Kevin stood with his back to the fire, his thumbs tucked into his trouser pockets. "Don't get too excited, Cecily dear. I've managed only a brief respite. I told Watkins that it was possible that Armitage had been ingesting arsenic over a period of time, and may have brought the bottle of whiskey with him. I told him I wouldn't know for certain until I'd conducted more tests, in which case I would report the results to him. He agreed that it would be better not to upset everyone by questioning them if the murderer was not among them. Inspector Cranshaw, I told him, would not appreciate that."

Cecily's smile of relief had grown wider with every word. "You didn't show him the bottle with our label on it?"

Kevin shook his head. "I told him I needed to keep the evidence for a couple of days to conduct my tests. If needs be, I'll just say I didn't notice the label until later."

"Kevin, you are a genius and an absolute angel. Thank you so much."

"Don't thank me. I'm not sure I'm doing you that much of a favor." Kevin turned, holding out his hands toward the flames. "Someone here in the Pennyfoot administered that poison, which means it's very likely you have a killer on the premises. I know you want to solve this yourself as discreetly as possible, and I have no doubt you will manage it somehow." He turned to look at her. "Just swear to me that you will be careful."

She rose, reaching out to grasp both his hands. "I'm always careful, Kevin. You know that. Just to be on the safe side, let's not mention this to Baxter just yet. I'll tell him when the time is right."

Kevin frowned. "I think he already suspects that it's murder."

"Maybe, but as yet he doesn't know I'm investigating it. You know how he is about me getting involved. He keeps holding that ghastly position over my head, threatening to take it if I don't stay out of trouble, as he calls it."

"Position?"

"I told you about it some time ago. Baxter has been offered a position abroad, overseeing the construction and staffing of new hotels in various spots in the world. He wants to take it, and I've managed to talk him out of it so far, but on condition that I stay out of police business once and for all."

Kevin's frown cleared. "Ah, yes, I do remember you telling me. So what are you going to do about it?"

She shrugged. "What can I do? I have to protect my guests and staff, and if that means hunting down a murderer, then that's what I must do."

"You can't just leave it up to the constable?"

Cecily rolled her eyes. "You saw him. He's little more than a child. I have no doubt at all that I'm far more experienced than he is in exposing a guilty person."

"You may well be right. I'll be able to give you a day or two, but that's all. I'm sure P.C. Watkins will want a report from me in short order."

"Then let's hope we can track down the killer by then." Cecily walked with him to the door. "I have a suspect in mind, and I'll be asking questions as soon as I can find the opportunity."

She said good-bye to Kevin and walked slowly back to the fire, her mind working feverishly. Sir Reginald had good reason to want Armitage dead, but that didn't mean he killed the man. Perhaps his wife could shed some light on the nature of her husband. It was imperative that she talk to her as soon as possible. In the meantime, there was one person she could talk to right away.

Leaving the library, Cecily hurried down the hallway to the bar. To her immense relief, the room was empty, the hour too early for the pre-dinner cocktails. Barry, the bartender, was busy polishing glasses and looked up with a smile as she entered.

"Afternoon, m'm. Come in for a nice drop of sherry, have you?"

Cecily sat down on one of the bar stools. "No, Barry, thank you. It's a little early for me to indulge."

Barry held up the glass and twisted it around to inspect it for spots. "Never too early for the good stuff, m'm."

"Speaking of which," she tried to look unconcerned, "how many bottles of our special whiskey do you have left? I wonder if we need to order more before New Year's Eve."

"Well, let's see." Barry put down the glass and turned around to study the shelves. "As a matter of fact, I've sold a few bottles in the last few days. People like to give them as Christmas presents, seeing as how they have the Pennyfoot name on them. It might be a good idea to order a few more. Just in case we run out." He turned back to look at her. "I'll take care of it, m'm, don't you worry."

"Thank you, Barry. I thought I saw Sir Reginald with a bottle the other day."

"Actually he bought a couple of bottles. Lady Bottingham was in here, too, asking for one. Bit bold of her, if I may say so. Oh, and a couple of the staff bought them, too."

In the act of getting up, Cecily paused. "Our staff?"

"Yes, m'm. The new housekeeper bought two bottles, and Samuel bought one."

Cecily blinked. "Samuel?"

"Yes, m'm." Barry frowned. "Is something wrong? There's nothing wrong with the whiskey, is there? I can have it all replaced if there's a problem."

"No, no, Barry." Cecily stood up and replaced the bar stool against the counter. "I was just making sure we had enough whiskey for Christmas, that's all."

His face cleared. "Very good, m'm. I'll be sure to order more, then."

She thanked him and left, an uneasy feeling growing in her stomach. What if the poison originated at the distillery? No, it couldn't be. People had been drinking the whiskey in the bar without ill effect. The poison had to have been added to one particular bottle that found its way to Archibald Armitage's room.

Samuel? In all her visits to the public house with her stable manager, she had never seen him drink anything except beer. . He must have bought the whiskey for a Christmas gift. Or . . . no! Samuel could not have poisoned the actor. She'd stake her life on it.

Beatrice Tucker? A possibility. After all, what did she really know about the temporary housekeeper, other than that she was thoroughly disagreeable and had little respect for anyone? True, Beatrice had brought good references, but they could be faked. Cecily had been too anxious to hire someone to waste time verifying them.

Beatrice had bought two bottles of the whiskey. Had she poisoned one of them, to pay the actor back for being rude to her, not realizing that it would kill him? Then again, Sir Reginald, who had argued so vehemently with the victim that Phoebe had been forced to hide, had also bought two bottles of the whiskey. That gentleman seemed a far more likely suspect, and she would have a conversation with his wife as soon as she could find her.

She made her way to the foyer, where Philip, the reception clerk, was dozing behind the counter. He jerked to attention when she spoke his name.

"Do you have any idea where I might find Lady Henrietta?" Cecily asked, with just a touch of irritation.

Philip was not a young man, though his balding head and pale eyes behind the glasses he wore made him look older than his actual age. He was, however, supposed to be at attention at all times, and more often than not, she caught him napping at his desk.

On more than one occasion Baxter had strongly suggested she replace the clerk with someone more attentive and efficient. Aware that the idea had merit, she also knew that Philip was widowed and had no living relatives. He would be absolutely lost without his position behind the reception desk. She simply couldn't bring herself to deprive him of his only interaction with the outside world.

THE CLUE IS IN THE PUDDING

He stared at her now, as if she'd asked for directions to the moon. "I beg your pardon, m'm?"

Cecily curbed her temper. "Lady Henrietta, Philip. The wife of Sir Reginald Minster. Do you know where I can find her?"

Philip frowned, apparently struggling to place the woman, then his brow cleared. "I've got it!" he announced, with a note of pride. "She's the lady with the frizzy hair and big nose. Never seen such a big conk. You can see it coming round the corner before you see her."

Cecily briefly closed her eyes. "Please, Philip. Do not talk about our guests in that manner. It is not only rude, someone could overhear you and repeat your unfortunate remarks to the recipient of your insults. We have a reputation to uphold, and I won't have it jeopardized by thoughtless comments."

Philip looked contrite. "Yes, m'm. Sorry, m'm."

"Do you know where Lady Henrietta might be?"

"Sorry, m'm. I haven't seen her since early this morning."

Sighing, Cecily made her way up the stairs. She should have known better than to rely on Philip's help. She would just have to find the lady herself and hope to get some answers. For right now, she was in a familiar place—racing against time to solve a murder, without a clue where to begin.

Gertie picked up a knobby potato and slashed at the peel with a knife. Her afternoon off was supposed to have started ten minutes ago, but Tucker the Terrible had insisted she finish peeling the potatoes before she could leave. Her twins were probably jumping up and down, waiting for her to fetch them for their afternoon walk along the Esplanade. Daisy must be biting her nails, too. The nanny was waiting for Gertie to take the twins so she could go Christmas shopping for them.

Gertie smiled, thinking about the presents she'd bought for her children. She'd been saving all year, a few pennies at a time, so she could buy them what they wanted. She even had a little left over, but now Tucker the Terrible was threatening to take money out of her wages to pay for that bloody gown.

Gertie chopped at the potato, taking off a large chunk. It went flying across the sink and bounced out, dropping to the floor. Ignoring it, she scowled. To blazes with the toff's gown. Christmas only came once a year and she was going to make it the best Christmas she could for her twins. She'd worry about paying for the blinking gown later.

Gertie sighed. How she missed Mrs. Chubb. She couldn't wait until Christmas was over and the housekeeper went back to where she belonged. Tucker was a nasty, bad-tempered witch, and for all she knew, a murderer as well.

Pinching her lips together, Gertie took another swipe at the potato. She knew where she'd like to put the knife. And it wasn't in another potato.

Behind her, she heard the housekeeper muttering something under her breath. The old goat was talking to herself again. Gertie knew what that meant. Beatrice had been at the brandy bottle again.

Just wait until Michel found out. He'd be tearing his hair out. If there was one thing the chef wouldn't tolerate, it was someone knocking back his brandy. Gertie smiled at the image. She enjoyed hearing Michel screaming at Beatrice Tucker.

The thought was hardly out of her head before Michel came storming out of the pantry. "Who steals my brandy?" he demanded, waving a half-empty bottle in the air. "Who dares to touch my bottle?"

Beatrice seemed to be having trouble with her tongue when she answered. "It's not really your bottle, Michel. It belongs to the kitchen. It's supposed to be for cooking."

"Then why are you drinking it?"

"I'm not drinking it."

"Your breath stinks of ze booze." Michel's voice rose. "I tell madam that you steal ze brandy."

Gertie turned so she could watch them out of the corner of her eye, while still slicing peel off the potato.

Michel was hovering over the housekeeper, eyes blazing. She seemed unfazed by the onslaught. In fact, Gertie observed, the housekeeper looked as if she was actually enjoying the exchange.

Beatrice peered up at the chef. "You are quite welcome to do that, Michel. I'm sure madam would also be surprised to know that her renowned French chef spends his free time in Wellercombe visiting a house of ill repute."

Michel looked as if he were about to be sick. He stared at the housekeeper in horror for several seconds, then let out a howl of anguish, dropped the bottle onto the table and dashed out of the kitchen so fast his tall chef's hat fell off and floated to the floor. Beatrice stared at it for a moment, then walked unsteadily across the room. Bending over to retrieve the hat, she hung onto the side of the table to steady herself. "Michel needs to calm down before he gives himself a heart attack." She stared at Gertie with glazed eyes. "He can be such a nasty fellow when he's in a bad temper."

Taking advantage of the housekeeper's brandy-mellowed mood, Gertie asked, "Was that true? What you said about the brothel?"

Beatrice winced. "I never like to use that word."

"How did you know about Michel being in one?"

The housekeeper wagged a sluggish finger. "Never you mind. I make it my business to know such things. You never know when they will come in useful. Such as just now. It shut Michel up in a hurry, didn't it."

"He's upset about the puddings," Gertie said. "He was up all bloody night making more of them. He's worn out."

Beatrice straightened her back, wandered over to the stove and laid the hat on the counter. "Michel should be more concerned about Archibald Armitage's death than his precious puddings." She hiccupped, and put a hand over her mouth. "Though if you ask me, the world is well rid of that man. After what he did to Lady Bottingham—he got off easy if you ask me."

Thoroughly intrigued, Gertie dropped the potato and knife on the counter and gave the housekeeper her full attention. "What did he do that was so bad, then?"

Beatrice swayed forward, caught herself and straightened.

"He ruined lives, that's what he did. Now he's gone, and he won't be hurting any more people."

Gertie raised her eyebrows, still somewhat surprised to find herself actually having a conversation with Beatrice Tucker. "How d'you know all that?"

"Someone told me. Someone whose life has been destroyed by that man. Archibald Armitage was a desh-picable person, and I, for one, will shed no tears over his death."

"I thought you flipping liked him. Wasn't that why you sent him up that slice of pudding?"

Beatrice drew herself up, looking for a moment like her old self for a few seconds before her shoulders collapsed again. "I always wanted to be on the stage. I just like being around actors, and talking to them. I thought if I was extra nice to Mr. Armitage he'd be nice to me."

She shook her head, as if to clear it. "What the blazes are you doing standing around here for? Aren't you supposed to be off this afternoon?"

Gertie didn't wait to argue with her. She dropped the knife and was out the door before the housekeeper could draw another breath. As she hurried down the hallway, the question buzzed in her mind. What was it the housekeeper had said? *He ruined lives, that's what he did..* Had one of those lives belonged to Beatrice Tucker?

She'd probably never know the answer to that one. In any case, she had more important things to think about. Like taking her twins for a walk. Forgetting her worries, she smiled in anticipation of the treat and headed for her room.

CHAPTER

❄ 7 ❄

Twenty minutes later, Gertie was out on the Esplanade, a small hand clutching each of hers as they battled against the stiff breeze blowing off the ocean. Across the street, lights from the numerous shops flowed across the pavement. All along the seafront, red ribbons adorned the railings that divided the road from the sands, and wreaths of holly hung from the streetlamps. The lamp lighter had already finished his work, and the lamps glowed like miniature moons against the dark sky.

Gertie paused to enjoy the view, then shivered as the wind flapped her skirts around her ankles, stinging them with icy fingers.

"Is it going to snow for Christmas?" James asked, looking

up at her with his free hand holding down the cap on his head.

Gertie looked up at the sky. "It might. It's bloody cold enough."

"I'm cold." He tucked his chin into his collar and stuck his hand into his pocket.

"I don't want it to snow," Lillian said, pulling on her mother's hand. "Father Christmas might not come if it snows."

"Course he'll come," James said on a note of scorn. "He comes in a sleigh, doesn't he. He doesn't care if it snows."

A small frown creased Lillian's forehead. "How does he drive the sleigh when it doesn't snow?"

Deciding it was time to change the subject, Gertie said hurriedly, "Remember our sleigh ride in the snow with Mr. Clive?"

"Yeah," James muttered. "I broke my arm."

"That's because you didn't do what you were told."

"I want to ride in the sleigh again." Lillian tugged on Gertie's hand. "Why can't we go on the sleigh again with Mr. Clive?"

"Because it's not snowing." Gertie nodded at the brightly lit stores across the street. "Look at all the Christmas stuff in the windows. Let's go and look." She started across the street, dragging the twins with her. She didn't want to think about Clive. She'd done her best to keep him out of her mind ever since she'd made the astonishing discovery of her true feelings for him.

She would not allow herself to indulge in those feelings

again. Too many times she had listened to her heart instead of her head and got nothing but pain and misery in return. There wasn't a man on earth who could change her mind about that. Not even the kindest, sweetest, most gentle man she'd ever met.

"Look, Mama! There's Mr. Clive!"

Lillian's voice jerked Gertie out of her thoughts. She stopped dead, staring at the big man waiting on the other side of the street. For a moment she wondered if she'd conjured him up in her mind, but then a loud shout and a clattering of hooves turned her head.

Coming right at them was a carriage, the driver straining on the reins to halt the snorting horse. Acting instinctively, Gertie shoved the kids as hard as she could toward the pavement, then closed her eyes as the flying hooves plunged toward her.

The next thing she knew, she was swept up in two strong arms and flung aside. From some distance away a shrill scream rent the air, and she felt the blast of wind as the pounding hooves and rattling carriage wheels thundered past her.

Then she was on the pavement, her twins clutching her arms and Clive smiling down at her, fear still hovering in his eyes. "That was a close one," he said, patting both children on the shoulder. "I thought you were all going under those wheels."

Shaking uncontrollably, Gertie managed a weak grin. "We might have done if it hadn't been for you. You always seem to be there to rescue us."

"I hope I'm always there."

The look in his eyes made her heart beat faster, and she quickly turned her attention to the twins. "Was it you that screamed?" she asked Lillian, who seemed about to burst into tears.

The little girl nodded. "I thought you were going to get runned over."

"I knew she wasn't," James declared. "When I saw Mr. Clive, I knew he wouldn't let nothing happen to her."

"You can bet your boots on that," Clive said, with a hint of laughter.

Gertie cleared her throat. "We were just going to look in the shop windows," she said. "Thank you ever so much, Clive. You saved my life. I always seem to be thanking you for something."

"There's no need to thank me. I consider it an honor and a privilege to be your friend." He winked at the twins. "Would you mind if I walk along with you?"

Yes, she minded. Being around him was unsettling, like she was off balance. She'd always been the one in charge— the one everyone relied on to get things done. With Clive, though, it was different somehow. With him she wasn't trying to be everything and do everything, because he was always so willing and ready to do things for her.

For a long time she had been a staunch supporter of the women's movement, holding on to her independence as if her life depended upon it. Women's rights were important, she'd always said. Men had had their own way for far too long. Now it was time women took over.

Yet, when she was with Clive, he made her feel something she'd never felt before. Like she was someone fragile to take care of and protect. With anyone else she would have scoffed at the thought. Big blinking clumsy Gertie—fragile? Hah! Yet with Clive it felt right. Strange, but right. What's more, she liked it. That's what was so bloody dangerous about it.

"He can come, Mama, can't he?" Lillian tugged her hand again. "I want Mr. Clive to come with us."

There didn't seem much Gertie could say at that, so she nodded, flashing Clive a quick smile. "Course he can come. It's a free country, isn't it?"

"Goodie!" Lillian skipped over to Clive's side and took hold of his hand. "Come on, Mr. Clive. I want to show you the dolly's house in the window down here."

"I want to show you some stuff, too!" James grabbed the big man's other hand and started dragging him down the crowded street.

Gertie shrugged and followed behind, watching her children skipping along on either side of Clive. There was nothing she could do about it now, she thought, so she might as well bloody enjoy it. She'd worry about her feelings later.

Cecily had barely entered her suite before Baxter demanded, "Have you heard from Prestwick yet?" He was seated in his usual spot in front of the fire, and peered at her over the top of his newspaper. "If not, he's taking a blasted long time to get around to ringing us."

Cecily hoped her husband didn't notice her guilty start.

"Oh, I'm dreadfully sorry, darling. I've been so busy I haven't had a chance to talk to you. Kevin finished his testing."

Baxter looked put out. "He was here?"

"This afternoon, yes." Seeing the dark look on her husband's face, she hurried on. "He brought his testing kit with him and got the results right away. You'll be relieved to know that the poison wasn't in the pudding after all."

Baxter shook the paper and carefully folded it. "If it wasn't the pudding that poisoned the chap, then what was it?"

She might have known she couldn't stall for long. "I . . . ah . . . I'm afraid there was arsenic in one of our special whiskey bottles."

Baxter stared at her for a moment, then closed his eyes and raised his chin. "Dear God, what did we do to deserve this?"

"Kevin summoned the constable. He was here this afternoon."

Baxter abruptly lowered his chin. "Northcott was here, too?"

"Not Sam, darling. He's away on holiday in London. This was his replacement. A very nice young man. Rather green behind the ears, I'd say, but—"

Baxter's voice rose to a roar. "Just when were you going to tell me all this?"

"Well, actually, I was going to tell you after we'd eaten our meal. I didn't want to spoil your appetite. You ate so little last night, and I'm quite sure you didn't have much to eat today."

"Of course I didn't eat much today. I prefer to eat with

my wife, and since I haven't seen you all day because you're too blasted busy talking to doctors and constables to even talk to me about something as important as murder, it's no wonder I haven't eaten much all day."

Cecily sighed. He had a point. She'd skipped lunch in order to finish the paperwork before the final Christmas rush and now all she wanted to do was eat a nice meal in front of the blazing fire. "I've ordered supper in our suite, darling. It should be here any minute. Why don't we wait until we've eaten to discuss this dreadful business? We will both feel more able to deal with it on a full stomach."

Baxter leaned forward. "I will not eat one morsel until you tell me everything that is going on. To begin with, I have to assume that you are taking on the task of finding out who murdered our guest, since you consider this constable such an inexperienced clot?"

"Well, not exactly. I just thought I might ask a few questions, that's all."

Baxter groaned, leaning back in his chair as if he was suddenly exhausted. "When, *when*, are you going to stop all this nonsense?"

Cecily looked down at her hands. In a small voice, she answered, "When people stop committing murder in our hotel."

"Country club." He said it wearily, as if he were tired of reminding her. "It's no longer a hotel."

"The Pennyfoot will always be a hotel to me. That's where it all started, remember?"

His expression softened at once. "Of course I remember. How could I forget?"

"Then you remember why I must do everything in my power to protect my people. We cannot allow a murderer to remain under this roof undetected."

"I was under the assumption that the constabulary is supposed to take care of criminals."

Cecily managed a smile. "We all know how well that goes. More often than not, Inspector Cranshaw has to step in—something I've managed to avoid for quite some time."

Baxter uttered a monstrous sigh. "I suppose you're right. But I don't have to like it. I must ask you once more to promise me you will not put yourself in danger as you have done so often in the past."

She hesitated. "I promise not to deliberately walk into danger."

He was about to answer when, to her relief, a tapping on the door stopped him.

Gertie answered Cecily's command, shoving open the door with her hip before carrying the heavy tray over to the low table in front of the fire. "Mrs. Tucker sent up some bread pudding for afters," she said, straightening her back. "She said Mr. Baxter didn't eat nothing midday and would be hungry."

Baxter eyed the tray with a jaundiced eye. "I trust there's no arsenic in it."

Gertie stifled a laugh while Cecily frowned at him. "That was uncalled for, Baxter."

"Yes, I suppose it was." He nodded at Gertie. "Forget I mentioned it."

"Yes, sir." Gertie curtsied and left the room, still smiling.

Baxter continued to stare at the tray as if it would jump up and bite him.

"The poison wasn't in the pudding," Cecily reminded him.

"We still don't know who killed the poor chap. That Tucker woman could have just as easily poisoned a bottle of whiskey as she could a pudding. What do we know about her, anyway?"

Excellent question, Cecily thought. Deciding that this wasn't the time to share her doubts about the temporary housekeeper, she murmured, "She came with very good references, darling." She got up and lifted a plate of roast pork and vegetables from the tray. Handing it to her husband, she added, "Besides, who in the world would want to kill you?"

Still frowning, Baxter took the plate from her. "One never knows these days. It seems to me it's easier to make enemies than it is friends. All this talk in Parliament about an impending war, an infamous serial killer lurking around London, not to mention a man murdered right here under our roof, is it any surprise that I wonder from where the next threat might be coming?"

Cecily felt a pang of anxiety. She lived with that thought most of her days, though always striving to ignore it. After all, although one must be ready to deal with whatever presented itself, whether good or bad, life should be lived one day or even one moment at a time. To dwell on what might be was almost as bad as dwelling on what might have been. One was in the future, the other in the past, and the only sure thing in anyone's life was the here and now.

Right now she was relaxing in front of a warm fire, her dear husband at her side and a plate of delicious food in front of her. For that moment in time, what more could she ask?

Instead of the anticipated snowstorm, the morning of the carol-singing ceremony dawned sunny and bright, though a thick frost had laid a carpet of glistening jewels across the bowling greens. As usual, Cecily spent these precious moments of respite in front of her suite's large window, gazing out at the peaceful scene of sloping lawns and the dense wooded land beyond.

It was a time to gather her thoughts and brace herself for whatever trials and tribulations lay ahead. Today she must do her best to find the person who had placed a poisoned bottle of whiskey in the hands of Archibald Armitage. Tomorrow was Christmas Eve. How long would P.C. Watkins wait before calling on Inspector Cranshaw to investigate the murder? Would he wait until after Christmas Day, mindful of disturbing the dour inspector's holiday?

She had so little time and so little notion where to begin. Lady Henrietta. She must begin there. Her husband was one of the last people to have words with the actor, and they were harsh words at that, according to Phoebe.

What better reason for revenge than the loss of a daughter?

It was as good as any place to start. Without further ado, she left the suite and made her way down the stairs to the foyer.

Philip jumped to attention when he saw her approaching the reception desk. "I was just about to send a message up to you, m'm," he said, when she reached him. "I told Lady Henrietta you were looking for her, and she said she'd wait for you in the library."

"Thank you, Philip." Cecily turned to leave, then looked back at him. "Was Sir Reginald with her?"

"No, m'm. I think the gentleman is in one of the card rooms. Shall I fetch him for you?"

"No, no. That won't be necessary." She left him, making her way to the library while she thought about the questions she needed to ask.

Lady Henrietta stood by the window, gazing out at the rose gardens when Cecily entered the library. At the sound of the door closing, the aristocrat turned to face her. "These gardens must look lovely in the summertime," she said, gliding gracefully toward the fireplace. "I will tell Reginald that we must come down here next year."

"We will be most happy to have you stay with us again." Wearing her professional smile, Cecily joined the woman by the fireside. "Sir Reginald is not with you?"

"No." Lady Henrietta held out her hands closer to the smoldering coals. "He is in a card room, I believe." She heaved a sigh. "That's all he does, nowadays. Gamble and drink." She shuddered, and passed a hand across her brow. "Forgive me. I should not discuss such matters with you."

Cecily sat down on a brocade chair and motioned Lady Henrietta to do the same. "There is nothing to forgive. Sometimes it is easier to talk to a stranger. Rest assured, nothing you say to me will be repeated."

Lady Ashley's dark blue gaze bore into her face. "I must admit, it would be a great relief to talk about it. Ever since the tragedy happened, our friends and relatives have been tiptoeing around us, deliberately avoiding all mention of it."

Cecily pretended to look puzzled. "I'm sorry, I don't . . ."

Lady Henrietta sat down abruptly on the chair. "Of course you don't. How foolish of me. I . . . we . . . lost our only daughter a few short months ago. In some ways it feels an eternity since I last looked upon her face, yet the day we found her, lying so still in her bed, is as painfully clear to me as if it happened yesterday."

Feeling a deep sorrow for the woman, Cecily leaned forward. "I'm sure it is. There is so little one can say at this time, except that time heals all wounds. Though one never quite forgets. I still remember the death of my first husband, but I can do so now without writhing in agony at the memory."

Her gaze strayed to the spot above the fireplace where the portrait of James Sinclair had once hung. Even now, she felt a spasm of nostalgia, not so much for the man she had lost, but for the woman she once had been. Her life had changed so much since James's death. Responsibilities and the constant pressure of her work had aged her, and she sometimes missed the carefree, fun-loving young woman of long ago.

"Oh, if only I was allowed to forget." Lady Henrietta's voice rose in anguish. "My husband is constantly harping on our loss, and this" she waved her hand at the vast room—"is the last straw. The moment Reginald read in the paper that Archibald Armitage would be spending Christmas here, he insisted that we come here so he could meet him face-to-face."

She stared at Cecily, her face white with distress. "Armitage was responsible for our daughter's death, you know. Maybe not in a criminal way, but most assuredly he was the cause behind it. Reginald said he would not be satisfied until he had given the man a piece of his mind and made him realize just how completely he had destroyed our family."

She started rocking back and forth, her hands clasped together. "As if that would bring dear Miranda back to us. I don't want to be within ten miles of that man, much less ten feet. There's no arguing with Reginald, however, once his mind is made up."

Cecily nodded in sympathy. She chose her next words carefully, unsure as to whether or not the lady knew that Archibald was dead. Although her staff was sworn to secrecy about hotel matters, now and then someone let something slip. A death in the hotel was always difficult to keep secret. "So did Sir Reginald have a word with Mr. Armitage?"

"Oh, yes." Lady Henrietta leaned closer to the coals. "I'm not sure how much it satisfied him, though. He is still muttering about the dratted man. He must have made an impression on Mr. Armitage, however, since we have not seen any sign of him since. He has not been taking his meals in the dining room, and I have seen nothing of him in the hallways." She looked hopefully at Cecily. "I don't suppose he has left the hotel?"

Cecily let out her breath. If Sir Reginald had poisoned the actor, it was obvious his wife knew nothing about it. Unless she herself was an accomplished actress.

Still treading carefully, she said, "As a matter of fact, Mr. Armitage is no longer on the premises. I hope that helps to make you feel a little less distraught."

"It does, Mrs. Baxter. Thank you for enlightening me. I was in dread of coming across that man. Especially with Reginald by my side. I have no stomach for confrontation of that sort."

"Not many people do." Cecily paused. "It is fortunate your husband is not of a violent nature. His argument with Mr. Armitage might have come to blows."

Lady Henrietta sighed. "I have to confess, I worried about the same thing. My husband can be . . . ah . . . unpredictable when angered, and I must say, I have never seen him quite so wrought up as he was two days ago. I only hope he has flushed it out of his system, so to speak, now that he has had his say. I, for one, will be perfectly happy never to hear that dreadful man's name again."

"It is no wonder he consoles himself with whiskey," Cecily murmured.

"Oh, Reginald doesn't drink whiskey nowadays. He doesn't have the stomach for spirits anymore. He prefers a good port or sherry. Though I must say, lately he does consume more than is good for him."

"Oh, I thought I saw him the other day with a bottle of whiskey. I must have been mistaken."

Lady Henrietta frowned. "I'm sure you were. Unless he was buying the whiskey for a Christmas gift for someone."

"My thoughts exactly." Cecily rose from the chair. "I must return to my duties. I trust that you will have a good day."

Lady Henrietta looked surprised. "But you haven't told me why you wanted to see me."

Cecily thought fast. "I merely wanted to know if you and your husband are comfortable in your room, and if there is anything else we can do for you."

A wan smile floated across the other woman's face. "Thank you, Mrs. Baxter. You and your staff are taking excellent care of us."

"I'm happy to hear that. Please let us know if there is anything else we can do."

"I will." Lady Henrietta got to her feet. "But now that I know that horrible man has gone, I'm quite sure the rest of our visit will be as pleasant as it could be under the circumstances."

Cecily was in serious doubt of that. Thinking over her conversation with the aristocrat as she headed for the foyer, she strongly suspected that the woman's husband had poisoned the actor in revenge for the loss of his daughter. Who else would have such a strong motive?

Sir Reginald had bought two bottles of whiskey, though he didn't drink the stuff. Had he bought them for Christmas gifts, or had one of those bottles been laced with arsenic and placed in Archibald Armitage's room?

Cecily was inclined to think the latter, but proving it was

another matter. Short of the gentleman actually confessing, there didn't seem to be any way to confirm her suspicions. Perhaps she should mention all this to P.C. Watkins. Then again, if he was unable to establish Sir Reginald as the murderer, no doubt the inspector would be called in. And that was something she was determined to avoid at all costs.

CHAPTER

❀ 8 ❀

Frantically tying her apron strings, Gertie hurried along the hallway toward the dining room. She was supposed to have been there half an hour ago to help Pansy lay tables, but the twins had taken longer than usual to get out of bed and put their clothes on. By the time she'd taken them their breakfast and settled them down with books to wait for Daisy to arrive, it was too late to have her customary cup of tea in the kitchen.

Disgruntled about that, she turned the corner, stopping short when she caught sight of Tucker the Terrible down at the other end. The housekeeper was in deep discussion with another woman. Shocked to recognize the slender figure of Lady Bottingham, Gertie drew back, ready to vanish around the corner if either woman looked her way.

133

She was intrigued to notice that the conversation between the two women appeared to be quite earnest, with each of them leaning forward and speaking softly as if afraid to be overheard. She had no idea the housekeeper was that well acquainted with the aristocrat.

The housekeeper's words came back to her. *Someone told me. Someone whose life had been destroyed by that man.* Had Lady Bottingham been one of the actor's victims? Could that have been the person who had told Beatrice about Archibald Armitage's foul deeds?

At that moment Beatrice half turned, sending Gertie back around the corner. The last thing she needed was to be accused of spying by Tucker the Terrible. She waited a few seconds, then noisily stomped back around the corner, almost colliding with the housekeeper coming from the opposite direction.

"For heaven's sake, child, lift up your feet when you walk." Beatrice's cheeks were flushed, and she seemed to be out of breath. "You walk like a dustman with a loaded sack on his back. Chin up, shoulders back, and swing your legs from the hip."

Having delivered her sermon, she stalked off, leaving Gertie fuming behind her. *Child?* She was the mother of twins and had been married twice, for heaven's sake. Where did the old cow get the nerve to call her a child, or worse, speak to her as if she was one?"

Muttering to herself, she hurried up to the dumbwaiter and grabbed the tray of glasses she'd sent up earlier.

Pansy was in the dining room, polishing the last of the

candlesticks. She answered Gertie's greeting with a grunt and wandered over to help her put out the glasses. The young housemaid looked as if she had her lips sewn together.

"Sorry I'm late." Gertie dumped the tray of glassware on the dining room table, making them rattle. "The twins were giving me trouble this morning. They're all excited about Father Christmas coming and won't listen to nothing I say."

Pansy mumbled something in response.

Gertie tried again. "I just don't know what to give Clive for Christmas. I keep trying to find out what he needs, but he doesn't seem to need anything."

Pansy took a sherry glass in each hand from the tray and stood them on the table next to the place settings. "You don't get people things for Christmas that they need. You get them what they want." Her sigh was loud enough to crack the glasses. "I'll never get what I want now, so I'll just be glad when Christmas is over."

Gertie gave her a sharp look. "You've been moping about all morning. What's wrong with you?"

Pansy shrugged. "I broke up with Samuel."

Gertie nearly dropped the brandy glass in her hand. "Wot? Whatcha go and do that for?"

Tears glistened on Pansy's lashes. "He doesn't want to marry me."

"Course he does. What'd you do? Have a bloody row with him? He just said that to make you mad."

Pansy shook her head. "No, he didn't. He said he wants to save up his money to buy a garage and then he'll think about getting married." She burst into tears, gulping out words between sobs. "He . . . thinks more . . . about his . . . bloody cars . . . than . . . he does . . . *me!*"

She wailed the last word so loud Gertie was sure Tucker the Terrible would come running. "Shshh!" She put an arm around Pansy's shoulders and gave her a squeeze. "Of course he doesn't. He just wants to be able to give you the best of everything and he can't do that without money. You should be happy he's willing to work hard to make a good home for you."

Pansy pulled away, hunting in her apron pocket for her handkerchief. "I don't want a good home and the best of everything. I just want a place to live where I can have a husband to take care of and babies. Like everyone else. What's the good of money if I'm too old to have babies?"

Gertie suppressed a grin. "You're just a baby. You've got plenty of time to have babies."

Pansy found her handkerchief and blew her nose. "I want them *now*, while I'm still young enough to enjoy them."

Gertie leaned toward her. "Believe me, you need to enjoy your life before you get tied down with babies. Once they come it's all bleeding work and worry."

Pansy sniffed. "Do you wish you never had the twins?"

Shocked, Gertie drew back. "No, course not. I love my babies and I'd never change that. I'm just saying, if you've got a choice, it's better to wait."

"Well, I don't want to wait." Pansy grabbed two more glasses and stomped over to the next table. "And I'm not going to, so there. I'm not wasting any more time on Samuel. Me and him is finished, and I'm going to find someone else who wants to marry me and give me babies. Someone like Charlie Muggins."

Gertie almost laughed. *"Charlie?* You must be daft. He's no good for you."

Pansy folded her arms, her eyes bright with resentment. "Why not? He's handsome and strong, and he likes me, so there."

"He's too handsy with the maids, if you ask me. They call him Octopus 'cos his hands are everywhere they shouldn't be."

Pansy's cheeks warmed. "Well, it would be different if he was married."

This time Gertie did laugh. "Don't bloody bet on it. You'd do better with Gilbert Tubbs than Charlie."

Pansy stiffened. "I don't think so."

"Why not?"

"There's something shifty about him. I don't trust him."

Gertie gave her a curious look. "Why? What did he do?"

Pansy looked over her shoulder. "Charlie told me that Gilbert got the job with Samuel so's he could mess up the brakes on Mr. Armitage's motorcar."

"Wot?" Gertie listened while Pansy repeated the conversation she'd had with Charlie. When her friend was finished, Gertie shook her head. "I think we should tell madam about this."

Pansy looked frightened. "No, no! Samuel would never forgive me if he knew I told anyone what Charlie said. He wants Gilbert to go into business with him mending motorcars."

"He wants to be partners with a bloke what wanted to

kill someone?" Gertie gasped. "He could be the one what poisoned Archibald Armitage."

"No, he's not. Samuel swears he's not. He says he knows Gilbert well and he'd never kill no one."

"I still think I should tell madam."

Pansy grabbed Gertie's arm. "Please don't. I don't want Samuel cross with me."

"I thought you broke up with him."

"I did." Pansy started crying again. "I don't know what to do."

Gertie put a motherly arm around her. "There, there, don't carry on. I won't say anything to madam for now, but if she doesn't find out who killed Mr. Armitage by Christmas Eve, I'll have to tell her then. I'll ask her not to say that you told me."

Pansy pulled away and went back to the sideboard, where she picked up a brandy glass in each hand. "Samuel will know I did." Head down, she wandered over to a table and placed the glasses on the white linen tablecloth.

Forgetting about Gilbert, Gertie watched her friend for a moment, saddened by Pansy's obvious misery. Being in love could be so flipping agonizing at times. Which was why she didn't want to be in love with Clive. Just thinking about him gave her such a pang she caught her breath. It didn't seem she had much to say in the matter. The best thing she could do would be to ignore it and hope it would eventually go away.

She'd read somewhere that love was like a flower. If you didn't nurture it, then it would die. So if she ignored her feelings for Clive, maybe they would die. Only that made her feel sad, too. Cursing under her breath, she put the brandy glasses down on the table and reached for two more.

Why did life have to be so bloody complicated? Why couldn't she just be happy with her twins and not keep feeling that she was missing something? Why hadn't she been born a blinking man? They never seemed to have all these bloody ups and downs, not knowing what they wanted from one day to the next.

Why couldn't she think of something to get Clive for Christmas that wouldn't give him the wrong idea? That was the real question. And she only had two more days to answer it.

"You look quite ravishing this evening," Baxter observed, gazing at his wife's reflection in her dresser mirror. "I swear you look younger every year when Christmas comes around."

Cecily smiled, though she eyed her husband warily. Her violet silk gown was new, and with its lace trim around the neckline and gleaming silver buttons marching down the bodice, she was satisfied that it achieved the dictates of fashion and suited her matronly figure.

Baxter, however, was not given to complimenting her so lavishly unless he was about to impart unwelcome news. "Thank you, my love. I must say, you look quite dashing yourself."

Baxter ran a finger around his stiff starched collar. In his black dinner jacket and bow tie he looked quite distinguished, if somewhat uncomfortable. "I know this is your favorite night of the season, and I have no wish to spoil it for you. I must ask you, however, if there are any developments in the investigation of Archibald Armitage's death."

Cecily's smile vanished. She had so hoped to solve the murder before the actual Christmas ceremonies began. In a little more than hour the carol-singing ceremony would begin. Tomorrow was Christmas Eve. What with the last minute preparations and Phoebe's pageant, there was hardly enough time to investigate a murder.

It looked very much as if she would have to hand the whole thing over to P.C. Watkins, and that would inevitably mean the intervention of Inspector Cranshaw.

She turned to face her husband and reached for his hand. "I'm afraid not, darling. It seems that the constables will have to take on the case."

"Well, I must say I'm rather relieved to hear that, although knowing that a murderer could be in our midst is most unsettling, to say the least."

"I agree. I do believe, however, that Mr. Armitage was his only target. Since any sudden departure is bound to arouse suspicion, he will simply lay low until it is safe for him to leave the premises."

"I hope you're right." He leaned in to drop a kiss on her nose. "I'll join you in the library in a little while. I'm going to stop by the bar first and make sure everything is in order. Don't get into mischief while I'm away."

She laughed, chasing her concern away. Tonight she would try to enjoy the ceremony and worry about the murder later.

She was almost at the bottom of the stairs when a lanky figure emerged from the shadows.

Cuthbert Rickling trotted toward her, one hand raised in welcome. He was a rather fragile-looking man, with a nervous twitch in his right eye that made him appear to be winking. "Mrs. Baxter! I'm so happy to have caught you. I was on my way to the library to set the stage for my choir and wanted a word with you first."

"Of course." She waited for him to reach her, wondering what he needed at this late hour. "Your choir hasn't arrived yet?"

"Oh, they are here. I left them waiting in the ballroom." He tugged the starched collar of his shirt as if it threatened to choke him. "I thought it would be more effective if they made a grand entrance, filing in one behind the other holding a flaming candle."

Cecily shuddered. "No candles, please."

She'd spoken sharply and he drew back, his eyebrows raised. "I beg your pardon?"

"I'm sorry, but I can't allow candles at the ceremony. The fire danger, you know."

Cuthbert frowned. "I assure you, Mrs. Baxter, there will be no danger. My choirboys are extremely well behaved and would never do anything—"

"I'm sorry, Mr. Rickling. I must insist. We once had a Christmas tree catch fire from lit candles, and it almost burned down the hotel." She still couldn't think about the time she had been trapped in the library and had come close to losing her life. That was something she just couldn't bring herself to tell him.

"Ah." His frown cleared, and he nodded so hard a wayward lock of hair fell across his forehead. Sweeping it back, he gave her a nod, one eye closing in a wink. "I quite understand, Mrs. Baxter. No candles. I promise." He turned as if to leave, then swung back to face her. "By the way, I . . . ah . . . understand you had an unfortunate death on the premises. I trust that won't affect the proceedings tonight?"

Cecily stared at him in dismay. "May I ask where you heard of it?"

Cuthbert looked confused. "Oh, ah . . . I overheard someone talking about it. One of your staff members, actually. I was in a hurry at the time and just caught a word or two. A famous actor, I believe?"

Sighing, Cecily gave up all hope of keeping the death quiet. It was inevitable that word would get around sooner or later. She'd hoped to keep the secret at least until after Christmas, but it seemed that wasn't to be. Everything seemed to be working against her this time, and there didn't seem to be much she could do about it.

Reluctantly, she answered Cuthbert's question with a quiet, "Yes, he was a famous actor. Mr. Archibald Armitage." There was no need to tell the choirmaster that Armitage had been murdered. That, at least, she hoped to keep quiet a while longer.

"Hmmm." Cuthbert shook his head. "I'm not familiar with the name. Then again, I don't have much to do with the stage these days. I'm much too busy managing the choir and attending to my duties at the library. I find that—" He broke off with a startled gasp. "Goodness, look at the time. I really must fly and get things organized."

He practically leapt toward the hallway and disappeared, leaving Cecily staring after him openmouthed. She had no time to dwell on his abrupt departure, however, as she heard a voice speak her name.

Turning, she saw Lady Bottingham sweeping toward her from the staircase, magnificent in a cream brocade gown sparkling with beads and sequins. A diamond tiara twinkled in her hair and a wide band of diamonds circled each gloved wrist. Cecily greeted her guest with a polite, "Good evening, Lady Bottingham. How glamorous you look this evening."

"Why, thank you, Mrs. Baxter. I'd like to return the compliment. Quite an exquisite gown."

Since her gown could hardly compare with that of her esteemed guest, Cecily thought that most generous of the woman. She thanked her, and asked, "Will you be joining us in the library for the carol-singing ceremony this evening?"

"Most assuredly. I've been looking forward to it all day." Lady Bottingham glanced over her shoulder and lowered her voice. "I just heard the news about Archibald Armitage. That must have been quite a shock for you."

Unsure how much the woman knew, Cecily trod warily. "Yes, it was. Quite unpleasant."

"I must admit, I can't say I'm altogether devastated. He was not a nice man at all, you know. Quite horrible, in fact, and not much of an actor, either. I never could understand how he came to be so well-known."

Cecily raised her eyebrows. "I wasn't aware you were so closely acquainted with Mr. Armitage."

"Oh, I wasn't! I mean, I—" She fanned her face with her hand. "He was quite famous on the stage and everyone . . . well, most people, I suppose . . ." She laughed—a nervous sound that seemed just a little too loud. "Well, I'm sure you know what I mean." She glanced at the grandfather clock in the corner by the stairs. "Goodness, I had better get along. I thought I'd stop by the bar on my way to the library. A drop of Christmas cheer will be good for me, don't you think?"

She rushed off without waiting for an answer, one hand holding up the hem of her skirt. Cecily shook her head, wondering why everyone she spoke to that evening seemed in such a great hurry.

She had to rather admire Lady Bottingham, however. It wasn't considered protocol for a lady to enter the bar unescorted. She had often done so herself, but as manager of the country club, she felt the position gave her special privileges and released her from some of the binds of etiquette. After all, as a working woman in charge of a large establishment, she was already breaking a barrier.

Lady Bottingham, on the other hand, was a socialite, and as such, was held in much higher esteem. Cecily rather liked the fact that the woman was not afraid to thumb her nose at propriety and go where she pleased. Women these days were beginning to make strides in their quest for equality, and she, for one, couldn't be happier about it all.

She was about to make her way to the library when yet

another voice hailed her from the front doorway. "Cecily, old bean! Jolly good to see you, what? What?"

Sighing, Cecily turned to greet the newcomer. "Colonel Fortescue! Good evening. I'm so glad you could come." She looked beyond him. "Is Phoebe not with you?"

Colonel Frederick Fortescue jerked a thumb over his shoulder. "Ran into Dr. Prestwick and his wife. Phoebe's out there nattering on the steps. Too blasted cold out there if you ask me, what?"

"It is, indeed, Colonel."

A chorus of voices from behind him turned his head. "Ah, there you are. I was just telling Cecily it's too blasted cold to be standing around on the steps."

Phoebe bustled in, followed by Madeline Prestwick and her husband.

Phoebe, as always, was the first to speak, rushing forward with both hands outstretched and a rustling of silk. Her face was almost hidden by the wide brim of her hat, which bore the weight of two white doves nestled in a bed of white feathers and surrounded by a cascade of silver fronds. The white fur collar of her navy blue coat hid her nose and chin and all Cecily could see was a pair of eyes staring earnestly into her face.

"Dear Cecily," Phoebe said in hushed tones, "how are you holding up? Did you find out anything more about that dreadful actor's death?"

Cecily gave a warning shake of her head. "Not now, Phoebe. Let us just enjoy the ceremony."

"Good idea." Madeline floated up to them, her wispy cotton gown swirling around her ankles beneath a heavy blue wool coat. "This is not a night to be talking about the dead."

"Well, you should know." Phoebe stared down at Madeline's gold sandals. "Where on earth did you get those things? Your feet must be frozen."

"Not at all." Madeline lifted a foot and wiggled her bare toes. "They are most comfortable, and they allow my feet to breathe."

"It seems to me your feet will breathe their last if you don't start wearing stockings." Phoebe looked back at Cecily for help. "Tell her, Cecily dear. She simply won't listen to me."

Madeline laughed, a melodious sound that seemed to echo throughout the foyer. "If I listened to you, Phoebe, I'd be bundled up to the chin like an aging Eskimo."

Phoebe sniffed. "Are you calling me aged?"

"Jolly good people, the Eskimos," the colonel boomed. "I remember when I was in the Arctic . . ."

"You were never in the Arctic, dear," Phoebe muttered, still sounding miffed.

"I wasn't?" The colonel looked confused for a moment or two, then his brow cleared. "Dashed if I wasn't. I was thinking about Africa, and the Pigmies. Jolly good people, the Pigmies. A bit on the short side, but dashed helpful fellows. I remember—"

Cecily hurriedly cut in. "Colonel, I do believe the ceremony will begin in a little while—"

"One night when I was on guard duty," the colonel said, blithely ignoring all attempts to shut him up, "I heard a rustling in the bushes. Thought it was a lion and picked up my rifle to shoot when this little fellow comes walking out into the moonlight."

"Freddie, dear . . ." Phoebe began, but her husband was in full stride and a herd of raging bulls couldn't stop him now.

"Half-naked, he was. Thought he was a child lost in the jungle. I rushed over to the little chap, picked him up and threw him over my shoulder. Imagine my surprise when I set him down in my tent and saw he had a gray beard down to his knees. He must have thought I was capturing him or something, as he screamed and came at me with a knife. If there hadn't been a couple of other chaps in there to stop him, I might not be standing here today. I always say—"

"Freddie, my precious," Phoebe said again, more loudly this time.

"Know your enemy before you invite him to supper." The colonel paused, his brow furrowed in a ferocious frown. "Dashed if I know what that means."

Phoebe raised her voice once more. "If you want to visit the bar before the ceremony begins, Freddie, I suggest you trot along now, or you won't have time to consume an entire glass of brandy."

The colonel looked startled. "By Jove, old girl, you're right. I'd better toddle along." Smiling at Cecily, he raised his hand in a salute. "Be right there, old bean. Looking forward to the show." He rushed off, leaving his wife to gaze after him with a sour expression.

"Really," she muttered. "That man couldn't exist without

his war stories and his brandy. I don't think he lives for anything else."

"Not even you?" Madeline purred. "How very disheartening for you."

"Oh, you know very well I didn't mean—" Phoebe broke off and turned back to Cecily. "I promised myself I wouldn't argue with her tonight. I shall go along to the library and wait for you there."

Aware of Kevin Prestwick standing a little apart from them, Cecily nodded. No doubt the doctor wanted a word with her, and without the busy ears of Phoebe listening in. She waited until her friend had disappeared into the hallway before turning to Madeline. "You didn't bring Angelina with you?"

"She's at home with her nanny." Madeline smiled. "I wanted to enjoy a nice evening with my husband tonight without worrying if Angelina was going to disrupt everything with her efforts to sing."

Cecily laughed. "She sings?"

"She tries to sing. Her nanny is always humming to herself and Angelina does her best to sing louder. The contest invariably ends with our daughter screaming at the top of her lungs."

"Take my word for it," Kevin said, moving closer, "if you value your sanity you do not want to hear our child's version of 'Silent Night.' It's anything but silent."

Madeline rolled her eyes. "He's right. I'm going to find a seat in the library before they're all taken. Are you coming, Kevin?"

"I'll be there in just a moment." He smiled at his wife. "Save me a seat. I just a need a quick word with Cecily first."

"Of course." With a wave and a smile, Madeline drifted off down the hallway, leaving a faint flowery scent in her wake.

"My wife spoils our daughter," Kevin said, shaking his head.

"I'm sure you do as well." Cecily took his arm and drew him into the corner behind the staircase. "Do you have any more news for me?"

"I was going to ask you the same thing." Kevin looked around to make sure they were not overheard. "P.C. Watkins paid me a visit this afternoon. He's most anxious to complete his report by the end of Christmas Day. If the case is not solved by then, he says he will hand it over to Inspector Cranshaw."

Cecily sighed. "I'm sorry, Kevin. I seem to be getting nowhere."

"What about the suspect you had in mind?"

"I'm still investigating him. I'm planning to talk to him this evening in the hopes he'll let something slip that will help me pin him down. Otherwise, I'm afraid I shall have to let P.C. Watkins and the inspector do their worst."

"I'm sorry, Cecily. I know how badly you want to avoid that. If there's anything I can do . . ."

"Thank you, Kevin. I'll let you know. Now go and join your wife in the library and enjoy the evening. I'll be along a little later."

She watched him leave, her spirits sinking. After all these

years of staying one step ahead of the inspector, she found it hard to accept defeat. Hoping to find a little cheer, she wandered over to the Christmas tree. Madeline had hung white porcelain bells on the branches. Every time someone opened the front door, the bells tinkled in the draft. Cecily loved the sound they made and touched the bells lightly with her finger so she could hear them.

Every year Madeline managed to find something different and unique to hang on the tree. She would search high and low, refusing to give up until she found just the right thing.

Cecily stared at the bells. Was she growing old? When had she started giving up before she'd hardly begun to fight? Where was that indomitable spirit that had seen her through so many difficult and dangerous times?

Angry at herself, she swung around. She still had a day or so left, however, and she would make the most of it. Even if it meant questioning every guest in the house.

With renewed purpose, she headed for the ballroom. First she would make sure that Cuthbert Rickling kept his word and had done away with the candles. Then she would stop by the bar and ask Barry for a list of everyone who had bought whiskey bottles in the days prior to Archibald Armitage's death and concentrate on those guests first.

One way or another, she would find the fiend who had poisoned Archibald Armitage and see that he paid for his crime. To blazes with Inspector Cranshaw. Cecily Sinclair Baxter was hot on the trail once more.

CHAPTER
❀ 9 ❀

"Well, look who's here," Samuel said, as Pansy walked into the stables.

"I didn't come to see you." She tossed her head. "I came to see Gilbert." The stink that always greeted her in the stables seemed even worse than usual, and she wrinkled her nose as she walked over to where the mechanic was washing down a motorcar. "Madam said to tell you to take Sir Percy Rochester's motorcar around to the front. He wants to take it out today."

Gilbert looked up with a smile. "Right you are, gorgeous. I'll have it there right away."

"Here," Samuel said, sounding cross. "I usually take care of Sir Percy's car."

Pansy sent him a look loaded with contempt. "Too bad. I'm asking Gilbert to drive it."

She looked back at the assistant. "Thank you, Gilbert."

Gilbert nodded and turned away.

Without looking at Samuel, Pansy marched out of the stables, her nose in the air. She'd gone only a few feet when Samuel caught up with her.

"Here, what's your hurry?" He caught hold of her arm. "I want to talk to you."

"Well, I don't want to talk to you." She tugged her arm free, her heart pumping so fast she thought she might faint. "You don't love me so why should I bother with you?"

"I never said I don't love you." He dug his hands in his pockets, his face a mask of misery. "Why can't you understand, Pansy? I want to be able to start our life off right, with all the things a wife should have, like a nice home and a motorcar to ride about in, and good clothes and—"

"What's wrong with my clothes?" She brushed her skirt with an angry slap. "I wear uniforms most of the time, but I have nice clothes for my time off."

Samuel rolled his eyes. "You know what I mean. Stop being such a ninny and try to see things my way. I only want what's best for you."

"I know what's best for me, and that's to get married and have babies. If you don't want that, then I'll have to look elsewhere."

A flash of anger crossed Samuel's face. "Well, stay away from Gilbert. He and I have got plans, and I won't have you messing things up for us."

Pansy dug her hands into her hips. "That's all you think about, Samuel. Your flipping plans. Well, if they mean that much to you, you don't need me, and you've got no right to tell me who I can talk to, so there. If I want to talk to Gilbert I will, and not you or nobody else is going to stop me." Afraid she'd make a fool of herself and burst into tears right in front of him, she turned and ran as fast as she could toward the kitchen door.

Arriving in the ballroom, Cecily found the choirboys mingling about, admiring the lavish decorations Madeline had used to adorn the vast room. Red and green twisted banners hung from pillar to pillar, and huge wreaths of holly and mistletoe clung to the walls. Enormous white paper bells dangled from the high ceiling beside strands of tinsel wafting in the draft.

Cecily shuddered to think of her friend perched high enough on a ladder to reach the ceiling. Madeline seemed to have no fear, always serenely confident in her strange powers to see her through the most difficult of tasks.

Cecily was not quite so convinced of her friend's immunity from danger. Even Madeline was not invincible, and believing that she was only made her more vulnerable. Cecily's thoughts were shattered when a group of young and enthusiastic choirboys started chasing each other across the polished floor.

Before Cecily could call out a reprimand, however, Cuthbert sprang into action. Wading into the fray, he cuffed the ringleaders behind the ear and ordered all of the boys to line up in front of the stage. "You will stay there," he told them, "until it is time to go to the library. If anyone even twitches his nose, he will be sent home in disgrace."

Until that moment Cecily had always thought of the choirmaster as a rather timid person. Pleased to discover he had a backbone after all, she walked over to him and waited for the boys to shuffle into a line before saying, "Most of the guests should be in the library by now. I would give them another ten minutes or so, then you can make your grand entrance."

She eyed the ragged line of boys and smiled. They looked quite festive in their white surplices and red sashes. She would make haste to talk to the barman so that she could be in the library when the choir made their entrance.

"I trust there will be no candles," she said, just to make sure, although she could see no sight of them anywhere.

"No candles, as I promised," Cuthbert assured her. "We will each be carrying a silver star instead. Mrs. Prestwick was kind enough to provide them for us." He pointed at a table by the stage, upon which sat a large basket brimming with over-sized white cardboard stars, studded with silver sequins. "They will represent the Star of Bethlehem. I think they will be most effective."

Pleased by the idea, Cecily beamed at him. "Lovely. I shall be looking forward to your entrance."

One of the boys sneezed, which earned a scowl from Cuthbert. Cecily left him to his task and hurried down the hallway to the bar. Lady Bottingham sat at a table in the far corner and lifted a half-empty glass at her as Cecily approached the counter.

There were several gentlemen seated at the bar, and every one of them leapt to their feet at the sight of Cecily. She felt awkward disturbing them, but her mission was too important to worry about such trivialities. "If you gentlemen would like to go to the library now, the choir will be making an entrance in just a few minutes."

There followed a general mumbling and muttering among the men as they quaffed down the remains in their glasses. All but one of them gave Cecily a nod and obediently filed out of the room. Lady Bottingham tripped out after them, waving at Cecily as she passed.

As Cecily might expect, the sole customer left standing at the bar flapped a hand at her. "Come and sit down, old bean. Take the weight off your feet, what? What?"

Cecily gave Colonel Fortescue a stern look. "Your wife is waiting for you in the library, Colonel. I really think you should join her."

The colonel picked up his glass and swallowed a mouthful of brandy. "I will, old girl. Just as soon as I've finished one more glass." He held up his hand and beckoned to Barry. "One more of these, old man, if you please."

Barry raised an eyebrow at Cecily and she shook her head. "I'm sorry, Colonel, but we are closing the bar now until the carol-singing ceremony is over."

"Oh, that's a blasted shame." He tilted his head on one side and gave her a sheepish smile. "I don't suppose you could slip me one more tiny sip, old bean?"

Cecily wagged a finger at him. "Now, now, Colonel, you know very well, rules are rules. I can't go making exceptions, not even for a good friend like you."

The colonel sighed, gave his empty glass a long look of regret, then wandered out of the bar.

"Are you really closing down the bar, m'm?" Barry asked, picking up the colonel's glass.

"Yes, I am. I thought it would be nice if you could join the rest of the staff in the library for the carol singing."

Barry's expression suggested he'd rather be behind the bar, but he gamely nodded. "Thank you, m'm. I appreciate it."

"Before you go, however, I'd like you to write a list of everyone you can think of who has bought a bottle of our special whiskey in the last few days. "

Barry frowned. "I'll try, m'm. Though I can't promise to remember everyone."

"Just do your best, Barry. Bring it to me in the library when you've finished." She left him staring after her and hurried back down the hallway to the library. The first strains of "God Rest Ye Merry, Gentlemen" floated down to her, alerting her that the choir had already made their entrance into the library.

Disappointed at having missed it, she reached the doorway just as Cuthbert Rickling rushed out of it. Stepping backward, she stared at his flushed face. "Goodness, Mr. Rickling, are you not well?"

Cuthbert appeared to have trouble swallowing. He tugged at his starched collar, and said hoarsely, "I'm sorry, Mrs.

Baxter, I am not feeling at all well. I must be catching a cold or something. I feel I must go home and lie down."

Seriously worried now, Cecily's first thought was the poisoned whiskey. "Dr. Prestwick is in the library. Would you like me to fetch him?"

"No, no, that won't be necessary." Cuthbert edged past her. "I'm quite sure if I just go and lie down, I shall be quite all right by the morning."

He sped away and she called out after him. "What about the choir?"

"I've left Malcolm in charge. He can manage quite well without me. Good evening, Mrs. Baxter." He had disappeared around the corner before the words were out of his mouth.

Cecily sighed. Malcolm, a veteran member of the choir, was quite capable of course, but he wasn't the professional that she had hoped would lead the choirboys. Frowning, she pushed open the library door. The soaring voices of the choir filled the room and she relaxed her shoulders. Even without the choirmaster, the singers sounded magnificent. She paused for a moment to take in the sight.

Flames leapt in the fireplace, where the mantel was almost hidden beneath an abundance of holly, cedar, and fir. The choirboys stood close to the Christmas tree, upon which swirling glass balls and silver angels glinted in the glow from the gaslights. A year earlier Madeline had visited a curiosity shop in Wellercombe and found some bright red velvet birds. She'd used them again this year, scattering them in abundance among the branches. They added a splash of color to the tree that was most pleasing to the eye.

Looking resplendent in elegant gowns, the ladies sat in rapt attention as the young voices rose in chorus. Lady Bottingham sat closest to the choir, a full glass of sherry in her hand and a rather fixed smile on her face.

The gentlemen remained standing, perhaps less enthused by the singing, but nevertheless respectful of the choir's efforts. Even Colonel Fortescue, looking a little like Father Christmas with his red nose and bushy white beard, stood silently watching the proceedings.

Cecily was pleased to see that most of her staff was in attendance, the women dressed in their evening black frocks and lace-trimmed aprons, their hair covered by white lace caps. Cecily couldn't help noticing that Samuel, looking quite distinguished in his uniform, stood on the opposite side of the room to Pansy. Apparently they were at odds with each other. Not a good way to start the festivities. She hoped they would resolve their differences before the big day. Christmas was no time to be quarreling with a loved one.

The thought lingering in her mind, she caught sight of her husband standing by the fireplace. His face bore a look of displeasure, and she felt a stab of guilt. No doubt he had expected her to be in the library when he arrived. She hurried over to him, and slipped her hand under his arm.

"I'm sorry, dearest," she said softly, so as not to disturb the enjoyment of the guests nearby. "I had to make sure the choirboys didn't carry candles, and then I stopped by the bar for a moment."

Baxter grunted. "You know how I despise these things if you're not here."

"I know, dear, but I'm here now." She pulled him closer. "I'm rather worried about Mr. Cuthbert. It seems he has taken ill."

Alarm flashed across her husband's face. "You don't think . . . ?"

To her relief, he left the rest of the sentence unspoken. She shrugged, murmuring, "I really don't know what to think. Perhaps I should ask Kevin to take a look at him." She glanced across the room to where Kevin stood at his wife's side. He seemed to be enjoying the music, a slight smile playing across his face.

Cecily switched her gaze to Madeline and felt a cold stab of shock. Her friend stood quite still, her eyes wide and staring, her features frozen into a mask. Cecily knew quite well what that meant. Madeline had slipped into one of her trances, and heaven only knew what she would do next.

As chief housemaid, Gertie wasn't required to serve the refreshments with the rest of the maids after the choir had finished their recital. Therefore it was her choice whether or not to attend the ceremony.

She'd fully intended to be there. The carol singing was one of her favorite parts of the Christmas festivities. She'd even ventured to join in the singing now and then, though quietly, afraid of sounding a sour note.

Just as she was about to leave her room for the library, however, Daisy had informed her that Lillian was not feeling well. Upon closer inspection, Gertie had to agree with her.

Her daughter was listless, lying on her bed with her favorite doll in her arms, instead of bouncing all over the place with excitement.

Worried, Gertie urged Daisy to take her place in the library. "I'd rather be here with Lillian," she said, when Daisy emphatically shook her head. "Besides, you've missed so many of the ceremonies taking care of the twins. It's time you had a turn. You'll love the singing—honest. It's so blinking beautiful with all the voices and everyone singing the carols and all the decorations."

"But I don't feel comfortable in there with all the toffs." Daisy laid a hand on Lillian's forehead. "She doesn't have a temperature. It's probably just a cold."

Lillian moaned. "My tummy hurts, Mummy."

Gertie gave Daisy a little push. "That settles it. You go. I'll stay here with the twins. You can tell me all about it when you come back."

Backing away toward the door, Daisy looked worried. "I didn't get an invitation."

Gertie grinned. "All the staff's invited, silly. You don't need an invitation."

Still looking worried, Daisy disappeared through the door.

Alone with her son and daughter, Gertie turned her attention to Lillian. "Now, where does your tummy hurt?"

Lillian put a hand on her belly. "Right here."

"You probably ate too many sweets today. I told you not to eat them all at once." Gertie tried not to panic. Being the mother of twins had taught her that children were inclined to exaggerate ailments if it meant getting extra attention.

Still, thoughts of seeing Archibald Armitage lying dead from poisoning were still fresh in her mind, and her daughter's pale face made her all the more uneasy. "I'm going to get some water from the kitchen," she said, picking up the jug from the washbowl on the nightstand. "You two lie still and don't move until I get back."

James looked up from where he sat on the floor, his hands busy with a pile of building bricks. "I'm not lying down," he said, giving his sister a scornful glance. "I don't have nothing wrong with me."

"You flipping well will have if you're not in the same place when I get back." Shutting the door firmly behind her, Gertie hurried down the hallway to the kitchen. Above her head she could hear the faint strains of a Christmas carol, though she couldn't make out which one it was.

A surge of regret caught her unawares. Much as she enjoyed the ceremony, it wasn't so much missing it that she minded. It was missing a few moments of sharing something really nice with Clive.

The minute the thought popped into her head, she shoved it aside. No, she would not think about Clive. Not tonight. It was the excitement of the Christmas festivities that was making her all soft and soppy about the man. Once the New Year started, bringing with it the long dreary nights of bitter cold winds and snow, she'd forget all about her daft feelings. The best thing she could do was stay out of his way, and then she wouldn't have to think about him at all.

Besides, right now she had a sick child to worry about. She was glad Dr. Prestwick was in the club. He'd be right there for her if she needed him.

Absorbed in her worry about Lillian, she filled the jug with water and started back up the hallway. She was halfway there when a familiar voice spoke her name.

She almost didn't stop. But then good manners kicked in and she slowed her pace. Glancing over her shoulder, she called out, "I'm sorry, Clive. Lillian's got a tummy ache and I don't want to leave her alone."

"I know." He caught up with her, taking the jug from her suddenly shaky hand. "I saw Daisy in the library and she told me about Lillian. I came down to see if I could help."

Drat the man. Why did he always make her feel like crying? She never cried. Not even when her heart was breaking. She refused to waste time shedding tears. It did no good. It never made her feel better. Pansy cried a lot and her eyes got all red and puffy. Made her look like a bloody clown. Who wanted to look like that?

She realized Clive was staring at her, waiting for an answer. "Oh, it's very kind of you, but really, I don't need no help. I'm just taking the water in case Lillian is sick and makes a mess."

Clive gave her a deep look that made her shiver inside. "Then you'll need someone to help clean up." They had reached her door and he pushed it open. "Besides, you'll need help with the carol singing."

She followed him into the room, trying to make sense of what he said. "What? I'm not going to the carol singing."

"I know." Clive grinned as James leapt to his feet and threw his arms around Clive's legs. "That's why I'm bringing the carol singing to you." He untangled himself from James's death grip and carefully stood the water jug beside the wash-bowl.

Turning to Lillian, he sat down gently on the bed. "Hello, little one. What's the matter with you?"

"I got a tummy ache." Lillian sat up and belched.

"Uh-oh." Clive opened the nightstand door and dragged out the chamber pot. Just in time as Lillian brought up her supper.

"Ugh!" James leapt backward, banging his elbow on the dresser. He let out a howl and Gertie rubbed it for him, all the time staring at Clive in dismay. "You don't think she's got what Mr. Armitage had?"

Clive raised his eyebrows. "What did Mr. Armitage have?"

"I feel better now," Lillian announced.

Clive looked at her. "Well, that's good. You must not have what Mr. Armitage had, whatever it was."

"Mr. Armitage is dead," James announced.

Gertie gasped. "How did you know that?"

Lillian shrieked. "Am I going to die?"

"No, no, of course not." Clive raised an eyebrow at Gertie. "Mr. Armitage was a very old man. That's why he died."

To Gertie's relief, Lillian's sobs subsided.

"I promise you, you'll feel much better in a little while." Clive got up from the bed. "I'll empty this. I'll bring back some milk from the kitchen. That'll help settle her stomach."

Gertie stopped him, reaching for the chamber pot. "You don't have to do that," she said, trying to take it from him.

"I know I don't have to do it." He gently pushed her away and stepped outside into the hallway. "I want to do it." He smiled at Lillian, who had slid off the bed. "I'll be back in a few minutes and we'll sing some carols. Would you like that?"

Lillian clapped her hands. "Yes! I want to sing carols."

James scowled, still holding onto his elbow. "I don't. Singing is sissy stuff."

Clive nodded. "All right, then we'll just have to have a contest to see who can sing the loudest."

James's face broke out in a huge grin. "Yay! That'll be fun!"

Gertie shook her head. "You'll be sorry you said that."

Clive grinned. "I'm never sorry to have an excuse to spend time with you and the twins. I'll be back in a minute."

He disappeared and she shut the door, fighting her mixed feelings. It was dangerous to have him there, especially in such close quarters as her tiny room. On the other hand, the children were there and they made good chaperones. She and Clive wouldn't have much chance to talk with Lillian and James hanging on to every word.

She quickly washed Lillian's hands and face and dried her with a towel. She washed James, too, for good measure, while he protested the whole time and wriggled out of her grasp before she was finished.

By the time she'd straightened everything up, Clive was back, carrying a bottle of milk and two cups. He put everything down on the dresser and grinned at the twins. "All right, it's time to celebrate. We'll all have a drink first then we'll sing."

He poured a small amount of the milk into each cup and handed it to the twins. "Here you go. Drink up and happy Christmas!"

James swallowed his all at once and held out his cup. "That's good. Can I have some more, please?"

"Maybe later," Gertie said firmly. "You'll be asleep if you drink any more."

"That was sort of the idea," Clive said, with a wink.

Gertie could feel her cheeks growing warm. She dropped her gaze and pretended to be very busy making sure Lillian drank her milk.

The next hour passed swiftly as Clive led them in singing carols, the twins contributing with gusto, even though they didn't know all the words. James was the most creative. Instead of singing, "The cattle are lowing, the baby awakes," he sang, "The cattle are blowing the baby away." When Gertie corrected him he insisted he liked his version better.

At that point, Clive decided it was time to tell the twins a story. Gertie found herself every bit as fascinated as her children in the story he told. It was one she'd never heard before, about a brother and sister who ran away to find Father Christmas, and instead found the stable where the baby Jesus was born and learned the true meaning of Christmas.

By the time Clive announced "The end," both children were dozing and within minutes were fast asleep.

Clive got up from the bed slowly and came to sit next to

her on the settee. It was a very small sofa, and although he wasn't exactly touching her, she could feel the heat of his body. Pressing herself as far as she could against the arm of the settee, she murmured, "That was a lovely story you told."

"I'm glad you liked it."

"I've never heard it before."

"That's because I made it up."

They had been talking in whispers, wary of waking the children. Gertie was so surprised by his answer, however, she forgot and raised her voice. "You made it up?"

James stirred, and Clive placed a finger briefly over his lips. "Yes," he whispered. "I made it up."

"Do you make up a lot of stories?"

He smiled, and as usual, her heart did a little dance. "I did once. I don't much anymore."

"Why not?"

"I suppose because I have no one to hear them."

"You do now." She paused, knowing this was her chance, yet unsure how to proceed. She so badly wanted to know more about him, yet if she pressed him for details, would that give away her feelings for him? Dare she take that chance? If only she had someone who could give her advice.

But she had no one. She'd never had that luxury. All her decisions had been made on gut feelings, and brought her nothing but heartache. How could she trust them now? Could she grab this chance to learn more about the man she loved, and perhaps set her on a road she didn't want to go down? Or should she send him away right now, and spend Christmas regretting what she'd given up?

Clive had once told her that he would wait for her to make up her mind about him. Men didn't wait forever, though. She'd found that out a long time ago. It was time to make a decision that would affect not only her, but the twins as well. Somehow she sensed she was at a crossroads, and whatever path she took now would seal her fate, one way or another.

CHAPTER
❀ 10 ❀

Cecily watched in frozen anticipation as Madeline continued to stare at some unseen vision. Kevin apparently hadn't noticed his wife's condition, his attention focused on the choir. Which was fortunate, since his scientific mind often clashed with Madeline's herbal remedies and uncanny sixth sense. He would not forgive a public display of her psychic abilities.

All Cecily could hope was that Madeline didn't make one of her dramatic announcements before she was fully awake. She had no doubt that her friend had picked up some kind of message concerning the murder and was now in the process of interpreting it.

Leaning toward Baxter, Cecily murmured, "I shall be

back in one moment." Before he could argue, she slipped away from him and made her way to Madeline's side. She had to squeeze in next to a rather stout matron who seemed disinclined to give up her space. Cecily gave the woman a sweet smile and whispered an apology.

Just as she was about to speak to Madeline, her friend raised her hand and pointed at the Christmas tree. "Beware, the danger is right there," she said clearly.

Cecily grabbed the hand and pulled it down. "Madeline. Not now."

Madeline blinked, shuddered, and looked at her friend. Her eyes still looked a little unfocused, and Cecily squeezed the hand she still held. "We'll talk later," she whispered.

Madeline leaned toward her. "Evil is near. Be very careful."

"I will." Cecily turned her head as the choirboys' voices rang out in a glorious final chorus and faded amidst a burst of applause from their appreciative audience. "I must go now. Will you be all right?"

To her relief, Madeline's smile chased the remnants of her trance away. "I shall be fine, Cecily. Go and take care of your guests."

Kevin leaned across his wife to say, "The choir was excellent, Cecily. They really added to the festive occasion."

"Thank you, Kevin. I'm happy you enjoyed it." Satisfied that the doctor had apparently not noticed his wife's brief episode, she felt comfortable in leaving them, though she gave the Christmas tree a thorough inspection as she passed by it.

Whatever had Madeline seen? There was nothing, as far as Cecily could tell, that was remotely sinister about the tree. Indeed, most of the decorations had been used before, with no ill effect. There wasn't a candle in sight. Cecily shivered. She had almost died in that very room when the tree had caught fire. Could Madeline have been seeing that again and confusing it with the present danger?

Promising herself she would talk to her friend later, she joined the group of choirboys at the windows. After directing them to enjoy the refreshments before they departed, she informed them that the carriages waited outside to take them home.

Samuel had already disappeared to supervise the footmen, while Pansy and the other maids were making the rounds of the guests. They carried trays loaded with vol-au-vents stuffed with shrimp, toast squares topped with pate, caviar and pearl onions, buttered toast rounds with ham and mustard, pickled onions on toothpicks and for the sweet tooth, coconut balls and cream fondants.

Sherry and port were in ample supply, and Cecily spied Lady Bottingham requesting a maid refill her glass as the string quartet took over from the choir and guests strolled around exchanging polite conversation.

Spotting Sir Reginald Minster and his wife in a corner, Cecily made her way over to them. Lady Henrietta seemed ill at ease and kept fidgeting with the sash of her pink silk gown. Sir Reginald, on the other hand, was apparently in good spirits, having no doubt consumed a fair amount of the port he held in his hand.

"Jolly good recital," he said, his eyes sparkling above his rosy nose. "We really enjoyed it, didn't we, Henny?"

Lady Henrietta opened her mouth to speak, but her husband continued in his rather strident voice, "Good voices, those choirboys. You can't beat a choir for singing carols. Makes it all the more significant—the religious aspect, you know. Am I right, Henny?"

Again Lady Henrietta attempted to speak, only to be thwarted by her husband's booming voice. "Shame about that chap dying, Mrs. Baxter. Must put a dampener on the proceedings, I imagine?"

Cecily flinched but managed to keep her expression indifferent. "Somewhat, Sir Reginald. I trust, however, that it will not spoil your holiday."

She watched his face carefully, trying to detect some sign of guilt. Sir Reginald, however, seemed quite unconcerned. "I have to admit, Mrs. Baxter, that from what I've heard, no one is going to miss that blighter. He caused a great deal of anguish for a good many people. Am I right, Henny?"

Lady Henrietta managed to murmur something unintelligible.

"I hope you enjoyed our special brand of whiskey," Cecily said boldly. As she expected, she received a puzzled glance from Lady Henrietta which she ignored. "We have it specially brewed for our guests."

"Oh, I'm sure it's excellent, but I never drink the stuff. Burns holes in my stomach." Sir Reginald nudged his wife. "Henny will tell you."

"I thought I already did," Lady Henrietta murmured.

Cecily rather rudely cut in. "Oh, I assumed the bottles you bought were for you."

Sir Reginald narrowed his eyes. "Actually, I bought them for gifts. Henny's brothers both enjoy whiskey. I bought them a bottle each. Right, Henny?"

"Oh, yes, yes." Lady Henrietta nodded, her tiara slipping in the process. Straightening it, she added, "Charles and Douglas will so enjoy the whiskey. We have sent the bottles to them by courier to make sure they arrive on time."

Cecily was about to respond when she caught sight of Baxter beckoning to her. "If you will excuse me," she said, "I must attend to my duties. I do hope you will enjoy the rest of your stay. The pageant will be held tomorrow night. I trust you will both attend?"

"Wouldn't miss it, would we, Henny?" Sir Reginald assured her, apparently having discarded his momentary pique at her questions.

Cecily left before his wife could get out an answer. Was Sir Reginald as innocent as he sounded, or was he lying, with his wife confirming his lies? She could of course, check with the couriers to see if they really did send out the bottles. It would however, be much quicker to search their room. Sir Reginald had bought two bottles of whiskey. Only one had been found in Archibald Armitage's room. If she found the other in Sir Reginald's room, instead of on its way to Lady Henrietta's brother, then she would have enough to confront him.

Baxter seemed perturbed when she reached him. "Barry gave this to me to give to you." He handed her a slip of paper. "He said to tell you he did his best."

Glancing at it, Cecily was about to respond when he added, "Look at Lady What's Her Name, over there." He nudged his head at the fireplace.

Following his gaze, Cecily saw Lady Bottingham standing perilously close to the smoldering coals and visibly swaying.

"I think she's had a touch too much to drink," Baxter said. "You might want to rescue her before she falls into the fire."

Cecily wasted no time in rushing over to the aristocrat. Grasping her arm she said gently, "Lady Bottingham, would you like to sit down? There's a sofa over there that's quite comfortable."

The other woman stared at her with bleary, bloodshot eyes. "I was cold," she mumbled. "Now I'm hot."

"Well, then, why don't we move away from the fire." Guiding her guest to the settee, Cecily managed to get her seated without arousing attention. "Can I fetch you a nice cup of tea?"

Lady Bottingham shook her head. "Thank you, no." She hiccupped, and put a hand over her mouth. Leaning forward, she looked earnestly up into Cecily's face. "I had a little drink."

"Yes, I can see that. Perhaps some tea will help clear your mind."

Again the aristocrat shook her head. Patting the empty seat beside her, she said carefully, "I'd like to talk."

Cecily glanced around the room, decided she could spare a moment or two, and sat down next to the woman.

"Nobody talks to me," Lady Bottingham said, speaking

in a whisper so soft Cecily had to lean closer to hear. "No one cares about me."

"Oh, I'm sure that's not true." Cecily smiled at her. "I care about you, for one, and I'm quite sure there are others."

Lady Bottingham's face screwed up, as if she were about to cry.

Alarmed, Cecily reached for her hand. "Perhaps I should escort you to your room?"

"Would you?"

"Of course."

The other woman's grip almost broke Cecily's hand as she helped Lady Bottingham to her feet. Holding her charge firmly under the elbow, Cecily made her way to the door. She caught sight of Baxter staring at her with anxious eyes and nodded at him, hoping that would convey that she had the situation well in hand.

Although somewhat unsteady, Lady Bottingham managed to mount the stairs without too much trouble, and they reached her room without mishap.

Cecily would have left her at the door, but Lady Bottingham insisted on her coming inside. Following the woman into the room, Cecily watched her sink onto the bed, one hand passing across her forehead.

"I must apologize, Mrs. Baxter," she mumbled. "I don't usually imbibe to that extent. I'm sure I shall pay for it in the morning."

"No doubt." Cecily smiled. "Perhaps it would be best if you retired for the night. A good sleep might help."

"Perhaps." Lady Bottingham uttered a shuddering sigh.

"It was seeing that man again. It was just too painful. I should have known better than to obey such a ridiculous impulse."

Cecily frowned. "I'm sorry. Is there someone here who makes you uncomfortable?"

"There was." The other woman's smile was a trifle lopsided. "Thankfully, he is dead now."

A shiver of shock ran down Cecily's back. "Are you, by chance, speaking of Archibald Armitage?"

"I am indeed." Lady Bottingham stared at her shoes. "He completely ruined my life, you know. Despicable man."

Deciding that she needed to hear more, Cecily walked over to an armchair and sat down. "I'm very sorry to hear that."

Lady Bottingham waved a weak hand at her. "Oh, it was my own fault. He'd promised marriage and I foolishly believed him. One night he plied me with brandy, took advantage of me at my most vulnerable, then having had his way with me, deserted me like a common harlot of the streets."

Completely taken aback, Cecily managed to murmur, "Oh, how positively terrible for you."

"Well, as I said, it was my own fault. For one brief moment I let my feelings override my good sense and have lived to regret it ever since. I cannot allow any relationship with a man, for no gentleman wants used goods. I am doomed to be alone the rest of my life."

"Have you no family?"

"I have." She sighed, a sound of utter despair that tore at

Cecily's heart. "I made the mistake of expecting them to understand and console me. Instead, they have disowned me. The one thing I can be thankful for was that the scandal was never made public. No one besides myself and my family knows of my indiscretion."

"That is, indeed, a blessing."

"When I read in the newspaper that Archie would be here for Christmas, I made a rash decision to come here and confront him. I felt there were things that needed to be said before I could put it all behind me. Now it's over. He's dead and I'm free at last to banish the memory of him forever."

Cecily hesitated, then asked gently, "I do trust you didn't do anything to hasten his demise?"

The aristocrat's eyes opened wide. "Whatever do you mean? Was it not a natural death?"

Her shock seemed genuine enough and Cecily hastened to reassure her. "An accident, perhaps. We're not certain of the cause of death." It was a half truth at best, but better than openly admitting Armitage was murdered. "How did he react to your confrontation with him?"

"There was no confrontation. I never got the chance to say anything. He died before I could speak to him, and perhaps I should be thankful for that." Lady Bottingham briefly closed her eyes. "Forgive me, Mrs. Baxter, but I have grown exceedingly weary. I feel I must lie down."

"Of course." Cecily rose swiftly and made her way to the door. "Will you be able to manage by yourself?"

The aristocrat's lips twitched in a rueful smile. "I am used to managing things by myself, Mrs. Baxter. Thank you for listening. I fear the sherry has made me less than prudent. I trust our conversation will go no further?"

"You can rest assured, Lady Bottingham. No word of what you told me will pass my lips." Cecily let herself out into the hallway, her thoughts riveted on her conversation with Lady Bottingham. Much as she wanted to believe the good lady innocent of murder, she had a strong motive for poisoning Archibald Armitage, and she was on Barry's original list of people who purchased the whiskey.

Kevin stood close by his wife's side when Cecily returned to the library. Madeline looked concerned and managed to whisper in Cecily's ear as she bid her good night, "Don't go there alone."

Puzzled, Cecily smiled and nodded. "You will be at the pageant tomorrow night?"

"Of course." Madeline tucked her hand under her husband's arm. "How could we possibly miss one of Phoebe's notorious presentations?"

Kevin rolled his eyes. "Must we?"

"Yes, dear. We owe it to Cecily to be there."

Kevin uttered an exaggerated sigh. "Oh, very well. If you insist."

Having settled that, Madeline gave Cecily a final wave and floated out of the room.

Cecily wasn't given much time to dwell on her friend's odd warning. The second the door closed behind Kevin Prestwick, Phoebe was at Cecily's side.

"I thought she would never leave." Phoebe fanned her face with a lace handkerchief. "I so wanted a word with you before the night was over. I have a new idea for the pageant and I wanted to know what you thought of it."

Cecily looked at her in dismay. "A new idea? But Phoebe, you had the final rehearsal yesterday. The performance is tomorrow night. You have no time for new ideas."

"Oh, don't worry, it will be quite all right. I've told the dance troupe to be here tomorrow afternoon for another rehearsal, so we'll have plenty of time."

Cecily had to wonder how the members of Phoebe's dance troupe would feel about giving up most of the day before Christmas just to please a whim of hers. "They agreed to that?"

"They had no choice." Phoebe tossed her head, endangering the doves clinging to the brim of her hat. "I told them if they weren't at the rehearsal not to bother coming to the performance."

"Isn't that taking somewhat of a risk? What if they don't come to either? You won't have a pageant to present."

A shadow of uncertainty crossed Phoebe's face. "Of course they'll come. They look forward all year to performing at Christmas in the Pennyfoot. It's the highlight of their year."

Cecily tended to doubt that, but she let it go. She was about to ask Phoebe what time to expect them when the colonel strolled up, stroking his mustache.

"I say, old bean. What's this I hear about an actor being murdered in his bed?"

Cecily glanced over her shoulder in alarm. The colonel's booming voice seemed to carry clear across the room. Thankfully, no one seemed to hear him. "I don't know where you heard that, Colonel, but I assure you, there is no need for alarm."

She glared at Phoebe, who shrugged her shoulders.

"Oh, I'm not worried, old girl." The colonel nudged her so hard she fell against the wall. "I've been around enough dead bodies in my time, what? What?"

"There are no dead bodies in this establishment, I promise you," Cecily said firmly. "Now, if you will excuse me—"

The colonel laid a heavy hand on her arm. "Reminds me of the time I was in India." He frowned. "I *think* it was India."

"Oh," Phoebe said breathlessly, "I simply must have another of those delicious fondants before we go." She darted off before Cecily could stop her.

Left alone with the colonel, Cecily took a deep breath. "Colonel, I—"

"Did you know," the colonel said, leaning so close to her she almost choked on the brandy fumes, "that in India millions died from the plague? Blasted bodies all over the streets. The stink was so bad we had to wear bandanas over our noses to keep from suffocating."

Cecily suppressed a shudder. "That must have been awful, Colonel, but now I—"

"One of our lads got the bright idea to cover his horse's nose with a bandana. The fool rode like the wind, until the bandana rode up over his horse's eyes and blinded it."

Cecily gave him a stern look. "That's all very interesting, but—"

"Shot the poor blighter head first into a cart of rotting onions. Took him days to get the smell out of his hair. No one would go near him until—"

"Ah, there you are, Cecily."

Cecily gazed up at her husband in relief. "Baxter. The colonel was just telling me—"

"I hate to interrupt, my dear, but it's time for us to escort the choirboys out to the carriages."

Only Cecily saw Baxter's wink. "Oh, of course. Please excuse me, Colonel. Duty calls."

The colonel looked disappointed. "Oh, of course, old girl. Don't worry about intruders. You can count on me. I'll take my trusty sword to the blighters." He brandished an imaginary sword and swept a plate of sausage rolls off the sideboard.

Cecily just had time to signal to one of the maids to clean up the mess before Baxter hustled her out of the room.

"I swear," he muttered, "one of these days that fool will go too far and land himself in an asylum."

"Oh, I do hope not." Upset at the thought, she headed down the hallway.

"What was all that about intruders?" Baxter asked, catching up with her.

"I have no idea. You know the colonel. He's always fighting off imaginary foes."

"Yes, well, one day, one of them might decide to fight back."

"You do realize," Cecily said, as they emerged into the foyer, "that the choirboys left a half hour ago?"

"I know that," Baxter said, leading her toward the stairs, "and you know that. The colonel, however, doesn't know that. I got you out of his clutches without hurting his feelings."

Cecily laughed. "I doubt there's much that can hurt his feelings. Most of what he hears goes right out of his head."

"Except the fact that an actor was murdered in his room."

Cecily stared at him. "You heard him say that?"

"I did. But then I was already on my way over to rescue you and my full attention was on the colonel. I doubt if anyone else heard him."

"I certainly hope you're right." Cecily wearily climbed the stairs, holding onto the banister rail for support. "The last thing we need now is to set off a panic."

"You're no closer to finding the culprit?"

"Not yet."

"Aren't you running out of time?"

She paused to look back at him. "I am. If I haven't solved this case by tomorrow, I'll have no choice but to hand it over to P.C. Watkins. He's been remarkably patient as it is, though I rather think he is at a loss how to proceed."

"Which only means one thing."

She nodded gloomily. "Yes. Inspector Cranshaw. Heaven help us." A thought struck her, and she turned so sharply she almost lost her balance. "Oh, goodness, I forgot to ask Kevin to look in on Mr. Rickling."

Baxter frowned. "Well, let's hope it has nothing to do with whatever killed Armitage."

Indeed, Cecily thought, once more climbing the stairs. The last thing they needed was another death on their hands.

"A penny for them."

Gertie started, aware she had been silent for far too long. "What?"

Clive smiled. "A penny for your thoughts."

"Oh!" The last thing she wanted was for him to know what she'd been thinking. Before she had time to think about it, she blurted out, "Who did you tell the stories to before? Was it your children?"

His face turned so sad she immediately wished she hadn't said anything. "Yes," he said softly. "My own children. And my pupils."

She didn't know what had surprised her the most—the fact that he had children, or the fact that he'd had pupils. "You were a teacher?" she asked, deciding that was the safer subject.

"Once I was, yes." He folded his hands between his knees and stared down at them. "I should have told you all this before, Gertie. I wanted to, but you are so undecided about your feelings for me, I suppose I was afraid that what I had to say would turn you completely away from me."

Her heart started thumping against her ribs. What was he going to tell her? That'd he'd hurt someone? Killed someone? No, that was daft. Her gentle giant would never harm anyone. Of that she was sure. "Tell me what?"

When he didn't answer, she laid a tentative hand on his arm. "You're my friend, Clive. Nothing you say can turn me away from you. Whatever it is, I'll understand."

His smile was rueful. "Your friend. Yes, I suppose I am."

She shifted on the couch, wishing she could say more and so frightened of saying the wrong thing. "So tell me."

He took so long to start she thought he'd changed his mind about sharing his secrets. While the seconds ticked by, she became even more conscious of him sitting so close to her. She felt a deep urge to get up, away from temptation.

"I was married once," he said, making her jump. "I have two children, both boys. They live with their mother and stepfather. I don't see them anymore."

"I'm sorry." She sought in her mind for the right thing to say. "It must be hard for you."

"It is." He raised his chin and stared at the ceiling. "I miss them." He looked back at her. "It was my fault, though. You see, I had a . . . problem with drinking. I don't remember when it started. I used to go down the pub whenever I felt unhappy, or lonely, or afraid."

She stared at him, unable to believe him capable of being afraid of anything. "What were you afraid of?"

He shrugged. "Of being a failure, I suppose. I had a lot of responsibilities. I married very young. I had just started teaching, and when the first baby came along my wife was ill for a long time. It seemed as if all the troubles in the world had been heaped on my shoulders. Everyone expected so much from me—my pupils, my headmaster, my wife, my children. It became overwhelming."

She nodded, aching to touch him and afraid to make the move. "I know that feeling."

He buried his head in his hands. "I'm not like you, Gertie. You are so strong. I was weak. I drowned my sorrows and before I knew it, the drinking had control of me."

She could tell what it was costing him to speak of it and impulsively touched his arm. "I'm so sorry."

It was a moment or two before he answered. "When I

realized it was costing not only my marriage but my profession as well, I tried to stop. The harder I tried, the worse the addiction became. Eventually I lost my job, and then my wife told me to move out. I lost everything that was important to me."

He lifted his head, and she saw the pain in his eyes. Her whole body ached for him. "That must have been so bloody awful."

Clive looked down at his hands. "I reached a low point when I stood on Tower Bridge one night, intending to jump in the river."

She gasped, one hand over her mouth. "Someone came along and saved you?"

"No." He cleared his throat. "I realized I had two choices. I could either jump, and everyone would be rid of me, or I could turn myself around, make something of my life and hope everyone would eventually forgive me."

She swallowed, hard. "I'm so glad you chose to live."

His smile sent waves of warmth right through her body. "So am I, now. I haven't touched a drop of drink since that night. There were a lot of times when I didn't think the struggle would be worth it, but I know now I made the right choice. If I'd jumped, I'd have only been remembered as a drunk and a failure. I hope now when I die, I'll be remembered for something much better."

"You will." She could hardly speak, her throat was so tight. "You're a good man, Clive, and you've been so bloody good to me and the twins. Thank you for telling me all this. I know it wasn't easy for you."

His gaze raked her face, as if he were searching her mind. "You don't think any less of me for hearing about my sordid past?"

"Course not." Her heart was thumping so hard she could feel the vibration in her chest. "I've made my mistakes, too, and paid for them. Nobody's perfect. What counts is what you are now, not what happened to you in the past."

He reached out, taking her by surprise when his fingers brushed her cheek. "My dear Gertie. Wise beyond her years."

"I don't know about that." On guard again, she drew back and he dropped his hand. "Do you miss teaching?"

He looked sad again. "Very much. I still do a lot of reading, though, to keep my mind active and inquisitive."

"You like to read?" She'd pounced on his words, realizing this could be the answer to what she could get him for Christmas.

"Very much."

"What do you like to read?"

"Anything I can get my hands on—history, science, classic fiction, poetry—I'll read just about anything."

"Have you read the books in our library?"

He smiled again. "Just about all of them."

She hadn't realized they'd been talking in normal tones until James said sleepily, "Has Father Christmas come yet?"

She shot off the couch as if she'd been doing something wrong. "He doesn't come 'til tomorrow night, and he won't come at all if you don't flipping go to sleep again right now."

James mumbled something and closed his eyes.

"I'd better go," Clive said, heaving himself off the couch. "Thanks for a lovely evening."

"I should be the one thanking you." They were whispering again, and she crept across the floor to open the door. "It was nice."

She looked up at him as he loomed over her. For a long moment he stared down at her, while she wondered if he would try to kiss her and what she'd do if he did. Then he said quietly, "Good night, Gertie."

She closed the door behind him and leaned against it, letting out the breath she'd been holding for the past few seconds. She had to make up her mind about Clive, one way or another. She couldn't go on letting him think he had a chance if she wasn't prepared to take a chance with him herself.

Tomorrow, she promised herself. Tonight she would sleep on it, and tomorrow she would make up her mind one way or the other and stick to it. She only hoped that the prospect didn't terrify her enough to keep her awake all night.

CHAPTER
❁ 11 ❁

Cecily arose early the next morning, anxious to search the guest room while everyone was in the dining room. Baxter had decided to go into Wellercombe to do some last-minute Christmas shopping, thus relieving her of the necessity to tell him of her intentions.

After making sure she was alone in the hallway, she entered the Minsters' room. After a hurried and somewhat guilty rummaging through drawers and wardrobes, she could find no trace of a whiskey bottle anywhere.

Feeling thoroughly frustrated, she backed out of the room into the hallway. She didn't notice Gertie until the housemaid spoke from directly behind her, startling her out of her wits.

"Is there something I can help you with, m'm?"

Caught red-handed, Cecily struggled to find an excuse as to why she was lurking around a guest room with no good reason to be there. Gertie, however, wasted no time in reaching a conclusion.

"Beg your pardon, m'm, but were you by any chance looking for something to help you find out who killed Mr. Armitage?"

Cecily glanced over her shoulder in alarm. "Hush, Gertie. We don't want to frighten our guests. So far nobody knows he was murdered. As far as I know, anyway."

Gertie nodded. "It's all right, m'm. Everyone's in the dining room. I did want to have a word with you, though."

"Come along to my suite, then." Cecily led the way to her door and opened it. "Mr. Baxter has gone into town, so we won't be disturbed."

"That's good." Gertie followed her into the room. "I know Mr. Baxter doesn't like you chasing after murderers."

Cecily pulled a face. "No, he doesn't. Now, what was it you wanted to tell me?"

"It's about Gilbert, the new stable lad?"

"Go on."

"Well, Charlie Muggins told Pansy that Mr. Armitage had done Gilbert out of a lot of money. Charlie wondered if that's why Gilbert wanted to work here. So's he could get his revenge on Mr. Armitage."

Cecily raised her eyebrows. "When did Pansy hear this?"

"It were two days ago, m'm. Charlie said that Gilbert told him he would like to mess with the brakes of Mr. Armitage's motorcar so it would end up in the ocean. Charlie thought he was joking, but now he's not so sure."

Cecily regarded her chief housemaid with a keen eye. "You think Gilbert might have decided to find another way to exact revenge on Mr. Armitage."

"It did cross my mind, m'm."

"Why didn't you tell me this before?"

Gertie looked down at her feet and traced the pattern on the carpet with her toe. "Pansy asked me not to tell you. She was scared that Samuel would be cross with her if he knew she'd told me what she'd heard."

"I see." Cecily frowned. "Well, I shall have to have a word with Samuel and Gilbert, but I'll try to keep Pansy's name out of it."

"Thank you, m'm. I know she'd appreciate that. So would I." She paused, then added a little sheepishly, "As long as we're talking about it, there's something else I should tell you. I heard as how Mr. Armitage hurt a lot of people, and Mrs. Tucker seems to know an awful lot about it, though she won't tell me nothing when I ask."

Cecily frowned. "Are you saying that Mrs. Tucker knew Mr. Armitage personally?"

Gertie shook her head. "I don't really know, m'm. But if she didn't, she knows someone who did. She told me that Mr. Armitage had ruined Lady Bottingham's life, and before that she told me that the Minsters had suffered at the hands of a scoundrel and I think she meant Mr. Armitage."

Cecily let out her breath. "Well, thank you, Gertie. You've been a big help."

Gertie looked worried. "I don't want to get no one in trouble, m'm, but I thought you should know what I heard."

"Don't worry." Cecily opened the door and ushered her housemaid outside. "No one will know we talked, and no one will be in trouble who doesn't deserve to be."

Gertie smiled. "Thank you, m'm. I feel better now."

She hurried off, leaving Cecily gazing after her, her mind a whirl of confusing thoughts. Lady Bottingham had been certain no one but her family had known about her indiscretion. She certainly wouldn't have confided in Beatrice Tucker, of all people. So who was the mysterious person who had told the housekeeper about the socialite's unfortunate relationship with the actor?

Could it have been Gilbert? He obviously had dealings with Mr. Armitage in the past. Had he inadvertently found out about the actor's involvement with Lady Bottingham and relayed the encounter to Mrs. Tucker?

She tried to remember what Gilbert looked like. A husky, fine-looking man. He seemed eager to please, if she remembered. No matter if he was the gossip or not, he had applied for the position with an ulterior motive. She didn't like that. She would have a word with Gilbert Tubbs, and the sooner the better.

"We need clean serviettes," Beatrice Tucker announced the minute Gertie walked into the kitchen. "Go and fetch the ones hanging on the clotheslines outside."

It was on the tip of Gertie's tongue to refuse. As chief

housemaid, it wasn't her job to bloody fetch linens off the clotheslines. She was about to inform Tucker the Terrible of that when it occurred to her that a brief respite from the housekeeper would be most welcome.

Without another word, she grabbed the laundry basket, marched across the kitchen and out into the yard. The skies had cleared for Christmas Eve, but the wind from the ocean stung her ears with the cold. She blew on her fingers to keep them warm as she crossed the yard. Just as she reached the clotheslines, she spotted Samuel on his way to the stables.

She dropped the basket, cupped her mouth with her hands and yelled, "Samuel! I need to talk to you!"

He paused, looking back at her as if deciding whether or not to ignore her, then, with a shrug, he trudged back across the yard toward her. "Watcha want?" he demanded when he reached her.

"I want to talk to you about Pansy." Gertie reached up and tugged on the wooden clothes-peg that held the serviette to the line. The linen was frozen stiff, and she had to crumble it in her hands to get it to fold.

"What about Pansy?"

Samuel had sounded wary, and she chose her words carefully. "She loves you, you know."

"She's got a funny way of showing it. Making eyes at Gilbert and ignoring me. What's all that about?"

Gertie reached for another serviette. "She's just trying to make you jealous, that's all. She doesn't have no bleeding interest in Gilbert. In fact, I think she's afraid of him. You should know that."

"No, I don't know that." Samuel dug his hands into his pockets. "She wanted to get married right now. I told her I want to have a business established before we got married. She doesn't want to wait."

Gertie pulled the serviette from the line and folded it. "Pansy will wait if she knows you really mean it about marrying her."

"I told her I would when I have enough money."

Gertie put her face up close to his. "Telling her ain't enough, twerp. Words are easy to say and forgotten later. She needs something more solid than bloody words."

Samuel frowned. "Solid?"

"Think about it." She tugged more serviettes from the line and dropped them in the basket. "That's all I got to say."

She didn't see him leave, but she heard his footsteps scrunching across the yard. Smiling to herself, she picked up the basket. She was so bleeding good at giving other people advice about their love lives. Why couldn't she handle her own?

The thought of Clive twisted her stomach in knots as usual, and she impatiently shoved his image out of her mind. She had the morning to get through before she could think about him. Then she was going into town to get him his Christmas present. She knew now what she wanted to buy for him. She just hoped she'd be able to find what she wanted.

Much as she hated to admit it, it felt good to be buying a gift for a man again. It meant she had someone else in her life besides her children. They meant the world to her, of course, but there were times when she needed grown-up company, and it was so lovely to have that again.

She didn't need to let it get all complicated. It was enough that she and Clive could have a laugh now and then, and to have someone to grumble to when things got her down. He seemed happy enough with that, so why go and spoil it all? What they had was perfect for her right now.

Humming to herself, she marched back into the kitchen and dumped the laundry basket on the counter.

Michel was at the stove, stirring a pot of soup. He looked up when she passed him and muttered, "What do you have to be cheerful about?"

She was feeling so good she did something unheard of for her. She threw her arms around him and hugged him. "Happy Christmas, Michel! I got a feeling it's going to be the best bleeding Christmas ever!"

Michel coughed, and Beatrice stared at her as if she'd lost her mind. "Stop horsing around and get those serviettes ironed. They have to be on the table in half an hour."

For once, Gertie kept her mouth shut. She picked up the basket again and whisked it out of the kitchen and down the hallway. It didn't matter if Clive never found out how she felt about him. She knew it inside, and that was all that mattered. It was her secret to cherish and hold inside her for as long as she needed. One day she'd tell him how she felt. When the time was right.

Cecily made her way across the yard, holding her thick shawl tight to her throat. The sunlight dazzled her eyes, but she could feel the cold in every bone in her body. Shivering, she hurried across the courtyard to the stable doors.

At first she could see nothing, but then her eyes grew accustomed to the darkness inside and she could see Samuel crouched down in front of one of the stalls, mixing grains with beet pulp. There didn't seem to be any sign of Gilbert, and she walked cautiously across the stable, pausing behind Samuel.

He must not have heard her, as he jumped when she spoke his name. Leaping to his feet, he caught the bucket with his foot, overturning it and spilling out the horse feed onto the ground. "Crumbs," he muttered, squatting down again. "I'd better clean this up."

He started scooping the feed back into the bucket with his hands, and Cecily looked around for a shovel. Spotting one leaning against the wall, she fetched it and brought it over to him. "Here, this might work better."

Red-faced, he took the shovel from her. "Sorry, m'm. I'm just not used to seeing you in here."

"I didn't mean to startle you, Samuel." She waited until he'd scooped up as much of the feed as he could and leaned the shovel against the wall. "I'd like a quick word with you," she said, looking around the stables. Horses poked their noses over the gates, while farther down a gleaming motorcar stood where a blacksmith had once worked at his lathe. There was no sign of Samuel's assistant, however. "Is Gilbert in here?"

"No, m'm. He's taken one of the motorcars out for a test run. The gentleman wanted some work done on it, and Gilbert obliged. He just wants to make sure everything's working right."

Cecily raised her eyebrows. "I wasn't aware that we did motorcar repairs."

Samuel's gaze didn't quite meet hers. "Er . . . we don't . . . usually, but Gilbert wanted to do the bloke a favor. I hope that's all right, m'm?"

"Well, yes, I suppose it is, as long as it doesn't interfere with his work here. Which reminds me. I hear that Gilbert applied for work here because he wanted to damage Archibald Armitage's motorcar."

Samuel's face registered shock, fear, and then anger. "Pansy told you that."

"No, actually she didn't. I heard it from someone else." Cecily gave her stable manager a stern look. "Is it true?"

Samuel folded his arms across his chest. "I don't know how true it is, m'm. But one thing I'm sure of. If Gilbert did say that, he didn't mean it. He must have been joking. He's just not the kind of person that goes around hurting people. I'm sure of that."

"I hope you're right." She paused, then added, "I understand you bought a bottle of our special label whiskey from Barry."

Samuel frowned. "Yes, I did. Was that wrong? Barry didn't say anything when I bought it."

"No, no, it wasn't wrong." Cecily paused again. How she hated having to question him in such a critical way. She trusted her stable manager above all her staff, but if she was to identify the killer, questions had to be asked.

Samuel was watching her, a mixture of hurt and confusion

on his face. She drew in a deep breath. "Samuel, Dr. Prestwick discovered arsenic in a bottle of our whiskey that was in Mr. Armitage's room. Do you mind telling me what you did with the bottle you bought?"

Samuel's face was white with shock. "You're not thinking I killed that actor?"

"No, of course not."

They exchanged a long look, while realization slowly spread across his face. "I gave the whiskey to Gilbert for a Christmas present."

Cecily nodded. "I thought so."

He started to speak, cleared his throat, and tried again. "No, I don't believe it, m'm. Gilbert didn't kill Armitage. I'd stake my life on it. He was happy the bloke was dead but—" He broke off, apparently realizing the implications behind his words. "I'm just making things worse for him, aren't I?"

"I'm afraid so. Don't worry, Samuel, if Gilbert is innocent, the truth will come out. I'm sure of it. I'll have a word with him later, and we'll see if we can sort all this out. Please send him to my office as soon as he returns."

She left, knowing she'd upset her stable manager and praying that she wouldn't have to hand Gilbert over to the constable. She knew, only too well, how it felt to be betrayed by someone she liked and trusted.

As she entered the foyer she saw Phoebe and the colonel talking earnestly to Philip, who seemed a trifle agitated, which was unusual for him. Hurrying over to them, she was just in time to hear the colonel say, "But I tell you, old chum,

I saw the blighter myself, lurking around the bushes in the rose garden."

"I'm sure you did, sir," Philip stammered. "But I'm quite sure it's gone by now."

"Really, Freddie," Phoebe began, but the colonel silenced her with a swift jerk of his hand.

"I'll take care of it for you, old chap. I'll take my trusty sword to it. Or better yet . . ." He fumbled in his belt. "What a dashed nuisance. I seem to have left my pistol at home."

Philip's eyes were wide with alarm, and Cecily decided it was time to intervene.

"What seems to be the trouble, Colonel?"

At the sound of her voice, the colonel swung around. "Oh, there you are, old bean. Just in time to witness the slaughter, what? What?"

Cecily glanced at Phoebe who lifted her shoulders in an elegant shrug. "He won't listen to me," she muttered.

"A bear!" the colonel shouted, throwing both hands in the air. "Big as a mountain. The blasted bounder was in the rose garden. Probably starving, by the look of his coat."

"Were you with him?" Cecily asked Phoebe.

Before she could answer, however, the colonel once more butted in. "No, she wasn't, thank heavens. I was on a leisurely stroll when I saw this great brute of a bear in front of me. I should've dealt with it right then and there, but I thought I'd better get back here and warn everyone." Once more he fumbled with his belt. "If only I'd brought my pistol—"

The front door opened just then, letting in a blast of wintry air that flipped the feathers on Phoebe's hat over her face. She

199

brushed them back, while giving her husband a look that plainly warned him he was going too far. "That's *enough*, Freddy! You know very well we don't have bears in Eng . . . oh!"

This last was directed at the newcomer who had entered the foyer. The gentleman towered above everyone, his broad shoulders and wide girth seeming to fill the room. The most striking thing about him, though, was his fur coat and furry hat pulled low over his forehead.

Even Cecily was taken aback at the sight of him, though she managed to murmur, "I think, Colonel, that this could be your bear."

The colonel took one look, grabbed his wife's arm and bolted for the hallway, yelling, "I need a drink!" Phoebe's boots scrabbled wildly to keep up with her husband, as, with one hand on her hat, she was dragged out of sight. Her voice floated back from the hallway, her words indistinct, but her temper unmistakable.

Cecily turned to the visitor. "Please forgive us, sir. The colonel means well, but sometimes he gets confused."

The gentleman pulled his hat from his head, revealing a shock of red hair that matched his bushy beard. "Quite all right, madam. I assume I'm speaking to Mrs. Baxter?" He'd rolled his *r*'s, revealing his Scottish accent, and Cecily smiled.

"You are, indeed, sir. What can I do for you?"

"I was just passing by and wanted to take a look at your fine establishment. I think this would be a bonnie place to bring the family next summer."

"Of course. I'm sure your family would enjoy it. The beaches are lovely in the summertime. I'll be happy to escort you myself on a tour of the Pennyfoot Country Club. Come this way." She led him to the hallway, praying nobody within earshot mentioned the death of Archibald Armitage. One way or another, she had to solve this murder before word got out in the newspapers. Or she'd be begging for visitors come next summer.

Gertie paused in front of the bookstore and stared at the display of books in the window. There were dozens of them, all shapes and sizes, some with bright covers and gold inscriptions on the spine.

James tugged at her hand. "Can we go to the toy store, Mama? Can we?"

"Oh, yes, let's!" Lillian danced a few steps down the street. "I want to look at the dolls."

"You'll have to wait, then." Gertie held out her hand to the little girl. "Come along, we're going in here."

James pouted. "All there is in here is stuffy old books."

Gertie looked at him in surprise. "You like books. You both love *Alice's Adventures in Wonderland*. I've read it to you a dozen times."

"I like trains better." James dragged his feet as Gertie pulled him into the store. "I want to go to the toy store!"

Gertie bent over until her face was close to his. "If you don't flipping behave and do exactly what I say, Father Christmas won't leave you any toys tonight."

Lillian punched him in the arm. "Yeah, so behave, James. I want Father Christmas to come tonight."

James muttered something under his breath and stomped into the bookstore behind his mother.

Letting go of their hands, Gertie picked up a book from a table close by. Its pale blue cover gleamed in the light from the gas lamps, and words were embossed in silver on the front and the spine. It would look lovely sitting on a bookshelf, she thought, then read the title. *Mrs. Bartholomew's Book of Etiquette.*

She hastily dropped the book back on the table. The last thing Clive needed was lessons in manners. There were so many books to look at her head spun with indecision. She wandered down an aisle between shelves crammed with titles she barely understood. Choosing Clive's Christmas present was a lot harder than she'd imagined.

"Can I help you find something?"

The voice came from behind her and she spun around to face an earnest young man staring at her through thick-rimmed glasses. Taken by surprise, she muttered, "I'm looking for a book."

"Well, you've come to the right place." The shop assistant smiled. "What kind of book are you looking for?"

Gertie looked around the shop, her stomach beginning to tie up in knots. "I dunno. It's for a Christmas present."

"I see. For a friend or a relative?"

"A friend." She gulped, wishing she'd thought of something less complicated for Clive's present.

"A good friend?"

Something in the way he said it caught her attention. She lifted her chin. "A very good friend."

"Ah." The assistant nodded and smiled. "Then may I suggest a book of poetry?"

Gertie let out her breath on a sigh. Of course. Why hadn't she thought of that? "That would be perfect. Where is it?"

The young man looked confused. "Where's what?"

"The pertry book."

"Oh." He waved a hand at the end of the aisle. "We have several. They're on the first and second shelves."

"Ta ever so." Feeling completely out of her depth, she rushed to the end of the aisle. A quick glance revealed two rows of books, all labeled as poetry. Feeling the assistant's gaze burning into her back, she grabbed one and tore back to the counter.

Without even looking at the title, she paid for it, grabbed the bag from the assistant and headed for the door. She was halfway through it when she remembered she'd brought the twins with her.

Cursing under her breath, she turned back into the shop. At that moment she heard a yelp from somewhere in the back of the shop, followed by a series of thuds. The next instant Lillian's familiar wail echoed throughout the aisles. "Mumm-e-e-e-e!"

Rolling her eyes, Gertie rushed in the direction of the cries, and a moment later found her daughter sitting on the floor, surrounded by books, while James did his best to scoop some of them up in his arms.

The assistant who had served her towered over both twins, eyes blazing. "What do we have here?" he bellowed, above Lillian's howls.

"So sorry," Gertie muttered, hauling Lillian to her feet. She glared at James. "Put those down. We're going home."

James obligingly dropped the books back on the floor and trotted off toward the door. Gertie managed a weak grin at the furious assistant and, dragging Lillian with her, fled after her son. Next time she went shopping, she vowed, she'd do it without the twins. She only hoped that the book she bought for Clive was a good one, or she was going to look like a proper ninny.

CHAPTER 12

Cecily finished her tour of the Pennyfoot Country Club in record time and sent off her prospective guest with a brochure and a tin of mince pies. She was on her way to her office when she heard strains of piano music and raised voices drifting down the hallway.

She hesitated for a moment, mindful of her meeting with Gilbert Tubbs, then decided she should probably look in on Phoebe's last-minute rehearsal, just in case the new idea turned out to be disastrous.

As she drew closer to the ballroom the voices sounded louder and more belligerent. Her heart sinking, she pushed open the door and stepped inside.

Phoebe was at the foot of the stage, throwing her hands

in the air while her hat tilted back and forth. Her yells were drowned out by the pandemonium onstage. Two of the dancers were actually fighting, pulling hair and clawing at each other's faces. The rest of the troupe stood around and watched. Some applauded and called out encouraging remarks while others covered their mouths with their hands, their eyes wide with apprehension.

Over in the corner, the pianist was still thumping away at the keys, his long hair bouncing on his shoulders as he jerked in time to the music. He seemed to be the only one in the room unaffected by the melee going on onstage.

Cecily hurried over to Phoebe's side and touched her arm.

Phoebe turned a red face toward her and yelled, "I have no control over these hooligans. I give up. There will be no presentation tonight."

Alarmed now, Cecily held onto her friend's arm. "Surely it can't be that bad?" She glanced up at the screeching combatants. "What happened?"

"I wanted to add a tableau to the presentation." Phoebe paused for breath, having been forced to shout to be heard. "A living Christmas tree. Five girls on the floor, three standing on their shoulders, then two, and then the angel at the top."

Cecily noticed now that all the dancers were dressed in various shades of green, except for one of the fighting women, who was dressed all in white.

"Everything was going just fine until Ada fell," Phoebe yelled. "She said Mathilda pushed her. Mabel said she should be the angel anyway because she's lighter. They started fighting and won't listen to me." She turned and screamed at the pianist. "For heaven's sake stop that infernal racket!"

The pianist, obviously offended, tossed his head and mercifully lifted his hands from the keys.

Cecily held up a finger at Phoebe then marched over to the door leading backstage. Moments later she walked out onto the stage. Ada was now on her back on the floor, while Mathilda sat on her, arms flailing wildly. The dancers jumped back when they saw Cecily, but the two fighters were too intent on killing each other to notice.

Cecily reached out and grabbed a handful of Mathilda's hair and pulled it hard.

"Ow!" The young woman swung around, her hand raised to swipe at the new threat.

Cecily stepped out of reach and crossed her arms. "This stops *now*," she said, "or you will both be out of the presentation. What's more, you will never be invited back again. Do I make myself clear?"

Both women nodded and scrambled to their feet. "It weren't my fault," Ada began, but Cecily silenced her with a quick jerk of her hand.

"I'm not in the least bit interested in hearing the lurid details. Not another word about it, understand?"

Cecily left the women mumbling among themselves and joined Phoebe out front. "I take it the Christmas tree tableau was your new idea?"

Phoebe nodded. "Yes, I thought it would make a wonderful festive finale and—"

"I suggest you cut it," Cecily said bluntly. "Stick with

what you already have rehearsed and hopefully there will be no more of this sort of disruption."

Phoebe raised her chin. "But I called a special rehearsal just for the tableau."

"Then use the time to perfect the original numbers." Cecily smiled in an attempt to soften her words. "It would be nice to have an accident-free presentation, don't you think?"

"Oh, absolutely." Phoebe glanced up at the dancers, who were now meandering about like lost souls. "If such a thing were possible."

"I'm sure everything will be just fine." Cecily patted her friend on the shoulder. "I have to get back to my office, but I know I'm leaving all this in good hands." She marched off before Phoebe could protest and headed for the door.

She was halfway down the hallway to her office when she saw Cuthbert Rickling turn in at the other end and hurry toward her.

"Oh, good afternoon," the choirmaster murmured when he reached her. "I'm sorry to intrude, Mrs. Baxter, but I left all my sheet music in your library last night. I was hoping I might retrieve it?"

"Of course!" Cecily waved a hand at the hallway behind her. "I'm fairly certain my maids would have left it there for you to collect, but if not, be sure to tell me and I'll ask my housekeeper where it might be."

"Thank you, madam, so very much. I'm much obliged." He hurried off, just as another figure appeared at the end of the hallway.

Cecily recognized the woman as she walked toward her. "Lady Bottingham? Is there something I can do for you?"

The woman seemed to be looking past Cecily's shoulder, a puzzled frown creasing her brow. She gave a little shake of her head and focused on Cecily. "Ah, Mrs. Baxter. I just wanted to ask what time the pageant will be presented tonight."

"Directly after the evening meal." Noticing that Lady Bottingham still seemed absorbed in something behind her, Cecily turned her head, just in time to see Cuthbert Rickling disappear into the library.

"I think I know that man," Lady Bottingham murmured. "I just can't remember where I met him."

"His name is Cuthbert Rickling and he's our local choir-master. Though I do believe he lived in London before moving to Badgers End."

Lady Bottingham nodded. "I know him from somewhere, though the name is not familiar. Cuthbert Rickling? No, I don't know the name. How odd. I could swear I've met the man somewhere."

"Perhaps he reminds of you of someone you know?"

Still frowning, Lady Bottingham muttered, "Perhaps. And yet . . ."

"Well," Cecily said brightly, "why don't we go to the library and you can meet him. Then perhaps you'll find out whether or not you've met before."

"That's a good idea." She followed closely on Cecily's heels as they walked toward the library. "I'm not usually so

Kate Kingsbury

persistent, but I do hate it when I can't remember something I should know."

Cecily laughed. "I find myself doing that more often these days."

Lady Bottingham paused, waiting for Cecily to open the library door, then stepped inside ahead of her. "I suppose one should become accustomed to these little inconveniences and be thankful for . . . oh!" She broke off and stared around the room. "Where did he go?"

Joining her, Cecily looked around in disbelief. The room was quite empty. It was as if Cuthbert Rickling had simply disappeared into thin air.

Pansy stomped across the courtyard, struggling to carry the loaded coal scuttles in each hand. Usually Gertie filled the coal scuttles. She was much bigger and tougher and didn't seem to mind the weight that dragged down Pansy's arms and shot pain across her back.

Gertie, however, was out Christmas shopping, and Mrs. Tucker had ordered Pansy to fetch the coal. Pansy had tried to argue that she wasn't strong enough to carry the scuttles, but the housekeeper, as usual, had simply waved a hand at the door and turned her back.

Another pain shot across Pansy's back, taking her breath away. Groaning, she dropped the scuttles onto the ground and stretched, one hand rubbing the sore spot. A stiff breeze caught her cap, lifting it off her forehead. She grabbed it and fiercely pinned it back into place.

Out of the corner of her eye she saw a figure turn the corner of the building and march toward her. Her stomach gave a treacherous flip before her temper overruled her heart.

Samuel was actually smiling as he drew closer, which did nothing to cool her resentment. Arms crossed, she glared at him. "Watcha want?" she demanded, letting him know she was in no mood for his nonsense.

He paused in front of her, his smile wavering. "I came to wish you a Happy Christmas," he said, his hands thrust deep in his pockets.

"Same to you."

She bent to grasp the handles of the scuttles but he was too quick for her. Snatching them up, he swung them easily back and forth. "I'll take these for you."

"Why?"

"'Coz they're heavy."

"I can manage."

"I know you can. I just want to help, that's all."

She tried to reach for the handles, but he backed away. "I don't want no favors from you," she muttered. "Give them to me."

Instead of handing them over, he put the scuttles down on the ground and stood in front of them. "I got something to say to you."

"I don't want to hear it."

"I've got a Christmas present for you. It's right here in my pocket."

Curiosity almost won her over, but her pride was stronger. "I don't want nothing from you, so there."

Kate Kingsbury

"You'll want this." He drew a small package from his pocket and held it up for her to see. "I know you'll want this."

Hope started fluttering deep inside, but she was too afraid to entertain it. "Well, you don't know everything, do you."

"Pansy." He stepped closer to her, and she had to struggle to breathe. "Here, just take this. Just look at it. If you don't want it, I'll go away, and I won't bother you anymore."

She stared at the package, every instinct in her body urging her to take it.

"*Please*, Pansy."

She'd never heard that tone in his voice before. Her hand seemed to have a mind of its own. It reached out and took the package from him.

Her fingers trembled so much she had trouble opening it up. The small box inside had a lid to it, and she slowly lifted it off.

Just at that moment the sun slid out from behind a cloud and sent a beam of light across the courtyard. It fell on the tiny box and filled it with such dazzling radiance Pansy was momentarily blinded. She lifted the diamond ring from its nest of velvet and stared at it. Dare she hope that it meant what she wanted it to mean?

Samuel stepped closer and took the ring from her. Tears spurted from her eyes as he knelt in the dirt, the ring in his hand and his heart in his eyes. "Pansy, I love you. Please say you'll marry me."

It was as if all her doubts, fears, and anger were released in one ear-splitting scream as she flung her arms around his

212

neck. Taken by surprise, he lost his balance and toppled over. She fell on top of him, laughing and crying at the same time.

Sitting together on the ground, he hugged her until her tears dried, then gently took her hand and slid the ring on her finger. "Now it's official," he said. "We'll be getting married just as soon as I have the down payment for a lease. Before next Christmas, I promise. We'll work together to build the business. If that's all right with you."

"It's more than all right. It's perfect!" She hugged him again. "I can't wait to tell everyone!"

"Well, we'd better get this coal to the kitchen before Mrs. Tucker gets her knickers in a twist." Sam climbed to his feet and pulled her up into his arms. "Happy Christmas, the future Mrs. Whitfield."

She clasped her hands and stared at the ring sparkling on her finger. She'd never seen anything so marvelous in all her life. "Mrs. Whitfield. It sounds wonderful."

Grinning, he dropped a quick kiss on her mouth, then hauled the scuttles up in his hands. "All right, then. Lead the way."

She skipped across the courtyard, feeling as light as a snowflake. Reaching the kitchen door, she turned to take the coal from him. "See you tonight?"

"Of course." He handed the heavy scuttles over. "We have a lot to celebrate."

"Happy Christmas, Samuel. I'm so happy."

"Me, too." He reached out to stroke her cheek. "Happy Christmas, Pansy."

She waited until he'd disappeared before carrying the scuttles into the kitchen. Although she was bursting to tell someone—anyone—she also wanted a few quiet moments to herself. To think about what had just happened and what it meant. *Mrs. Whitfield*. She was going to be a wife and mother. She'd be scrubbing her own floors instead of someone else's. No more waiting on tables, making up all those beds or cleaning silver. No more Pennyfoot.

She dropped the scuttles on the grate next to the stove. *No more Pennyfoot.* The country club and all the people in it had been her home and family for so long. How she would miss them all.

The thought tempered her happiness for just a moment, but then she felt a surge of excitement. She was going to be married and have children of her own. In less than a year. She uttered a little squeal of joy, and then realized Michel and Mrs. Tucker were watching her as if she'd gone out of her mind.

She opened her mouth to make her stupendous announcement, then closed it again. No, she would tell Gertie first. Gertie was like an older sister to her, and she would be happy for her. Hugging herself, she ignored the stares and marched across the kitchen. This was going to be the very best Christmas of her life.

Cecily stared in disbelief at the empty room. "I saw Mr. Rickling come in here moments ago," she murmured. "How very odd."

Lady Bottingham looked around. "Perhaps he's hiding?"

"Why on earth?" Cecily shook her head, unable to accept such a ridiculous idea. Nevertheless, she walked around the room, peering behind the furniture just to make sure. Just as she was about to pass the French windows, she felt a draft across her face. Upon further inspection, she saw that the doors were slightly ajar.

Staring out at the rose garden, she murmured, "I do believe Mr. Rickling chose to leave through here."

"I wonder why?" Lady Bottingham joined her in front of the windows. "There isn't much to see out there this time of year, is there?"

"I wouldn't think so." Cecily stared at the doors for several moments, turning everything over in her mind. Turning to her guest, she murmured, "If you will excuse me, Lady Bottingham, I have an urgent meeting to attend. I do hope you will enjoy the pageant tonight. Mrs. Carter-Holmes usually presents very good entertainment, as long as one doesn't expect too much professionalism. She and her cast are strictly amateur, but what they lack in expertise they make up for in enthusiasm."

Lady Bottingham smiled. "It sounds like my cup of tea. I'm looking forward to it."

Cecily followed her out the door, her mind still feverishly working. Cuthbert Rickling seemed to have a habit of making abrupt exits. Each time, it seemed, whenever Lady Bottingham was present. It seemed as though he was deliberately trying to avoid the lady. Which brought up some very interesting questions.

She parted company with Lady Bottingham in the foyer and headed down the steps to the kitchen. There was something she needed to ask her temporary housekeeper. Pushing open the kitchen door, she saw Michel at the stove and Mrs. Tucker at the kitchen table. The maids were apparently attending to their duties elsewhere, and Cecily wasted no time in seizing the moment.

"Mrs. Tucker, would you please step outside with me for a moment?" Without waiting for an answer, she marched across the room and out of the back door. The housekeeper followed her, stumbling over the step in her haste.

"What is it, m'm? Is there something wrong?" She looked fearfully over her shoulder. "Not another murder, is there?"

Irritated to discover that the woman knew Archibald Armitage had been murdered, Cecily shook her head. As usual, the grapevine had been busy. "No, thank heavens. There's something I must ask you, however, and it concerns some of our guests."

Beatrice's frown deepened. "Is it Lady Henrietta? Has she been complaining? Is it about the gown that Gertie ruined? I already told Gertie she would have to pay for another one."

Cecily raised her eyebrows. "Gertie ruined Lady Henrietta's gown?"

"Yes, m'm. She's clumsy and careless, that one. Spilled sherry all down the front of the gown and Lady Henrietta was most upset. She said it was a Paris original and irreplaceable. I told her we would give her another one."

216

"Did you now." Cecily folded her arms. "Gertie is supposed to buy a Paris original from out of her salary?"

"Yes, m'm. I thought it only right."

Cecily leaned forward. "Mrs. Tucker. *I* couldn't afford a Paris original. Could you?"

"Well, no, m'm. But then I didn't—"

"Then you have no right to expect my chief housemaid to produce such an outrageous sum of money for what was no doubt a simple accident. In future, I suggest you be a little less generous with your compensation to strangers." She paused. "I assume that Lady Henrietta is a stranger?"

The housekeeper looked puzzled. "Pardon, m'm?"

"I mean, were you acquainted with Lady Henrietta before this week?"

"Why no, m'm."

"And Lady Bottingham? Are you acquainted with her?"

Beatrice's frown deepened. "We have spoken on occasion. Lady Bottingham asked me for an extra blanket for her bed. Other than that, I don't know her at all."

"I see." Cecily glanced out toward the ocean. She could see the horizon over the top of the gate and the faint smudge of gray above the blue water. Clouds were gathering, probably bringing rain, or maybe even snow if it got any colder.

Turning back to the housekeeper, she said quietly, "Then tell me, Mrs. Tucker, how you heard about Lady Bottingham's unfortunate relationship with Archibald Armitage. Lady Bottingham told me that no one but she and her family knew about it."

The housekeeper's cheeks grew red. She stared down at the tips of her shoes poking out from under the hem of her skirt and nervously traced a circle with her foot. "I . . . ah . . . I'd rather not say, m'm."

"Your loyalty is admirable, but entirely misplaced. I insist that you tell me the name of your informant."

The housekeeper's lips trembled. "I don't want to get no one in trouble, m'm. He's a nice man and I'm sure he meant no harm. I swore I wouldn't tell no one else about it, and I haven't. I—"

"Mrs. Tucker." Cecily hardened her voice. "I simply won't take no for an answer. I have to know who it was who gossiped about Lady Bottingham. I would hate to have to give your agency an unfavorable reference."

Beatrice's eyes opened wide. "Oh, please don't do that, Mrs. Baxter. I need to work. I have no one to take care of me."

Considering the housekeeper's unfortunate temperament, that came as no surprise to Cecily. "Very well, then, I suggest you tell me the name of the person who appears to know so much about Archibald Armitage."

Beatrice hesitated a moment longer, apparently struggling with her conscience, then blurted out, "It was Mr. Rickling, m'm. I've been acquainted with him ever since I met him in church a few weeks ago. We were sharing a glass or two of whiskey the other night and I happened to mention Lady Bottingham. I don't think he would have said anything if he hadn't been a little fuzzy in the head with the drink."

Cecily let out her breath, sending a puff of steam into the air. "Thank you, Mrs. Tucker. I appreciate your candor."

"You won't say anything to Mr. Rickling about this?" The housekeeper wrung her hands. "He and I have become friends, and I'd hate to lose that."

Stunned at the thought of the rather sedate choirmaster befriending someone like the outspoken, brash housekeeper, Cecily took a moment to answer. "Rest assured, Mrs. Tucker, Mr. Rickling will never know you spoke to me about this."

Beatrice's features relaxed in relief. "Thank you, m'm. I'm much obliged. Will that be all?"

"Yes. Thank you." Cecily preceded her into the kitchen, acknowledged Michel's salute with a wave of her own and hurried out the door into the hallway.

So Cuthbert Rickling knew Lady Bottingham well enough to know about her secret involvement with Archibald Armitage. Yet the woman hadn't remembered where she'd met him, so obviously she hadn't imparted the knowledge herself.

Which could mean only one thing. Mr. Rickling must have obtained the information from another source—the only other person who would have told him. Namely, Archibald Armitage himself.

Then again, the choirmaster had proclaimed no knowledge of the man when she'd mentioned his name. It would appear that Cuthbert Rickling had lied, and she would very much like to know why.

CHAPTER
❋ 13 ❋

Having reached the foyer, Cecily headed for the reception desk. Philip was slumped in his chair as usual and started up as she spoke his name.

"Sorry, m'm." He ran a hand over his sparse hair. "I was just about to straighten up the desk." He reached for the heavy ledger that contained the signatures of the guests and shifted it over an inch.

Cecily curbed her rebuke. Receptionists were hard to find in Badgers End. "Have Samuel bring a carriage round to the front door as soon as possible. Tell him we'll be going into town."

"Yes, m'm. Right away, m'm." Philip settled his spectacles a little more firmly on his nose and reached for the telephone.

Cecily headed for the stairs and started to rapidly climb them. As she reached the first landing she saw Lady Bottingham stepping down the next flight toward her. Passing each other on the landing, the aristocrat acknowledged Cecily's smile with one of her own.

"I'm off to do a bit of last-minute shopping," she said, gathering up her skirt in readiness for the next flight down. "I do love to shop on Christmas Eve. There's such an air of excitement and merriment among the people."

Cecily nodded in agreement. "Not to mention the last-minute bargains."

Lady Bottingham laughed. "There's that, too, I suppose."

Cecily turned to leave, only to be halted again by Lady Bottingham's next words.

"Oh, by the way, I remembered where I'd seen that gentleman who disappeared in the library."

Turning back, Cecily waited.

Lady Bottingham shook her head. "I should have remembered, of course, but I've tried so hard to blot out all those memories. His name is not at all familiar. In fact, I'm almost certain he used a different name when I knew him."

Hardly able to contain her impatience, Cecily asked quietly, "So where did you meet him?"

"He was a friend of Archie's. Or I should say, a former friend. The gentleman was also an actor and doing quite well on the stage from what I remember. That is, until he suddenly fell apart at a rehearsal. The director was Richard Tidewell, one of the best in the country. Your choirmaster got his lines all mixed up and caused an uproar onstage.

Everyone was laughing at him. The director fired him, and from what I heard, he was so mortified by it all he left the profession. Actors can be so terribly sensitive, you know."

"That's awful." Cecily felt a surge of sympathy for Cuthbert Rickling. Becoming the laughingstock of his profession must have been devastating.

"Yes. It is." Lady Bottingham stared into the distance, as if reliving another moment in time. "I remember there were rumors that Archie had stolen the heart of the gentleman's lover and that's why he fell apart and left the stage. How true that is I couldn't say." Her face grew bitter. "Though, knowing Archie, I wouldn't be at all surprised if it were true."

Cecily watched Lady Bottingham descend the stairs. Had Archibald Armitage really stolen away Cuthbert Rickling's lover? Rickling's name had been on the list of people buying whiskey from the bar. But then so had numerous other people, some with just as strong a motive for the murder.

Though none of the other suspects had worked so hard at concealing their past relationship with the victim. It was obvious that Cuthbert Rickling had gone out of his way to avoid meeting up with Lady Bottingham. Was it because he knew she would recognize him and remember his past association with Archibald Armitage? Was it possible Mr. Rickling had more to hide than the others?

Now it was all the more imperative that she have a word with the choirmaster, and as soon as possible. It was quite likely that he would be at the church, preparing for the midnight Mass. She would go there first, and if he was not there, she would have to pay a visit to his home. No doubt Phoebe's son, Reverend Algernon Carter-Holmes, would direct her to the choirmaster's house.

Baxter was not in the suite when she arrived, much to her relief. She hated lying to him, which more often than not she'd been forced to do while pursuing a villain. Telling Baxter the truth about her activities usually ended up in an argument, and she did her best to avoid that.

After pulling on her heavy wool coat and green velvet hat, she wound a red scarf around her neck and picked up her fur muff for good measure. She passed no one on the stairs and arrived in the foyer just as Samuel appeared in the doorway. He wore his cap pulled low over his forehead and the wool earmuffs Pansy had bought for him last Christmas.

Hurrying across the lobby, she half expected to hear Baxter calling out her name. It was with relief that she stepped out into the chill of the afternoon. The clouds were drawing in and had already turned the ocean into an angry gray.

"It looks like we'll have snow for Christmas again," she observed, as she followed Samuel down the steps to the carriage.

"Yes, m'm." He opened the carriage door for her and offered his hand.

Ignoring the offer as usual, she clambered up and settled herself on the creaking leather seat. The interior of the carriage smelled of damp upholstery. The cold quickly numbed her fingers, and she tucked them inside the muff. Her nose felt as if it had been dipped in ice. She wriggled her toes inside her boots, trying to keep the circulation going.

"Where to, m'm?" Samuel asked, sounding somewhat impatient. "Philip just said you were going into town."

"We're going to St. Bartholomew's," Cecily said, her teeth beginning to chatter. "Do get going, Samuel, before I freeze to death."

Instead of jumping to obey as he normally did, her stable manager stood staring at her. "The church, m'm?"

"Yes, Samuel. The church. I need to speak with the choirmaster."

Samuel frowned. "But the service isn't until midnight."

"I know that. I'll be attending it as usual. However, I need to speak with the choirmaster now." She peered down at him. "Are you all right, Samuel? You look a little out of sorts."

"No, m'm. I mean, yes, m'm. The church it is." He slammed the door shut so hard it rocked the carriage. The bay in front snorted and stamped his feet, as if startled by the sound. The carriage rocked again as Samuel swung up into the driver's seat.

Cecily leaned back as the carriage lurched forward, its wheels rattling on the hard ground. Something was wrong, she was sure of it. She and Samuel had shared many adventures together and she knew him almost as well as she knew her husband. If she wasn't hot on the trail of a murderer she'd stop the carriage and insist that he tell her what was concerning him so.

She couldn't spare the time right now, but just as soon as

the opportunity arose, she would find out what was causing her stable manager to act so strangely.

Gertie arrived back at the Pennyfoot just a few minutes before Daisy, who had also been out Christmas shopping. "I have to be back on duty in half an hour," Gertie said, as the nanny helped her take off the children's coats, hats, and boots. "There's something I want to do before then."

"Go right ahead." Daisy hung the coats up in the wardrobe. "I'll be taking the twins to supper soon."

Thanking her, Gertie grabbed her apron and the package from the bookstore and tore off down the hallway. She took the stairs two at a time and arrived in the foyer out of breath and thankful she was still wearing her coat. No doubt Clive would be outside somewhere in the cold.

Philip was dozing behind the counter, and she slammed her hand down on the bell. He leapt to his feet, blinking at her as if he didn't recognize her. "What can I do for you, madam?"

"I'm not a madam, you flipping twerp. It's me, Gertie."

"Oh, it's only you." He sat down again, looking grumpy. "I thought you were one of the guests. We have to get brighter gaslights in here. It's too dark to see properly."

"You'd see a lot bleeding better if you kept your flipping eyes open." She leaned across the counter. "I'm looking for Clive. Do you know where he is?"

Philip gave her a sour look. "What'd you want him for?"

"None of your bloody business. Do you know where he is or not?"

"Not. Though I should think he's gone home by now."

A wave of disappointment almost overwhelmed her. She was about to turn away when Philip added, "He's coming back tonight, though. He has to be here to help with the Christmas pageant."

She felt like hugging the frail little man. "Oh, that's right! I'd forgotten that. Thank you, Philip!"

Without waiting for a response she dashed back across the foyer to the stairs. She'd see Clive tonight and give him his present. She should have known he wouldn't go home without seeing her. After all, he'd told her he had presents for the twins, and he hadn't given them to her yet.

Skipping down the stairs, she decided she now had time to wrap the book. A gift was always nicer if it was wrapped. Hoping she wouldn't run into Tucker the Terrible, she hurried down the hallway to her room.

She could hear the twins arguing before she opened the door. Daisy sat on the edge of the bed and looked at her in surprise when she walked in. James and Lillian were in the corner, arguing about whether or not they should leave the window open for Father Christmas.

"He won't come at all if you two don't stop flipping squabbling," Gertie said as she sank onto the bed next to Daisy. "Leave the window shut. It's blinking freezing out there."

"But what if—"

Gertie cut off James's protest with a swift flip of her hand. "He'll find his way in, no matter what."

"Yes, silly," Lillian said, her voice laced with scorn. "He comes down the blinking chimney."

227

"Here!" Gertie swung around to glare at her daughter. "What have I told you about using those words?"

Lillian crossed her arms and raised her chin. "But you use them!"

"I'm a grown-up. You're just a little girl. Little girls and boys don't use those words if they want Father Christmas to bring them presents."

James jigged up and down, his face growing pink. "Father Christmas is coming tonight!"

"Yes, if you're both as good as gold." Gertie frowned at her children. "Now sit down quietly and behave. It's almost suppertime and then you'll be able to see the Christmas pageant, and after that it will be time for bed."

"And then Father Christmas comes!" the twins chorused together.

"Only if you're good." Gertie rolled her eyes at Daisy. "I don't envy you taking care of them tonight. They're wound up tighter than a blinking watch spring."

Daisy laughed. "They'll be good. They know what will happen if they're not."

Taking the warning to heart, the twins dropped to the floor and began playing with some brightly colored marbles.

Gertie held up the paper bag that contained Clive's book. "I have to wrap this before I go to work."

"There's some wrapping tissue left in the wardrobe." Daisy moved to get up but Gertie stopped her with a hand on her arm. "I'll get it. You need to save your energy for the twins tonight." She stood up, carrying the bag with her to the wardrobe.

A few sheets of green and red tissue lay on the shelf. After a moment's thought, Gertie decided on the red, tied up with silver string. She pulled the paper from the shelf and laid it on the dresser, then took the book out of the bag.

Turning it over, she read the title and uttered a gasp of dismay. "Oh, blinking crumbs!"

Daisy looked up at her. "What's the matter?"

Gertie swallowed. "I bought this book for Clive." She held it up for Daisy to see. "I didn't look at the title. I just wanted a book of poems for him."

Daisy squinted. "What does it say? I can't read it from here."

Gertie stared at the book as if it would jump up and bite her. "It says, *Love Poems for Your Loved One*."

Daisy grinned. "That should make Clive a very happy man."

Gertie groaned. "No, no. I can't give this to him." She looked at Daisy, feeling very close to tears. "What the blinking blazes am I going to do now?"

Staring out of the carriage window, Cecily spotted a few snowflakes drifting down through the trees as Samuel parked the carriage in front of the church gates. She waited for her stable manager to open the door, hoping that she could get her business over with quickly and get back to the warmth and comfort of the country club.

Once more she declined the offer of Samuel's hand and alighted onto the hard ground. She was relieved to see the flickering glow of candles and gaslights in the stained glass windows. It meant someone was inside.

Pushing open the doors, she stepped into the foyer. The smell of candle wax mingled with the fragrance of pine—a familiar aroma that always reminded her of her escape from the burning library of the Pennyfoot Hotel.

She shuddered as she walked quickly down the aisle toward the pulpit. Shadows danced across the walls and along the rows of pews on either side of her. The main hall appeared to be empty. Whoever had lit the candles had to be somewhere in the rear of the church.

She turned to speak to Samuel and saw to her amazement that he was not standing behind her, as she'd expected. Frowning, she retraced her steps and opened the doors again.

Samuel was sitting on his driver's seat in the front of the carriage. Irritated now, she called out to him. He turned his head at her shout and raised his hand in response, though he made no effort to climb down from his perch.

Muttering under her breath, Cecily marched down the path and out through the gate. "Samuel Whitfield, get down from that carriage this instant."

The stable manager leapt to the ground, causing the bay to make snuffling noises as it shuffled its feet. "What is it, m'm?"

"Why didn't you follow me into the church?"

Samuel looked at the church as if he'd never seen it before. "Oh, I thought you wanted to go in there by yourself, m'm. Sorry."

"If I had wanted to go in alone I would have ordered you

to wait for me here. Usually you are practically attached to my heels when I go somewhere." She peered at him from under the brim of her hat. "What on earth is wrong with you, Samuel? You seem to be in another world. Are you not well?"

Samuel cleared his throat, peered up at the darkening sky, and blinked. "It's starting to snow."

"I'm not moving another inch until you tell me what is troubling you." Cecily moved closer. "You're keeping something from me. I can tell."

"No, m'm. That is . . . ah . . . yes, m'm." Samuel cleared his throat again. "I'm sorry, m'm. I'm just a bit fuzzy, that's all. It's not every day a man gets engaged to be married."

Cecily opened her mouth, closed it again, then let out a squeal that echoed all the way down the lane. *"Married?* Samuel! Is it Pansy? Yes, of course, it's Pansy. Who else would it be? Oh, I'm so happy for you!" Forgetting herself entirely, she threw her arms around his thin shoulders and hugged him.

Samuel seemed shocked by her embrace and quickly moved away from her. "Thank you, m'm. I'm happy you're happy. Of course, you do know that means I'll probably be going after my own business next year. I promised Pansy we'd be married before next Christmas, and I won't marry her unless I'm in business for myself."

"Oh." Deflated, she drew back. "Well, of course, but Samuel"—her voice wobbled and she quickly controlled it—"I really don't know what I shall do without you. You have been such a good worker, an excellent stable manager, but more than that, you and I have shared so many interesting situations. I've come to rely upon you to aid and abet me, as it were, and even to protect me when needs be."

Samuel's grin was replaced by a frown. "I know, m'm. I did think about that. A lot. But one of these days you'll be giving up chasing after villains, and you won't need me anymore. Whereas Pansy needs me now, and I want to build a life with her."

"Of course you do, Samuel. Take no notice of a silly old woman. Get married, build your business, and have lots of children. I know you'll make a great father. Now come along, we have business to attend to, and a Christmas pageant to see when we get back to the Pennyfoot."

Fighting ridiculous tears, she led the way back up the path to the church doors. Samuel was like a son to her. Her own two sons lived abroad, and she barely heard from them from one year's end to the next. They were both busy with their lives and families, and seldom had time to write. She had replaced them with Samuel, and now she was losing him, too.

It was all very sad, but the natural progression of life, and she was the last person in the world to stand in his way. She wanted him to be happy, and to be happy for him. Pansy would make him a good and loving wife. She couldn't ask for anything better for him.

Shaking off her melancholy, she once more pushed open the doors of the church and stepped inside. There was still no sign of anyone in the main hall, and she turned to her stable manager. "Go into the rear of the church to see if Mr. Rickling is here. If not, ask whoever is here for Mr. Rickling's address. I would really like to speak to him before this evening."

Samuel gave her a sharp look. "Does this have anything to do with the murder of that actor?"

She did her best to look innocent. "Why would you think that?"

"Because you're here to question the choirmaster." Samuel fixed her with a stern stare. "Does Mr. Baxter know you're here?"

She patted his arm. "Now don't fret, Samuel. We shall be in and out of here before anyone knows we're gone."

"He doesn't know, does he." Samuel wiped his brow with the back of his hand. "You know I'll be the first one he blames when he finds out. He's threatened to give me the sack if I let you get into trouble again."

"Oh, piffle. He'll never do that. As I've reminded you many times, I'm the manager of the Pennyfoot Country Club and I'm the one who decides who shall work for me. Besides, I have no intention of getting into trouble, as you so succinctly put it. Now run along and see if you can find Mr. Rickling. I just want to ask him a question or two, that's all."

She watched him trudge down the aisle and disappear out of sight. Poor Samuel. She'd led him into so many scrapes in the past, and he'd never once complained. Where was she going to find another stable manager willing and able to follow her into danger without question?

Seating herself in one of the pews, she mulled over his words. *One of these days you'll be giving up chasing after villains, and you won't need me anymore.* Perhaps this was a sign. Perhaps it was time she did give up trying to solve murders and let the constables do their job.

Baxter would be elated, and she'd be released forever from the threat of him taking a job overseas—something he so far had refused to give up entirely. She'd miss the excitement and the challenge of following clues and the thrill of bringing a miscreant to justice. She wasn't quite ready yet to settle down in an armchair and sew away the rest of her life.

She would have to find something else to do. Perhaps write a book about her adventures. She'd certainly had enough of them.

So deep was she in her thoughts she didn't notice the gentleman entering the pew until he sat down beside her. His presence startled her, and she turned to him so suddenly her muff slid off her lap. "Why, Mr. Rickling!" She smiled at him. "How quiet you are. I was hoping to find you here."

He was watching her, his gaze intent on her face as if he were trying to read her mind. "You wanted to see me?"

"Yes, I did." She glanced toward the altar, hoping to see Samuel emerge from the shadows beyond. "I wanted to talk to you about Archibald Armitage." She saw it then, in his face. The hatred and bitterness in his eyes shocked her.

"What about him?"

His tone of voice warned her, and she felt a quickening of her pulse. He looked different somehow. All traces of the meek, nervous choirmaster had disappeared. The man next to her was stronger, forbidding, *dangerous.* Of course. The man was an actor, after all. It had been easy for him to hide his true nature behind a façade.

Madeline's words came back to her, chilling her to the bone. *Don't go there alone.* But she wasn't alone, was she? Samuel couldn't be too far away. She made an effort to sound indifferent. "I was just wondering why you professed to have no knowledge of him, that's all."

He didn't answer her, but just kept staring at her with that evil gleam in his eyes.

Unnerved, she said the first thing that popped into her head. "You did know him, didn't you, Mr. Rickling. You knew him quite well, in fact. I believe he was responsible for the loss of your acting career."

"He was responsible for a lot more than that." Rickling raised his chin for a moment. "You know, Mrs. Baxter, you should really curb that incessant curiosity of yours. It could get you into trouble one of these days."

She might have smiled at that, had she been less anxious. "I manage to take care of myself, Mr. Rickling. I was merely curious as to why you went to such trouble to hide your association with Mr. Armitage."

"I think you know the answer to that." His smile was pure evil, transforming his face from a mild-mannered choirmaster to something far more menacing. "Unfortunately, I cannot allow you to inform anyone else of that fact."

Again Cecily heard Madeline's voice. *Beware, the danger is right there.* She'd been pointing at the Christmas tree at the time. No, not the Christmas tree. Madeline had been pointing *at the choirboys.*

Cecily slid away from Rickling along the bench. "I'm not the only one who knows about it. Lady Bottingham—"

"Ah, yes, the dear Lady Bottingham." He shook his head. "I shall have to take care of her, too. That's the problem when you get rid of someone. There's always a loose end or two."

Horror was making her skin crawl. Once more she sent a searching glance beyond the altar.

"If you're looking for your stable manager," Rickling said, slithering toward her, "I'm afraid he can't help you. He's taking a nap right now."

A whimper escaped her lips. Dear heaven, had she finally overstepped her mark? Why did she always act before she thought things through? Was Samuel dead? She couldn't bear the thought of it. "If you've hurt Samuel—" she began, but once more he cut her off, this time by grabbing her arm.

"You're in no position to threaten me," he snarled, his fingers biting into her flesh. "You are a busybody, Mrs. Baxter, and now you will pay the price. You and your pathetic little stable manager. You should have minded your own business. Armitage deserved to die, in the worst way possible. A young girl took her own life because of him. A woman I loved with all my heart. He had to pay for that."

Cecily stared at him. "You were in love with Sir Reginald Minster's daughter?"

For a moment she saw pain and vulnerability in his face, then it was once more replaced by the mask of evil. "The world is better off without Archibald Armitage. But you couldn't leave it at that, could you. You're causing me a great deal of trouble, and now I shall have to get rid of more people. Come."

She tried to resist as he dragged her down the pew, but he was surprisingly strong for his lean build. Her feet scrabbled for a hold as he hauled her past the altar and through a door in the rear of the church.

Still struggling to free herself, she noted two more doors they passed as Rickling hauled her along a dark, narrow hallway and into a tiny office. Shoving her over to a wardrobe, he opened the door and shoved her inside. "You can stay here while I decide what to do with you. I have no qualms in killing men, but I have no taste for slaughtering women. I shall have to think of a merciful death for you and your precious Lady Winifred Bottingham."

With that, he slammed the door and clicked the lock, leaving her in the musty darkness.

CHAPTER

❀ 14 ❀

Gertie paused at the top of the stairs to catch her breath. It wasn't often she got an urgent summons from Mr. Baxter. Usually when she did it meant trouble, and that was something she could do without right now. She had a hundred things to do before she could join Daisy and the twins at the pageant.

Meeting Clive, for one, and giving him his present. Every time she thought about it, her stomach jiggled around and she felt dizzy. If only she'd had time to go back to the store and exchange the book for a more suitable one. How was he going to react when he saw the title?

Would he think her too brazen and pushy? What if he got embarrassed and turned away from her? Perhaps it would be better not to give him anything. But that would make her look stingy. No, she had to give him something and the book was the only thing she could give him.

A door suddenly opened beside her and Baxter's furious face peered out at her. "Gertie! Where have you been? I called for you ten minutes ago."

"Yes, sir. Sorry, sir." She dropped a curtsey. "What can I do for you, sir?"

"You can tell me if you've seen my wife lately. I've been looking all over this dratted hotel for her and I can't find her. We're supposed to go to that dismal pageant together tonight and she should have been back by now, getting ready for supper."

Gertie frowned. "I think she left to go into town. I saw Samuel waiting with a carriage at the front door."

"When was that?"

"Earlier this afternoon, sir, when I went shopping."

"Did you see Mrs. Baxter in town?"

"No, sir. I went shopping along the Esplanade. I didn't go into town."

Baxter shook his head. "All right. I suppose she'll be back when she's ready. If you see her, though, please tell her I'm waiting for her here. Tell the others to keep an eye out for her, too."

"Yes, sir." Relieved that she wasn't in trouble after all, Gertie sped back to the stairs. She was late herself now, and Mrs. Tucker would probably be screaming her head off, wanting to know where she'd been. She had dinner to serve and dishes to be done before she was free to go to the pageant.

Her afternoon off had come and gone, and now she wouldn't get another one until after Christmas. She was tired already just thinking about it.

Reaching the foyer, she waved at Philip and dashed across to the kitchen stairs. Just as she reached them, a tall, bulky figure barred her way. Clive's deep voice seemed to penetrate right through her bones.

"What's your hurry, Gertie? Not trying to avoid me, are you?"

"N-no, of course not." Why was it she stammered every time she was around him?

"Good, because I was hoping to catch you. I came back early so that I could give you the twins' Christmas presents. Though we'll have to find somewhere to hide them until after they fall asleep."

Her stomach was flopping around so fiercely she was sure she would be sick. "I'd love to see them, Clive, but I'm already late in the kitchen. Can we meet later?" She swallowed. "I have something to give you, too."

"I was going to suggest I bring the toys to your room later tonight, when the twins are asleep, but I wasn't sure if you'd like that."

"I'd love that." She couldn't seem to get her breath and her voice sounded funny when she added, "The children are going to the pageant, though, so it will be late by the time they're asleep."

"The later the better." He stepped aside to let her pass. "Until tonight, Gertie."

She was too agitated to speak and could only manage a

241

brief nod before dashing down the stairs so fast she almost tripped at the bottom.

Arriving at the kitchen door, she paused to get her breath. She had to get ahold of herself. She couldn't go tearing in there like some nut-head from the asylum. Everyone would notice and want to know what was up with her. This was something she couldn't talk about to anyone.

She stood for a moment longer, filling her lungs with air, then walked into the kitchen. Michel was at the stove as usual, throwing sliced carrots into a boiling pot of soup. Two of the maids stood at the dumbwaiter, loading trays of canapés. Another maid was helping Mrs. Tucker form lumps of marzipan into roses to put on the trifle.

The housekeeper looked up at Gertie and yelled, "Where in blazes have you been? You're needed up in the dining room. One of the maids took sick and has gone to bed. Get up there at once and help serve the dishes, and for heaven's sake straighten your cap. You look like a street urchin."

Gertie turned tail and burst through the door into the hallway. She'd rather be in the dining room anyway, she told herself as she stomped back up the stairs. It might help settle her mind and her stomach. As for bossy old Tucker the Terrible, if it wasn't Christmas she'd tell that old woman what she really thought of her.

The dining room was buzzing with conversation when she walked in. Candles flickered on every table, throwing shadows across the holly and ivy centerpieces. The huge chandelier hanging from the ceiling sent a soft glow across the white tablecloths, while swathes of red and green velvet ribbons colored the walls.

Catching sight of Pansy on the other side of the room, Gertie skirted the tables to reach her. Trays of canapés sat on the sideboard and Pansy thrust one of them at her. "Thank goodness you're here," she said, sounding out of breath. "We're getting behind on everything. These need to go to the tables over there." She nodded at the windows, where several couples sat waiting.

Gertie took the tray and was about to leave when Pansy added, "I've got something important to tell you. Meet me outside in the hallway when all these have been served."

Taking a good look at her friend, Gertie couldn't tell whether it was good news or bad. Pansy's face was flushed, but then it always was when she got really busy. Her eyes were sparkling, too, but that could have been either excitement or temper.

"Go!" Pansy said, giving her a little push. "They've been waiting ages for those."

Gertie went, threading her way through tables to reach the windows. She was supposed to be the one giving orders and normally she would have bristled at Pansy's arrogance. Tonight, however, was different. Tonight she had more important things to worry about. Like the chances of Clive taking her gift the wrong way and getting offended.

The niggling worry started again in her stomach, and she did her best to ignore it as she approached the windows. After placing a dish of canapés on each table, she carried the empty tray back to the sideboard and grabbed another one. What was it Pansy had to tell her? Was it about Mr. Armitage? In all the excitement of everything she'd almost forgotten about the murder.

Thinking about the murder reminded her of madam. She'd forgotten to tell them in the kitchen to watch out for her. It wasn't like madam to be late for a meal. Normally she'd be right there in the dining room, joining her guests for the Christmas Eve banquet.

Gazing around the dining room, Gertie could see no sign of madam or Mr. Baxter. That was strange. She forgot about it again in the next moment, though, as Pansy rushed up to her and grabbed her arm. "We're finished when you've emptied that tray. I'll wait for you outside. Hurry! The soup will be here any minute."

Gertie rushed over to the last tables and deposited the dishes, then still carrying the tray, slipped out of the door into the hallway.

Pansy was jogging up and down, hugging herself as if she were cold.

"Whatever's the matter with you?" Gertie demanded.

Before her friend could answer, the bell at the dumbwaiter rang out a summons. Pansy sent a desperate look in that direction then blurted out, "Samuel asked me to marry him. I'm engaged!"

Gertie screamed. "What? Bloody hell! I don't believe it." With one arm she hugged Pansy's thin body so tight her friend called out in protest. Letting her go, she added, "Did he give you a ring?"

Pansy nodded. "It's in my pocket." The bell sent out another strident demand and she jumped. "We'd better get the soup. I'll show you later."

"Why aren't you wearing it?"

"I didn't want anyone to know until I'd told you about it."

Gertie followed her to the dumbwaiter, her heart bursting with joy for her friend. Pansy and Samuel had been through a lot together, and Gertie was happy that Samuel had taken her advice and finally proposed.

If only she was as good at managing her own life. Right now she was so topsy-turvy she didn't know which way to turn. One minute she felt like bursting with happiness and the next she was down in the dumps worrying about that stupid book. She'd be glad when she could give it to Clive and get it over with so she didn't have to worry about it anymore.

Carrying the heavy tureen of soup through the dining room door, she concentrated on getting it to the sideboard without spilling it. Pansy had gone ahead of her and was waiting for her put the tureen down.

"Look!" Pansy pulled a ring from her pocket and held it up. "Here it is. Isn't it beautiful?"

"Let me look." Gertie took the ring from her and held it up to the light. A flash of brilliance from the square cut diamond almost blinded her. "It's blinking gorgeous. You're a lucky girl." She went to hand it back but as Pansy reached for it her hand shook and somehow the ring fell from her fingers. Before either one of them could grab it, the ring rolled out of sight underneath the nearest table.

Gertie's heart sank when she saw Sir Reginald and Lady Henrietta seated there. "Cripes," she muttered. "Now we're in trouble. We'll have to wait until they leave before we can get it."

"I'm not waiting," Pansy wailed, and dived to her knees. Crawling forward, her head disappeared underneath the table.

Gertie froze for a moment, then sprang into action. Leaping over to the table she plastered a smile on her face. "Good evening, Lady Henrietta. I trust you are enjoying your meal?"

The woman looked startled, and without answering, glanced at her husband. Sir Reginald grunted something under his breath.

Gertie struggled to keep her smile going, even though her face felt like it was being stretched like a starched collar. "Is there anything else I can get for you?"

Sir Reginald scowled. "We haven't had our soup yet. How much longer do we have to wait?"

"Oh, I'm sorry. I'll get it to you right away." Gertie stuck her foot under the table, hoping to give Pansy a nudge to get out of there.

Instead, Lady Henrietta uttered a little yelp." You kicked me!"

Hastily withdrawing her foot, Gertie stammered, "I'm dreadfully sorry. I was just—" Out of the corner of her eye she saw Pansy rapidly scrabbling backward across the carpet, one hand holding up the ring. "I'll get your soup now, m'm."

Still baring her teeth in a smile, Gertie backed away and then made a dash for the sideboard. "Look what you did," she muttered, as Pansy slipped the ring on her finger. "I'm already in trouble with her. She'll be complaining to madam next."

"Sorry." Pansy grabbed the soup ladle and started spooning soup into a bowl. "But I didn't know you were going to kick her. Why'd you do that, anyway?"

"I was trying to kick you." Gertie sighed. "The way this bleeding day is going I'll be lucky if I get through the rest of it alive. Everything's going wrong."

Pansy stared at her. "What's the matter? Has something happened?"

"Not yet." Gertie filled two bowls with soup and picked them up. "But I've got a nasty feeling that it's going to."

Pansy looked scared. "Another murder?"

"No, nothing like that." Gertie turned to face the tables. "Just maybe the end of my hopes and dreams again."

Pansy opened her mouth to answer, then made an odd sound as she stared past Gertie's shoulder.

Gertie turned her head to see what her friend was looking at and saw Gilbert standing in the doorway, frantically beckoning to them.

"What does he want?" Pansy put down her bowl of soup. "I hope he's not cross with me for telling Samuel what he said about Mr. Armitage."

"I'll go and see what he wants," Gertie said, handing over her bowls of soup. "I'll get rid of him. He has no business coming in here after you." She marched across the room to the door, glad to have an outlet for her bad mood.

Gilbert had retreated into the hallway and she pushed open the door, ready to give him a piece of her mind.

Before she could say anything, Gilbert grabbed her arm. "Is Mrs. Baxter in there?"

"No, she's not." Seeing the worried look on Gilbert's face, she added, "Is something wrong?"

"I dunno." Gilbert sent a hunted glance over his shoulder. "She told me to meet her in her office. I've been in there waiting for her. I was supposed to be off an hour ago. My mum's waiting for me to come home for dinner."

Gertie stared at him, all the anxiety of the past few hours coming to a head. "That's not like her. Something must have happened to her. You'd better go and tell Mr. Baxter. I'll go down to the kitchen to see if anyone's seen her down there."

Gilbert dashed off and Gertie hovered in the dining room doorway for several seconds, torn between helping Pansy and finding madam. She looked across the room and saw Pansy flapping a frantic hand at her.

Deciding that she owed Pansy an explanation, she tore back to the sideboard. "I have to go down to the kitchen," she said, cutting off whatever Pansy was about to say. "I'll be right back."

"But—"

"Sorry, I've gotta go." She sped off again, narrowly missing a maid carrying a tray of dirty dishes. She didn't stop until she arrived at the kitchen, heart pumping and chest heaving.

Both Michel and Mrs. Tucker looked up as she burst into the kitchen. She got the words out, despite her lack of breath. "Has anyone seen Mrs. Baxter?"

"Not since the midday meal." Mrs. Tucker put down the

spoon she was using to dollop crème Chantilly on the top of the trifles. "Why? Is something the matter?"

Gertie looked at Michel. "Have you seen her?"

"I have not." The chef walked toward her, still holding a jug of cream. "Why ze big fuss? She is a busy woman, *non?*"

Gertie glared at him. "Busy here in the hotel, yes. The problem is, she's not here in the hotel. Mr. Baxter can't find her, and she was supposed to be in the dining room having dinner with him. She's kept Gilbert waiting in her office for over an hour. She *never* does that. Something must have happened to her."

"Like what?" Mrs. Tucker sounded impatient and Gertie turned her glare onto the housekeeper.

"How the bloody hell do I know? I'm going to tell Mr. Baxter that nobody's seen madam and he'll know what to do." Without waiting for an answer, she turned tail and flew out of the kitchen and back up the stairs.

Just as she reached the foyer, she saw Baxter hurrying down the stairs, followed closely by Dr. Prestwick. She ran to meet them, her stomach turning at the look on Baxter's face. "I've asked everyone," she said, as he paused at the foot of the stairs. "No one's seen madam since midday, when she left to go into town with Samuel."

Baxter nodded, his mouth a thin, grim line.

Dr. Prestwick stepped down beside him. "Thank you, Gertie. You can run along now. We'll take care of this."

"Yes, sir." Not sure if that was at all reassuring, she turned to leave.

"Oh, and Gertie?"

She turned back.

Dr. Prestwick gave her an encouraging smile. "Try not to worry. I'm sure there's a simple explanation. Most likely a breakdown of the carriage or something. There's no need to alarm anyone."

"Yes, sir. Thank you, sir." Feeling only slightly better, Gertie lifted her skirts and made a mad dash once more to the dining room.

Pansy frowned at her when she got back. "What was all that about? What's wrong?"

"Nothing. Madam's a bit late coming home, that's all." Gertie grabbed the last two bowls of the soup. "I'll get these. The main course is probably on the dumbwaiter by now."

"Crumbs. We'll never get all this done in time for the pageant."

"Course we will. Go and get the next dishes. I'll be there in a minute." Carefully she carried the soup to the last table, aware of her hands trembling enough to spill the soup. After safely placing the bowls in front of the hungry guests, she tore off to the door and out into the hallway.

Pansy was already lining up plates along her arms and Gertie helped her place the last one on her wrist, then started lining up plates along her own arm. Telling herself to calm down, she carried the plates back to the dining room. Everything was happening at once. She was facing a possible change of her life tonight, Pansy was now engaged to be married and madam was missing.

She didn't want to think about the murder, because that brought up the possibility that somehow the killer had done away with madam, and that was unthinkable. She hoped that Dr. Prestwick was right and that something had gone wrong with the carriage.

One thing kept hammering in her head. Nobody had mentioned seeing Samuel. He had left with madam, which meant he was missing, too. If something bad had happened to them, she couldn't bear to think how Pansy would feel. All she could do was hope and pray they both came home safely. For if not, it would be a terrible Christmas for them all.

Alone in the darkness, Cecily did her best not to panic. Rickling had given her a brief respite, and she had to make the most of it. Thoughts of what might have happened to Samuel held her frozen for several moments, then she deliberately shut the awful visions out of her head.

She couldn't think about Samuel right now. She had to concentrate on getting out of there. Survival first. Unless she escaped, she was powerless to help her stable manager, always supposing he was still alive to save.

The idea that he might be alive and suffering spurred her on. She ran her fingers down the wardrobe door until she found the lock. It seemed like a simple one, fastened by a key on the other side.

Had Rickling left the key in the door or taken it with him? She peered down at her feet, hoping to see a thread of light at the bottom of the door. She could see nothing but blackness. Squatting down, she ran her fingers along the bottom edge, but the gap was far too narrow to bring a key through.

She stood up again, and raised her hand to her hair. In her favorite books about Sherlock Holmes, she'd read that it was possible to open a lock with a hairpin. She wasn't exactly sure how to do it, but she'd always been a firm believer in providence and it had served her well in the past. Praying that it would do so this time, she stuck the prongs of the hairpin into the lock.

What seemed like hours later, she flexed her sore fingers and stretched her aching back. The lock remained stubbornly closed and no matter how she wiggled the hairpin, nothing happened except that now the prongs were twisted and bent.

Refusing to give up, she patted her hair to find another hairpin while she tugged the damaged one out of the lock. It refused to budge and, muttering under her breath a word of which her husband would most certainly disapprove, she wrestled with it, wriggling it back and forth to get it out.

Suddenly she heard a click, and to her utter joy and amazement, the wardrobe door swung open. Momentarily blinded by the light, she stumbled out into the room, mindless of who might be waiting for her.

Fortunately the office was empty, and she paused for several seconds, straining her ears. No sound penetrated the silence, and she crept toward the door. Rickling had to be around somewhere, perhaps waiting for her around the corner, ready to pounce on her.

The thought unnerved her, and she clutched her skirt with nervous fingers as she opened the door and slipped out into the hallway. The flickering gas lamps sent shadows dancing along the wall, causing her heart to leap in alarm as she stepped carefully toward one of the doors she'd passed earlier. A loud creak under her feet almost gave her a heart attack, and she waited, heart pumping frantically, until she was sure Rickling hadn't heard her and come running.

Samuel had to be somewhere in one of the rooms. She wouldn't consider the possibility that he was already dead. Samuel had to be alive. She could never live with herself if he wasn't. As for Rickling, he could be with Samuel right now. The thought spurred her on.

She reached the door and twisted the handle. It opened to reveal a closet crammed with brooms, mops, buckets, and cleaning supplies. Quietly she closed the door and advanced on the next one. She paused for a moment, her ear close to the panels, but could hear nothing from the other side. There was a key sticking out of the lock and she turned it, slowly, making as little sound as possible.

The door swung open. The room beyond was in darkness, but light from the gas lamp behind her spilled into the room. There in front of her was a huddled shape lying on the floor.

"Samuel!" Though she'd whispered his name it sounded as loud as an alarm bell, and she quickly slipped inside the room and closed the door behind her. She couldn't see a thing in the darkness, but she dropped to all fours and crawled toward the still figure.

Her hand bumped against a body and heart still thumping; she shook Samuel's shoulder. A soft moan answered her. Almost crying in relief, she whispered urgently, "Samuel?

Are you hurt?" The second the words were out of her mouth she knew how stupid that sounded. Of course he was hurt. Why else would he be lying there?

She tried again. "Can you get up?"

This time he didn't answer and she felt along his back to his head. Her fingers came away sticky and her stomach flipped over. "Hold on, Samuel. I'm going for help." She started to get up, then sat down again. She couldn't leave him there.

No one would come to the church from now until midnight Mass. That was several hours away. If she left to find help, by the time she got back Rickling might well have killed Samuel. On the other hand, if she stayed there, they could both be killed.

She needed a weapon of some sort. She'd noticed earlier that right across from the room she was in was a built-in shelf in the wall containing a pair of heavy vases. Maybe one of those would be heavy enough to use as a club.

Quickly she got to her feet and carefully opened the door. The hallway was empty and she rushed over to the shelf and lifted one of the vases from its perch. Weighing it in her hands she decided it was heavy enough to do some damage if she brought it down hard enough on Rickling's head. The trick was to reach high enough to hit him.

Deciding she'd worry about that when she came to it, she carried the vase back into the room and closed the door. No sooner had she done so, she heard footsteps creaking along the ancient floorboards in the hallway.

Rickling was coming back.

CHAPTER
❋ 15 ❋

The pageant had already started by the time Gertie joined Daisy and the twins at the back of the ballroom. Pansy sat farther along in the back row of chairs, anxiously staring at the doors. Gertie knew what that meant. Samuel hadn't returned with madam yet. She could see no sign of Baxter or Dr. Prestwick. They had to be out looking for them.

She crossed her fingers tightly in her lap and closed her eyes. Talking to God wasn't one of her strong points, but right now it seemed like a good idea. She had barely started praying when Lillian nudged her.

"What's the matter, Mama? Are you not feeling well?"

"I'm feeling just fine." Gertie smiled at her daughter. "The pageant will be starting any minute, and then we have to be quiet, don't we."

Lillian nodded and pressed her lips together.

Daisy got up from her chair and edged toward Gertie. "Do you mind if I leave now? I still have some things to do tonight."

"No, course not." Gertie put a hand on the nanny's arm. "Thank you for taking such good care of the twins."

Daisy smiled. "My pleasure, I'm sure. Happy Christmas, everyone." She waved good-bye to the children and disappeared down the aisle.

Just then the lights dimmed, and the curtains swept open to reveal two of Phoebe Fortescue's dancers dressed as Mary and Joseph. It was the first time in many years that Phoebe had put on a nativity play. Gertie had to wonder if it was a sign, and if so, was it a good one or bad?

She made herself concentrate on the play, and kept her fingers crossed—this time in the hopes that Phoebe's presentation wouldn't end in the usual disaster. So engrossed was she in the performance, she didn't notice Clive entering the ballroom until he came and sat down beside her.

He leaned toward her and whispered, "Happy Christmas, Gertie."

From that moment on she entirely lost the rest of the play. All she could think about was the book she was going to give him and how he would react to it. She had just about made up her mind not to give it to him when all pandemonium broke out onstage.

The angel was delivering the proclamation of Jesus's birth when a live sheep wandered onto the stage. The Three Wise

Men shrieked, and stumbled over each other to get out of the startled animal's way. In doing so they barged into the structure representing the stable and set the whole thing toppling to the ground.

The confused sheep darted this way and that, while Phoebe stood at the edge of the stage screaming, "What idiot numbskull brought that wretched beast in here?"

Colonel Fortescue then appeared on the opposite side of the stage, waving his arms and shouting, "Tally ho, old bean! How do you like my surprise?"

Polite titters and louder guffaws erupted throughout the audience as Phoebe advanced on her husband, her hat bobbing up and down as she yelled, "*You* did this? Whatever gave you such a harebrained idea? Get this animal off my stage. *This minute!*"

The curtains hastily drew together, amid a burst of applause from the appreciative audience. Gertie could feel Clive shaking with laughter, and in spite of her worries, giggled along with him.

Lillian tugged at her sleeve, wailing, "What will happen to the sheep, Mama?"

"He'll be all right, kitten," Clive said, leaning across Gertie to pat Lillian's head. "I'll go and see that he gets home safely. Happy Christmas, to both you and James."

James leaned forward, his gaze anxiously searching Clive's face. "Will we be seeing you tomorrow?"

Clive turned to look into Gertie's eyes. His face was inches from hers, making her squirm. "Will they be seeing me tomorrow?"

"Well, if you come by, they will." She grinned at him. "I don't have to be on duty until eleven."

Clive nodded and turned back to James. "Then I'll see you in the morning. I hope you'll let me play with the toys that Father Christmas brings."

Lillian jumped up and down on her chair. "I hope he brings us lots of toys!"

"You can play with every one of them," James promised.

"Then I'll definitely be there in the morning." Clive got up, leaning over to whisper in Gertie's ear, "I'll call on you in about an hour."

"Perfect." She watched him leave, and for a brief moment felt so warm and happy she forgot about the book. Until James asked, "Is Father Christmas coming to see Mr. Clive, too?"

With a jolt of anxiety she answered, "Of course. He'll be bringing Mr. Clive a very big surprise."

Lillian's eyes opened wide. "Do you know what it is? Will he like it?"

"I bloody hope so," Gertie murmured, "or I'm going to be really disappointed."

James frowned. "Why's that?"

"Never you mind." She got up, pulling Lillian up with her. "You two have got to get to bed. You have to be asleep by the time Father Christmas gets here, or he won't leave you any toys."

Lillian yawned and rubbed her eyes. "I'm sleepy now."

"Good." She grabbed James's hand and led the two of them to the door. Up onstage, a confused group of Phoebe's dancers were taking awkward bows, while most of the audience was filing out of the room.

Another of Phoebe Fortescue's infamous presentations gone wrong. Gertie would have felt sorry for her, except she knew that the reason Phoebe's audience was so large every year was because they anticipated a fiasco and couldn't wait to see what would happen next.

If she didn't know the fussy little woman better, Gertie would have suspected Phoebe of deliberately staging the disasters, just to keep the spectators coming.

Just as she reached the door Pansy came rushing up to her, her eyes wide with anxiety. "Samuel didn't come to the pageant," she said, her voice choking on the words. "He promised he would. Do you think he's changed his mind about asking me to marry him?"

Gertie hesitated for a long moment, wondering if it would be worse for Pansy to think Samuel had changed his mind or for her to know he was missing. She decided the former would be worse. Looking down at James she said sternly, "I want both of you to go straight to the room and wait there for me. Straight there, do you understand?"

James nodded.

"You know what will happen if you don't go straight there, don't you?"

James nodded again.

"We'll go there," Lillian piped up, "or Father Christmas won't come."

"Right. Off you go." Gertie watched them leave and

turned to Pansy. "That's one of the reasons I love Christmas. I have something I can use to threaten them. Once Christmas is over I'm on my own again."

Pansy couldn't even conjure up the vestige of a smile. "I don't know what to do. Should I go looking for him? Maybe he had to work late in the stables." She looked around the room. "I didn't see madam or Mr. Baxter, either."

Gertie drew a deep breath. "That's because madam is missing. She didn't come back from town this afternoon."

Pansy's eyes widened even more. "What? Where is she, then?"

"Nobody knows." Gertie waited for the rest of it to sink in, her heart aching in sympathy as she watched the realization dawn in Pansy's eyes.

"Samuel was with her?"

"Yes, but I'm sure they're all right. You know madam, she always takes care of herself."

Pansy's face hardened. "Not before she gets Samuel into lots of trouble. She went after whoever killed Mr. Armitage, didn't she?"

"I don't know." Gertie laid a hand on her friend's shoulder. "Don't worry, luv. Mr. Baxter and Dr. Prestwick are out there looking for them and I know they'll be all right."

"They'd better be." Looking close to tears, Pansy turned to the door. "I'm going to wait up for them. All night if I have to." She disappeared through the door and down the hallway, leaving Gertie to stare after her.

Poor Pansy. Gertie shook her head. What a Christmas

Eve. Madam and Samuel missing, and she about to wreck a friendship she'd come to depend on and cherish.

Wandering down the hallway to her room, she tried not to give in to the panic rising in her chest. In an hour she'd have to give the book to Clive. She was certain now that the gift would change everything. He would take it as encouragement and expect things to be different between them. Was she ready for that? If she wasn't, and let him know that, would he finally give up on her?

The thought of that devastated her. Opening the door, she saw the twins sitting on their beds, waiting for her. They would be affected by what happened tonight, as well. What would they do if things went bad between her and Clive? They'd never forgive her, that's what.

Why did life have to be so bloody complicated? Just when she'd decided that she would never let herself get involved with another man, she had to go and fall in love with one.

Was she doomed to be disappointed and hurt again, as she had been so often in the past? Or was this time the magic one—the one that would last and make her happy for the rest of her life? Was it too much to hope that it would happen for her and the twins? They had only known one father, and for such a short time. Something told her that Clive would be a wonderful father to them.

She closed her eyes and once more talked to God. First she prayed for madam and Samuel's safety, and then she prayed that whatever happened between her and Clive tonight it would all come out right. Then she put the twins to bed and settled down to wait for his visit.

Feeling around in the darkness, Cecily's fingers collided painfully with the back of a chair. She had to shuffle her feet along the floor as she blindly carried the chair over to the door, in an attempt to avoid stepping on Samuel as she passed.

She wasn't quite as far over as she'd thought, and her foot stabbed him. He grunted, and the sound both alarmed and relieved her. At least he was still alive. "Sorry, Samuel," she whispered, then continued on until her foot came in contact with the door.

The footsteps were close, and she hurriedly placed the chair against the wall and felt around on the floor for the vase. This time her sense of direction was more accurate, and her hand closed over the neck of the vase almost right away.

She heard the rattle of the key in the lock and hurriedly climbed onto the chair. On the other side of the door she heard Rickling's exclamation. No doubt he was wondering why it wasn't locked.

Raising the vase above her head, she waited, praying that he wouldn't notice it was missing from its place on the shelf and realize she was holding it as a weapon.

The door slowly opened, and Rickling stuck his head inside the room. "I know you're pretending to be unconscious," he said, as the light fell on Samuel's still figure. "I don't know how you unlocked the door, or why you're still here, but it doesn't matter. You won't escape me now. You and that dratted nosy parker you brought with you are both destined for the churchyard. I've got two empty graves waiting for you, and no one will ever think of looking for you there. You needn't worry about your horse. I chased him off. He's probably taken the carriage home by now." He chuckled at his own cleverness, then took a step inside the room. In one hand he carried a rope, in the other a knife.

Cecily waited no longer. She raised her hands, then brought the vase down as hard as she could on Rickling's head.

The vessel shattered in a dozen pieces, scattering across the floor. The sound brought a groan from Samuel, and his eyes flickered open.

To Cecily's horror, Rickling just stood there as if paralyzed, then slowly turned to look up at her. A trickle of blood crept down his face as he stared at her, his eyes burning with rage. He raised a hand as if to strike and she cringed, waiting for the blow. Then his eyes glazed over and he fell to his knees. He started to speak, but before he could finish the word, he toppled over and was still.

Shaking so hard her teeth chattered, Cecily climbed down from the chair and rushed over to Samuel. "We have to get out of here," she said, shaking his arm. "I don't know how long we have until he wakes up again. Can you get up?"

Samuel nodded. He tried to sit up, groaned and laid back, holding his head.

Cecily felt dreadfully sorry for him but her sense of urgency compelled her to be firm. "Try, Samuel. I'll help."

She hooked her arm under his and hauled him into a sitting position. "Come on, you're nearly there." She hauled on him again and he held up his hand.

"I'll get there. Just give me a minute."

"We don't have a minute." She glanced at Rickling, who lay on his side, eyes closed. "I'm afraid he'll wake up and attack us again."

"Let him," Samuel said grimly. "I'll be ready for him this time."

"You're in no shape to be heroic." She hooked both hands under his arms and tugged. "If I have to drag you out of here, you're going now."

Samuel shook his head, groaned once more, then dug his heels into the floor. With an almighty heave Cecily got him to his feet, where he stood for a moment, swaying back and forth.

"Just a few steps," she urged him, holding onto his arm. "So we can lock the door on this dreadful man."

Samuel looked down at Rickling and snarled, "I hope his head hurts worse than mine."

"I'm sure it does." She dragged him to the door and out into the hall. Leaving him propped up against a wall, she quickly slammed the door and turned the key in the lock.

"I have to ring for the constable. I think there's a telephone in the office. Will you be all right until I get back?"

Samuel nodded, then winced, once more holding his head. "I'll be fine."

Still worrying about him, Cecily hurried down the hallway to the office. Spotting the telephone on the wall, she rushed over to it and lifted the receiver. The operator answered right away.

"This is Mrs. Baxter, from the Pennyfoot Country Club. Please put me through to the constabulary," Cecily said, doing her best to calm her voice.

"The station is closed," the operator answered. "Unless this is an emergency your business will have to wait until after Christmas."

"This *is* an emergency." Cecily's fingers tightened on the receiver. "Please put me through to the constable on duty."

"He asked me not to disturb him unless it was a matter of life or death."

Cecily took a moment to control her temper. "Do I have to ring Inspector Cranshaw? I'm sure he'll be interested to know one of his constables is not taking care of his duties."

The operator paused, then said quietly, "I'll put you through to P.C. Watkins's home."

"Thank you." Cecily waited, one foot tapping the floor, while a series of buzzing and whistling went on down the line. Then a male voice demanded, "P.C. Watkins. What do you need?"

Frowning, Cecily answered, "This is Mrs. Baxter, and I need you to come to St. Bartholomew's church right away."

"Is this a joke? If so, it's not very funny. I'm trying to enjoy Christmas with my family."

Losing her patience, Cecily raised her voice. "This is not a joke. I have your killer, Constable Watkins. The man who poisoned one of my guests in the Pennyfoot Country Club. He tried to kill me and my stable manager. I have him locked in a room in the church and I suggest you get here right away to arrest him, or do I have to call Inspector Cranshaw?"

P.C. Watkins stammered into the telephone. "No, no. I'll be there right away. Keep him locked up until I get there."

"No need to worry about that. I have no intention of doing otherwise." Shaking her head, Cecily hung the receiver back on the hook and returned to where she'd left Samuel in the hallway.

She found him slumped on the floor, his back resting against the wall. "Samuel! What's wrong? Is it your head?"

Samuel looked up at her, his face pinched with pain. "It hurts, and I'm a bit light-headed. I feel like I'm floating off the floor."

"Oh, my." She squatted down beside him. "I'll have Dr. Prestwick take a look at you as soon as we get back to the Pennyfoot. I—" She broke off and stood up. "Oh, my, I wonder what time it is. I had better ring the Pennyfoot and let everyone know we're all right. They must be wondering where we are."

Once more she left Samuel and went back to the office. This time the operator put her through right away. Cecily waited while the telephone rang once, twice, three times and kept on ringing without an answer. *Where is Philip?*

She looked around the office and spotted a small clock perched on a shelf. One look at it and she cried out in horror. It was much later than she'd thought. She must have been locked inside that wardrobe for hours. The evening meal at the Pennyfoot would be over by now. The pageant was probably coming to a close as well. Baxter must be out of his mind with worry.

Of course. She'd given Philip the night off, thinking there would be few, if any, telephone calls until after Christmas. Everyone else was most likely at the pageant. The only other telephone was in her office and no one would be in there.

She would just have to wait until P.C. Watkins arrived to arrest Cuthbert Rickling. Without a horse and carriage neither of them was going anywhere for a while. All she could hope was that Baxter would forgive her for this latest escapade.

Baxter had long ago given up any hope that his wife would lead a normal life. He blamed the dratted women's movement and all the controversy over equal rights. It had turned women into autonomous adventurers with a thirst for excitement and a belligerence that was entirely unladylike.

Although he would die rather than admit it, he rather liked Cecily's feisty nature, even if it did land her into trouble more often than was comfortable. As for women's rights, he didn't know why the government didn't just hand them the vote and be done with all the nonsense. If half of them possessed the intelligence of his wife, the country might well be better off with their contributions.

Right at that moment, however, he was not at all happy with Cecily's penchant for danger and excitement. Having searched the town with Kevin Prestwick in vain, he had returned to the Pennyfoot only to find the carriage they'd sought standing in the middle of the courtyard, with the bay hanging its head and steam gushing from its nose.

At first his heart had leapt with relief. Cecily had returned home safely after all. Then the realization had hit him. Had Samuel been with her, the bay would have been snug in its stall, and the carriage put away in the stables.

He had wasted no time bounding up the steps to the front door. The foyer was quite empty. Even Philip was not in his usual position behind the reception desk. Cecily must have sent him home.

Kevin halted behind him, his voice strained with anxiety when he said, "She's not here, is she."

Baxter glanced at the grandfather clock in the corner. "Take a look in the ballroom, just in case she's there. I'm going up to the suite. Meet me back here."

Kevin nodded and disappeared down the hallway. Baxter's stomach felt like an angry ocean churning away inside him as he swiftly climbed the stairs. The unaccustomed exercise took a toll on his knees, and he was hobbling by the time he reached the door of the suite.

One look inside told him what he'd feared. Cecily had not arrived home. What in the world had happened to her? He sunk on the bed, burying his head in his hands. It was all his fault. He should have been more strict with her. Not allowed her to go chasing after criminals. Obviously that's what she'd done this afternoon, and it appeared that she had ended up in serious trouble. He would have to call the constabulary and ask for their help.

THE CLUE IS IN THE PUDDING

A wave of fear took his breath away. *Dear God, don't let anything bad have happened to her.* He fought against the vision of her lying in some dark alley, her throat cut and her life's blood trickling down the road. *No, not Cecily.* He simply couldn't live without her. Raising his chin, he once more appealed to the heavens. "It's Christmas, for pity's sake," he whispered. "Let her come home to me. I can't lose her now."

An urgent tapping made him jump. Dashing at his eyes with the back of his hand, he rose and stumbled over to the door to open it.

Madeline stood in the doorway, with Kevin peering over his shoulder. "Is she not here?"

Baxter shook his head. "I'm going down to the foyer to ring the constabulary. Then I'm going out again to look for her."

"I'm coming with you." Kevin silenced his wife's murmur of protest with a raise of his hand. "I'll have one of the footmen take you home, Madeline. Our nanny will be wondering where you are, and you should be with little Angelina tonight."

"I suppose you're right." Madeline looked at Baxter. "Don't worry, Cecily will be all right. The Lord is taking care of her in his house."

Alarmed, Baxter stared at her. "I hope you don't mean—"

"She means nothing." Kevin gave his wife a little push. "Go home, Madeline. I'll be there as soon as possible."

Madeline turned to leave, and glanced at Baxter over her shoulder. "Look for her there." She was gone before he could ask her again what she meant.

"You know Madeline," Kevin said, with a smile of apology. "She means well, but she relies entirely too much on her visions and dreams. It's best to take whatever she says with a grain of salt."

Baxter shook his head. "I'm inclined to agree with you, old man, but I have to say, there are some things about Madeline that defy explanation. In any case, I'm going down now to ring the constabulary. I truly appreciate your help tonight, but there's no need for you to stay. It's Christmas, and you should be home with your wife."

"I'm not going home until I know that Cecily is safe." Kevin turned and started walking toward the stairs.

Baxter followed him, his mind whirling and his stomach feeling as if it were on fire. He had to cling to the banister rail on the way down and felt quite weak by the time he reached the foyer. He managed to get over to the reception desk without stumbling and reached for the telephone. After dialing for the operator he waited. And waited. The only sound in his ear was the insistent buzzing on the line. Burning with frustration, he slammed the receiver back onto its hook.

Kevin raised his eyebrows in silent question.

"They're not answering," Baxter said, his voice hoarse with the strain. "They must have gone home for Christmas."

Kevin rolled his eyes. "Come on, let's get out there and look for them."

Baxter lifted his hands, a feeling of utter helplessness almost overwhelming him. "Where? We've looked everywhere. How—?"

A voice from across the foyer interrupted him. "Mr. Baxter?"

Baxter scowled at the footman hurrying toward him. "Not now, Charlie. I'm busy."

"This is important, sir." Charlie halted in front of him, his eyes wide and full of concern. "I thought you should know. I've been trying to find Mrs. Baxter to tell her, but I can't find her anywhere."

Baxter brushed weary fingers across his eyes. "Tell her what?"

Charlie glanced at Kevin, then lowered his voice. "Samuel told me earlier today that Mr. Armitage had been poisoned by arsenic in a bottle of whiskey."

Baxter sent a quick glance around the foyer. "I hope you haven't repeated that to anyone. Samuel knows better than to spread gossip like that."

Charlie shook his head. "No, sir, I haven't told anyone. I didn't think that much about it at the time, but then I remembered a short while ago that Mr. Rickling had asked me to take up a bottle of whiskey for Mr. Armitage. He said to tell Mr. Armitage it was a Christmas gift from an admirer."

Kevin uttered a startled curse, while Baxter stared at Charlie. "Rickling? The choirmaster?"

"Yes, sir." Charlie looked uncomfortable. "I don't know if it means anything but—"

"The house of the Lord," Baxter muttered. He surged forward, heading for the door.

Behind him, Kevin called out, "Where are you going?"

Baxter shouted over his shoulder. "The house of the Lord. Madeline said to look for Cecily there. She's with Rickling in the church!" He didn't wait for an answer but went leaping down the steps, praying as he'd never prayed before.

CHAPTER

❀ 16 ❀

Gertie had been waiting for the knock on her door for what seemed like hours. Even so, she nearly jumped out of her skin when at last she heard the light tap. Glancing at the twins to make sure they were fast asleep, she crept over to the door and opened it.

Clive stood outside, a huge doll's house in his arms. At his feet stood a castle, its battlements filled with knights in armor, each holding either a lance or bows and arrows. Both toys were so exquisitely crafted, Gertie shoved a hand over her mouth to muffle her cry of delight.

"How did you carry them both down here?" she asked, as she stooped to pick up the castle.

"I made two trips." He followed her into the room and

carefully lowered the doll's house to the floor at the foot of Lillian's bed. The children had hung pillowcases on the bed-posts, and Gertie had already filled them with toys and sweets. She placed the castle at the bottom of James's bed and squatted down for a better look.

The walls of the castle had ivy growing up them, and windows in the turrets. There was a courtyard in front, with double gates that opened, and inside the castle she could see tiny furniture and colorful banners on the wall.

Lillian's dollhouse had curtains at the window, and was also furnished with miniature chairs, tables, a bed and ward-robe. Two little dolls sat in the sitting room side by side, and a small dog lay in front of a fireplace.

Gertie breathed out a sigh. "How do you do this? It's so . . ." She sought for a word to describe what she saw and could find only one. "Perfect."

Clive grinned. "I hope they like them."

"I know they will." She got up and signaled him to take a chair. Sitting down in the other one, she said quietly, "Thank you, Clive. You are so clever. Why don't you start up a business as a toy maker? I know you could do really well at it."

He studied her face long enough to unsettle her. "You know, I might just think about that."

Now she was sorry she'd said anything. The thought of working in the Pennyfoot without the possibility of bump-ing into Clive now and then was too depressing to even consider.

"I brought something for you, too." He dug in his vest pocket and drew out a small box. "Happy Christmas, Gertie. I hope you like it."

She took it from him, trying not to let him see her hand shaking. "Thank you! Can I open it now?"

There was laughter in his voice when he answered her. "Of course. I was hoping you would open it while I'm here."

She slowly lifted the lid, aware of her heart thumping madly in her chest. She wasn't sure what she expected to see. Something carved in wood, most likely. A serving spoon, perhaps, or an ornament for her mantelpiece. What she saw when she opened the box was so unexpected, she could hardly breathe.

Nestled on a bed of red velvet lay a gleaming gold bracelet engraved with silver swirls. She was afraid to touch it. Never in her life had she ever owned such a beautiful thing, and she was half afraid it would vanish if she put a finger on it.

She was quiet for so long, Clive leaned toward her, his voice now taut with anxiety. "Is something wrong?"

"No, not at all." She looked up, her words threatening to choke her. "It's bloody gorgeous."

Clive grinned. "Here, let me put it on you."

She gave him the box and held out her wrist. His fingers were warm on her arm as he fumbled with the catch, and she thought she would faint by the time he'd fastened the bracelet.

He sat back and tilted his head on one side. "It looks very nice on you."

She lifted her wrist and studied it, wishing she could find the words to thank him properly. The last thing she had expected from him was jewelry. Especially something this nice. She knew he didn't have much money, and the thought of him spending it on her like this was so overwhelming she almost cried. Considering the fact that she hardly ever cried, that was quite a shock to her system.

"It looks bleeding beautiful and I can't wait to show it off." She smiled at him, putting her heart into it. "Thank you ever so much, Clive. It's the nicest thing anyone has ever given me."

"Then you deserve to be spoilt."

She stared at the bracelet for several seconds more, then jumped to her feet. It was time, and she couldn't put it off any longer. Her heart was racing so fast she felt dizzy as she went to the dresser and picked up the package she'd wrapped for him.

"Here," she said, thrusting it at him. "Happy Christmas, Clive."

He took it from her, and carefully undid the string and unwrapped the paper. He took so long she thought she would scream. At last he took out the book with a murmur of appreciation. "A book! You couldn't have given me anything better. Thank you, Gertie." He turned it over then, and read the title out loud. *Love Poems for Your Loved One.*

The silence that followed seemed as thick as a fog. Gertie sought frantically for the right thing to say, but everything she thought of seemed only to make things worse.

Finally Clive spoke. "Am I your loved one?"

Everything hung in the balance with her answer. She opened her mouth to tell him the whole thing was a mistake and she hadn't even read the title before buying the book. Then she saw the hope in his eyes and the words died before they were ever spoken. Feeling as if she were standing on the very edge of a high cliff, she whispered, "Of course you are."

His smile dazzled her, and she blinked. Hard.

Clive looked down at the book and opened it. He began to read out loud, though softly, so as not to awaken the children. " 'How do I love, thee? Let me count the ways.' "

Overcome by the beauty of the words flowing over her, Gertie closed her eyes. *Let this moment never end, and I'll be content the rest of my life.* She opened her eyes again to find Clive watching her with an expression she'd never seen on him before. It took her a moment to realize he was about to kiss her, and when he leaned forward, she hesitated, just for a second. Then she leaned forward to meet him, and in that moment she knew where her heart belonged. Come what may, she would follow this man to the ends of the earth.

"You know, Samuel, we really should stop all this nonsense." Cecily studied her stable manager, concerned by his pallor. "If you keep getting hit on the head like this, your brain will be addled."

Seated on the floor with his back propped up against the wall, Samuel managed a weak grin. "I think it's a bit late to worry about that, m'm."

Cecily shook her head. "No, really, I mean it. You have

been a good and faithful servant all these years, and you've risked life and limb for me too many times for me to remember. You've been rendered unconscious far too often, and it's time this stopped."

Samuel's face registered dismay. "Are you giving me the sack, m'm?"

"Great heavens, no! Of course not." Cecily edged herself down the wall until she was sitting next to him on the floor. "I'm saying that I've been entirely too selfish all these years, expecting you to accompany me on these wild pursuits that generally end up with you getting injured. If we keep this up, you could very well be permanently damaged, or worse. Now that you have a future wife to think about, I simply can't allow you to put yourself in harm's way anymore."

Samuel's frown deepened. "But who will take care of you if I don't? Who will help you hunt down these scoundrels and bring them to justice?"

Cecily smiled. "I'm not sure I'll be doing any more scoundrel hunting myself, but if I do, I'll find someone else to assist me." Seeing his forlorn expression, she hastened to add, "Not that I could ever replace you, Samuel, but I'm sure I can at least find someone halfway decent."

"If you don't mind me saying so, m'm, perhaps it's time you gave up chasing after criminals altogether."

"I think that's a very good idea."

The deep voice had come from down the hallway. At the sound of it, Cecily scrambled to her feet, just in time to see her husband rushing toward her, his arms outstretched.

Enclosed in his embrace, she felt a moment of weakness, and had to fight against shedding a tear. "I'm so glad to see you, darling," she murmured, when she could speak without faltering. "The constable should be here any minute. Mr. Rickling is locked up in that room." She nodded at the door. "I'm afraid he'll have rather a nasty headache when he wakes up."

Baxter let her go and stepped back to look at Samuel. "What about him?"

"He has a headache as well." She looked past Baxter, relieved to see Kevin Prestwick standing there. "Perhaps you could take a look at him, Kevin?"

Kevin nodded and squatted down in front of Samuel.

Looking up at her husband, Cecily asked, "How did you know we were here?"

"Madeline. She told me to look for you in the house of the Lord. Charlie Muggins told me that Rickling had sent up a bottle of whiskey for Armitage. I put two and two together."

She grinned. "Clever. Perhaps I should enlist your help more often."

"I think not." He looked grim. "Do you have any idea how I felt when I realized you were missing?"

"I'm dreadfully sorry, darling." Cecily patted him on the arm. "I'm perfectly all right, as you can see. That dreadful man shut me up in a wardrobe, but I managed to get out. She gazed at the lone vase sitting on the shelf. "I'm afraid I broke the other vase."

Baxter glanced at the vase. "You did? How did that happen?"

"I smashed it over Mr. Rickling's head."

Baxter rolled his eyes. "You will be the death of me, wife of mine."

"Piffle." She gave him a serene smile. "Think how bored you'd be if you didn't have me to worry about." She glanced over at the doctor, who was leaning over Samuel. "How is he?"

"He'll live." Kevin turned back to Samuel. "You'll have to lay quiet for a few days, young fellow. You have probably got a concussion."

"Oh, dear," Cecily murmured. "I'll see that he gets plenty of rest."

Heavy footsteps from down the hallway caught her attention. "Here's the constable now." She smiled at P.C. Watkins as he trudged into view. "Good evening, constable. I'm so sorry to bring you out here on Christmas Eve. Your prisoner is locked in that room." She pointed at the door. "He may be sleeping still."

The constable gave her a sharp look. "How do you know he killed your guest?"

"Oh, he told me." She nodded at Samuel. "He told my stable manager as well. He also planned to kill us both. I think that should be enough to put him in prison, don't you?"

Baxter grunted. "He was going to kill you?"

"Well, yes, dear, but he didn't get the chance."

Baxter put both hands on his head as if he would tear out

his hair. "Thank the Lord for that. I really don't know what I would do without you."

"I have no intention of you ever having to find out." She slipped her hand under his arm. "Now take me home, darling. We have a Christmas to celebrate."

Mrs. Chubb paused at the gate that led into the Pennyfoot Country Club's courtyard. Rows of dazzling white sheets hung from the clotheslines, flapping in the brisk sea breeze. Overhead, fluffy clouds scudded across a pale blue sky, promising a sunny afternoon. She could just see the corner of the stables from there. Tess was chasing her tail while a couple of ducks waddled past, apparently unfazed by the big dog's antics.

Mrs. Chubb smiled with satisfaction. She was home again and everything was as she left it. Still smiling, she hauled her bags across the yard and up to the kitchen door.

When she opened it, the first person she saw was Gertie standing at the sink. Her cap sat askew on her head as usual, allowing strands of her dark hair to float about her face. Normally Mrs. Chubb would utter a familiar phrase. *Gertie, straighten your cap and for heaven's sake do something with that hair!*

Today was different, however. She'd been gone for two weeks, and much as she loved being with her daughter and grandchildren, she couldn't wait to get back to work in the surroundings she knew and loved.

So, instead of yelling at Gertie, she put a foot inside the kitchen and said loudly, "Well, I must say, it's good to see you're all still working hard."

Three faces turned in her direction. Pansy stood on the other side of Gertie, and Michel was at the stove, waving a wooden spoon at her.

Gertie was the first to speak. Rushing toward the housekeeper, arms outstretched, she screeched, "Chubby! You're home! Am I bloody glad to see you."

"Welcome home, Mrs. Chubb," Pansy called out, her face wreathed in smiles.

"It's about time you were here," Michel said, doing his best to hide a grin. "This place, it is a mess without you, *n'est-ce pas?*"

"He's bloody right." Gertie grabbed one of the housekeeper's bags and linked arms with her. "Come on, I'll help you take this to your room. I've got blinking lots to tell you."

Mrs. Chubb allowed herself to be dragged through the kitchen and down the hallway. Opening the door, she looked inside and sighed. "The nicest thing about going away," she said, as she walked into her room, "is coming home and finding nothing has changed."

Gertie followed her in and dumped the heavy bag onto the bed. "Well, I wouldn't exactly say that."

Mrs. Chubb dropped her bag on the floor and sat down on the edge of the bed. Something in Gertie's voice had alarmed her and she looked up anxiously at her chief housemaid. "What do you mean? Nothing's happened to madam, has it? Or anyone else?"

Gertie sat down beside her. "Madam's fine, though she nearly wasn't. The new choirmaster at St. Bartholomew's killed one of our guests and madam went after him at the church and he almost killed her and Samuel and now Samuel's getting over a concussion and has to be really careful and he just got engaged to Pansy and—"

"What?" Mrs. Chubb grabbed Gertie's arm. "Pansy's engaged to Samuel?"

Gertie grinned. "Out of all that, all you heard was that Pansy got engaged?"

"No, of course not." Mrs. Chubb collected her thoughts. "It's awful that someone died, of course, but it's not the first time Mrs. Baxter has done battle with a murderer, and it is the first time Pansy has got engaged." She thought about that for a moment or two. "When are they getting married?"

Gertie shrugged. "I dunno. Pansy said it will be sometime this year. Samuel promised they'd be married before Christmas." She put her head on one side. "How's your daughter? Is she better?"

"Much better, thank you." Mrs. Chubb shook her head. "Our little Pansy getting married. I can't believe it. How we'll miss her."

"And Samuel as well." Gertie sighed. "He's going into business for himself with Gilbert Tubbs."

"Who's Gilbert Tubbs?"

"He's the new stable boy. He and Samuel are going to open up a garage to repair motorcars."

"Oh, my."

"We really, really missed you." Gertie settled herself more comfortably on the bed. "The old bat that took your place was a miserable cow. She yelled at us all the time and she made Michel mad when she drank his brandy and we were all bloody glad when she left."

Mrs. Chubb squirmed as guilt washed over her. "It sounds as if you had a miserable time. I'm sorry you had to put up with all that."

Gertie shrugged. "Oh, it was all right. We all had a good time in spite of Tucker the Terrible. Did you have a nice Christmas?"

"Very nice. My daughter was feeling a bit better by Christmas Day and the children enjoyed all the toys they got. I must say, though, I missed being here for Christmas." She shook her head. "So much happened while I was away."

"Well, that's not all."

Alarmed again, Mrs. Chubb looked up at her. "What else? Don't tell me someone else is leaving."

"Clive might be leaving before too long."

Gertie's voice had sounded funny, and Mrs. Chubb gave her a sharp look. "Clive? Where's he going?"

"He's thinking of going into business, too. He wants to open a toy shop in Wellercombe."

"Goodness." Mrs. Chubb fanned her face. "Here I was thinking how nice it was that nothing changes here and now I go away for two weeks and the whole world changes." She gave Gertie another scrutiny. "You're keeping something back."

To her surprise, Gertie actually looked bashful. She

couldn't ever remember Gertie being shy about anything, unless . . . "Wait a minute, are you and Clive . . . ?"

She didn't need an answer. She could see it in Gertie's face.

"It's nothing serious," Gertie said hurriedly. "Not yet, anyway. We're going to take things really slowly. We have the twins to think about and there's a lot of stuff we have to sort out before we know for sure, but right now"—her grin spread all over her face—"things look bloody good."

Mrs. Chubb held out her arms and wrapped them around Gertie's shoulders. "He's a good man, Gertie," she said softly. "I hope things work out for you."

"So do I," Gertie muttered. "It's about bleeding time."

"I must say," Baxter said, as he unfolded his newspaper, "it's good to have Mrs. Chubb back again."

"Why, darling, I didn't know you'd missed her so much. I'll have to tell her. She'll be most appreciative." Seated across from him in her favorite armchair, Cecily stretched out her feet to warm them in front of the fire. This was her favorite part of the day, spending the evening with her husband alone in their suite.

Baxter gave her a withering glance. "You have to admit, that Tucker woman was most unpleasant. I've never heard so many complaints from the staff."

"She is rather an unhappy woman." Cecily watched the yellow flames licking the coals. "I had a long talk with her just before she left. I was reluctant to give her anything more than a lukewarm reference, but after chatting with her, I changed my mind. After all, she was extremely competent and efficient. The kitchen ran like clockwork all through Christmas and New Year's Eve."

"Even though half the staff threatened to walk out."

Cecily smiled. "They didn't mean it, my love. It was just the pressure of the work."

"More like the pressure of that woman's tongue." Baxter yawned behind his hand. "What made you change your mind about the reference?"

"It was what she told me. Her mother died when she was born and her father couldn't take care of her. She grew up in an orphanage and her biggest dream was to become an actress. She said she was always pretending she was performing on a stage. Personally I think it was an attempt to escape from the miserable world she lived in."

"That could well be." Baxter pursed his lips. "I suppose that sort of life could make one miserable enough to take it out on others."

"Especially when all her attempts to become an actress met with nothing but rejection." Cecily shook her head. "It really hurt her badly. To make matters worse, her husband of a few years left her for a younger woman. She sought solace by immersing herself in the theater, going to plays when she could afford to, and associating with actors as much as possible. That's how she befriended Cuthbert Rickling. She recognized him as a former actor when she saw him in church."

"I'm surprised Rickling wanted anything to do with her."

"I was surprised about that at first. Then I started thinking. Rickling must have known Archibald Armitage was going to spend Christmas at the Pennyfoot. It would make things easier for him if he befriended someone working here. Someone who could tell him what room Mr. Armitage would be in, for instance."

"Ah!" Baxter nodded. "That makes sense."

"Anyway, I sent Mrs. Tucker off with good references, so she should have no problem getting another job. I'm just glad it's all over and now we can relax for a while."

"Make the most of it. The summer will be upon us before long." He shook the newspaper and opened it.

She laughed. "I always enjoy the start of a new year. Everything seems fresh and full of promise. A chance to start again, so to speak."

He peered at her over the top of his newspaper. "To start what again?"

"Oh, I don't know. Everything and anything."

"Well, just as long as it's not another murder."

Cecily looked at him in alarm. "Don't even mention the word. I have no wish to find another dead body in this hotel."

"Country club."

"Whatever." She smiled at him. "Don't you find it exciting to contemplate what the New Year might bring?"

"Not at all. I find it somewhat intimidating."

She had to laugh. "When has anything ever intimidated you?"

He lowered the newspaper to his lap. "Every time I rush to your side, never knowing if I'm going to find you dead or alive."

Her smile faded. "I'm sorry, darling. I know I give you cause for worry, but I always have the best of intentions."

"I'll put that on your gravestone." He sketched words in the air with his finger. "She died with the best of intentions."

She got up from her chair and bent over him. "Don't be so morbid, my love. I have no intention of dying anytime soon. I feel in my bones that this is going to be a wonderful year. After all, we have a wedding to look forward to, and maybe two."

"Two? Who else besides Pansy is getting married?"

Cecily smiled. "No one yet, but you never know."

He grunted and raised his newspaper again. "Weddings are for women. Men would much prefer just to go off and get married somewhere quiet without all that fuss and palaver."

"Piffle! You know you enjoy them as much as I do." She dropped a kiss on his forehead. "No matter what the year might bring, one thing is certain, there will be another Christmas celebration at the end of it. In spite of everything."

"Well, I suggest that next Christmas, you forbid any live animals on the stage. I got tired of listening to footmen whining about having to clean up after one more of Phoebe Fortescue's disasters."

Cecily sighed. "I rather regret I missed all that."

"I don't." He looked up at her, and she was surprised to see real concern in his eyes. "I hope I never have to go through all that worry and fear again. I really don't know what I would do without you."

This time she kissed him on the mouth. "Please don't

worry, my love. It appears I have a guardian angel watching over me. I always seem to get out of those situations."

His smile warmed her heart. "Then I hope he or she is always there for you. As I am."

"I know. Happy New Year, darling. Just think, we have a whole year before you have to worry about Christmas again."